Wakefield Press

Sunburnt Veils

Sara Haghdoosti was born in Iran, grew up in Sydney and is currently based just outside Chicago. It generally takes her ten minutes to answer the question, 'Where are you from?'

She got her start in organising at the Australian Youth Climate Coalition and then went on to work at GetUp!, Change. org, the Mozilla Foundation and founded Berim ('Let's go' in Farsi) – a non-profit that worked to support change-makers in Iran. She's currently the Deputy Director at Win Without War.

Her writing has appeared in the *Sydney Morning Herald*, *The Punch* and *The Drum* and she's also been a panellist on ABC TV's *Q and A*.

Sunburnt Veils

SARA HAGHDOOSTI

Wakefield
Press

Wakefield Press
16 Rose Street
Mile End
South Australia 5031
www.wakefieldpress.com.au

First published 2021

Cover designed by Liz Nicholson, Wakefield Press
Cover illustration by Isabelle Seretis
Edited by Jo Case, Wakefield Press
Typeset by Michael Deves, Wakefield Press
Printed by Finsbury Green, Adelaide SA

ISBN 978 1 74305 776 6

NATIONAL
LIBRARY
OF AUSTRALIA

A catalogue record for this
book is available from the
National Library of Australia

For Ilya,
you may not know what a Fae Warrior is, but it's cool –
cause you're way better than one anyway.

Chapter 1

'Are you sure about this, Tara?' Mum asked, tucking a stray strand of hair out of my face and into my hijab.

Seriously? She wanted to bring this up today after avoiding it for all this time? Nope. No way I was taking the bait. 'Don't hate on the galaxy print. It's uni – I can finally unleash the nerd.'

Mum pursed her lips the way she always did when I was being deliberately difficult. She held my gaze for a moment before returning to scrolling through emails on her iPhone. 'I can give you a ride in.'

I shoved my feet into my black ballet flats. 'It's not kindy.'

Mum sidestepped me to the hallway mirror and ran her pinky along the side of her mouth, wiping away the tiniest smudge of her fire-truck red lipstick before nodding approval at her reflection. 'I must have gotten confused by the backpack.' The smile she flashed me was magazine-cover worthy.

It wasn't fair – with her olive skin, tailored pantsuit and perfectly styled hair, Mum was an Aussie Amal Clooney. It was impossible not to feel like a 'before' photo standing next to her. I ignored her comment and grabbed my sparkly purple backpack.

Mum zipped it up, then pulled me into a hug that said, *I love you despite your terrible taste in shoes.* 'Have an amazing day, okay?'

'Bye!' I rolled my eyes. She blew me a kiss before opening the door.

Wait, I almost called after her, but stopped at the last minute. It didn't matter. Even if she tried, it wouldn't be the same.

For my first day of uni, Maman Noosheen, my grandmother, would have been ready with the Quran on a tray next to a glass of water. She would have made me kiss the holy book and walk under it, then thrown the water after me. Was it an Iranian thing, an Islamic thing, or something older? I wasn't sure. Never asked her. Instead, every year at the start of school, I'd said, 'Maman, I'll be late, this is silly'.

'Then you'd better hurry so I don't splash you,' she'd tease. *Khoda* (God), I missed her. How had it been more than a year already?

I didn't want Mum to notice anything amiss, so I plastered on a smile and gave her an overly enthusiastic wave. I let my shoulders sag after the door clicked shut, then stepped in front of the hallway mirror and slapped on some sunscreen and lip balm.

Mum has one of those faces that old Renaissance dudes would have killed to paint – not hot, but straight-up beautiful. Me? I have brown skin, a slightly crooked nose, almost black eyes and a squarish face. Mum says I look distinct, *striking* even – but that's just a nice way of saying that nothing really fits together.

Make-up doesn't suit me, so I don't wear it. My eyes are already too big for my face. Add eyeliner, and well, they go full raccoon. Lipstick makes my lips look weird, and way more people tell me I look good when I wear lip balm than when I wear gloss. People used to remember me for my hair: frizzy curls that floated around my face like a cloud.

Mum argues that I just don't put in the effort. Look, she isn't totally wrong. If I have to pick between finishing reading a trilogy and shoving what looks like a medieval torture device near my eyes to curl my lashes – well, it ain't much of a choice. Besides, ever since *Game of Thrones* went mainstream, the 'Arya' look is totally in – so really, I'm not a slob, just fashion forward, *dahling*.

I wish I slayed like Arya though. When it counted, I fell just short. I grabbed my keys and gave the tiny sword keyring, a miniature of Arya's Needle, a squeeze. It still hurt to think about the night our results came out. I know only twenty people get straight into med at Sydney Uni. To have a shot, you have to get an ATAR of 99.95, ace an interview and nail some sort of written assessment. I'd topped all my classes and thought I'd killed the exams. I almost crashed my Mac refreshing when the ATARs were released. Mum cheered when my score of 98 loaded on the screen, but I crawled into bed and cried.

I could have gone somewhere else, but I'd watched Josie Alibrandi running through the Quad and dreamed of doing the same. I'd gone to every single open day since Year 9. Studying med at Sydney was my dream and I wasn't giving up on it. So Plan A was – ace the first year of my Med Sciences degree (sounds like the same thing but you don't get a stethoscope at the end), get high distinctions, retake the UCAT and get into med through the back door. Yeah, that was rarer than a leaked Harry Potter manuscript – but not totally impossible. Plan B was to get high distinctions, take summer school, finish the three-year undergrad way early and then apply for the graduate program while everyone else was still figuring out how to navigate campus. I nodded to myself, renewing my vow that one way or the other, I was going to make it happen. I could already imagine Carrie Bickmore introducing me on *The Project*. 'Now we have Dr Lutkari on the show to explain more about her incredible work . . .'

I glanced at my phone. Mitra was supposed to pick me up in two minutes, which meant that I had at least ten before she showed up. So I grabbed my book from my backpack, headed to my room and curled up on the window seat. The princess pretending to be a spy was about to be caught by the guard who was also obviously her soulmate. I snuggled into my puntastic 'it's going *tibia* great day' pillow and let myself fall into the book's world. Just as they were totally going to kiss for the first time, tyres screeched outside, followed by mad honking.

I looked out the window and literally laughed out loud. I live two blocks away from Bondi Beach because back in the day, Maman Noosheen thought it was silly to live surrounded by concrete if you could be next to the ocean. It's one of those leafy streets where all the houses are pastel colours: the kind of street you see in watercolour paintings that tourists buy at the Bondi markets. Mitra was all technicolour. *Kill Bill* on a *Home and Away* street.

I shoved my book in my backpack and headed out to conquer the last hurdle standing between me and my dream.

Mitra got out of her 1970s Datsun and moved to the passenger door, gesturing at it like a *The Price is Right* model. She hadn't changed her look for uni one bit. It still looked like she used sharpies as eyeliner. Her curls sprawled in different directions, and the gold chain around her neck was as big as it was fake. Her usual uniform of ripped black jean shorts, faded singlet and gold sequinned sneakers popped against the yellow car.

'What do you think of Dee?' She leaned against the car and picked flecks of muck from under her nails like she didn't care about my answer. But I knew when she was just playing tough. She'd told me a billion times about how special this car was – a Datsun 510 (apparently that means something to car aficionados).

I ran my fingers over Dee's hood and let out a whistle. 'Can't believe this is the same burnt-out car you bought a year ago.'

Mitra knocked on Dee's roof. 'Amoo Ali inspected every inch of her, said he'd never seen a Datsun in better shape. Besides, with this classy paint job,' she patted the hood, 'you can spot us from space.'

If aliens were looking down on us, they were probably rubbing their eyes at the sight. 'It's very you,' I said. Loud, inappropriate and damn cool. My smile evaporated as I opened the passenger door and the *doomph doomph* of her electronica hit me. I flipped the switch to AM and dialed the knob to ABC Radio.

The calm voice of a female newsreader declared, 'Sydney remains on high alert after police arrested a Middle Eastern man who attempted to detonate an explosive device at Central Station yesterday.'

'What, you're an eighty-year-old nana now?' Mitra buckled her seatbelt and flipped the radio back to FM. Electronica punched from the stereo again. I looked back. Her backseat was covered in clothes and make-up, as well as wires from rigging up various electronics.

'Still?' I looked over at her. Ever since the second week of Year 7, Mitra would walk out of her house with her parent-approved, perfectly ironed, longer-than-anyone-else's uniform on. Round the corner from school, she would slather on make-up, liberate her curls and pile on the bling. Then she'd flash half the neighbourhood to change into her white-out stained, totally crinkled uniform (short enough that it got glares – but not notes – from teachers) that she'd nicked from a secondhand bin. She was like a low-fi spy who shifted identities every day, and her backseat held the evidence.

'What? The parents are a bit more chill now that I'm in uni, but they didn't morph white overnight. Mum bought me that thing – ' she pointed to a crumpled bubblegum-pink dress that would have looked too girly on Hello Kitty, let alone Mitra, ' – and gave me an evil-eye necklace so big you could probably spot it from the moon.'

I choked on my laugh as Mitra swerved the car in an illegal U-turn. She turned up the music and bopped her head up and down, drumming her fingers on the steering wheel. The clanging of her bangles somehow offset the hammering electronica.

Once we were crawling in traffic, I pulled out the Welcome Week activities guide I'd printed out the night before. 'I don't think we're going to make the breakfast meet-and-greet.'

'Don't be such a priss,' Mitra said, adjusting the rear-view mirror and double-checking her lipstick. 'You can't fail at Welcome Week. It's a giant party.' She puckered her lips and blew a kiss before adjusting the mirror to show the road. 'Unless you keep up that nonsense.'

Scoffing, I folded my arms and glanced out the window as we drove past the giant neon Coca-Cola sign that marks the end of Kings Cross and wove through the high-rises and old sandstone buildings of downtown Sydney. I was bad at parties. That wasn't the only thing that made me nervous about uni. Telling people you believe in God is almost like declaring you have an imaginary friend at our age. With the hijab, I might as well have been wearing an 'I believe in God' billboard on my head. I fiddled with the edges of my scarf.

'It's gonna be fine. Besides, slinking around doesn't suit you.'

'I don't slink,' I said. Even when Maman Noosheen had died last year, I hadn't. Instead, I dove into work, spending every minute I could studying, to push the memory of her on the kitchen floor out of my head. When it did creep in, I'd end up curled up in bed crying for hours. Which was *something*, yes, but not *slinking*.

'Not since you put that on, you don't.' Mitra's side eye was so fierce it probably could have won Olympic gold. So maybe I *had* slunk around after Ryan, but that was two years ago. She was trolling me, trying to get a rise, so I poked my tongue out at her and turned to look out the window.

Mitra turned off the music and and I turned back to see what was up. She wound up her window and kept her eyes on the road. Two dozen police officers were patrolling outside Central Station. One of them was talking into a walkie talkie and pointing to the roof. Others were scanning the area or walking around, hands on belts. They set my teeth on edge.

Mitra held her breath as we drove by and exhaled like she was in yoga class once we were past them. It reminded me of what high school had been like at first. Mitra couldn't sit still and the teachers all came down on her hard. She got kicked out of class every other day and was outside the principal's office so often that she bragged the decrepit blue couch there had a groove of her arse-print. The first time we sat a test, she almost got suspended because everyone assumed she cheated, which was a load of bull. It took a few more runs for them to realise that she kept mucking around in class because she was bored. She picked engineering because she wanted to build toys that would make James Bond jealous. Of course Mitra would do it, because Mitra could do anything.

The parking fairies smiled on us and Mitra pulled into a spot off Glebe Point Road. Grabbing my bag, I realised Mitra's wallet was jammed between our seats and rescued it as I popped out of the car. 'I got your wallet!'

She shrugged, grabbed her debit card from her back pocket and fed it to the machine. She lost her wallet a few times a day and had started keeping her debit card in her jeans so she wouldn't end up stranded.

We walked through the gates and followed the smell of frying onions and sausages up the cobblestone path to the sprawling green lawns in front of the sandstone quad. Hundreds of white tents spanned out in semi-circles from a central temporary stage. A guitar solo sliced through the air. Mitra tweaked the air in front of her, playing along.

People darted about us, dancing, singing and handing out bright leaflets. A handful of cops stood around, bobbing to the music or looking bored.

'Is that normal?' I asked Mitra, nodding towards the police. She was about to reply when a group of guys wandered in front of us dressed as medieval knights, casually hauling papier-mâché mace and swords.

'Ain't nothing normal about this place,' she replied, as a girl with a pixie cut and fluoro-green shirt bounced towards us. Pixie girl laughed, dipped a wand into a vial, and blew bubbles in our faces, before twirling and yelling, 'welcome!' as she bounced away. The knights moved toward a tent wrapped in a fake dragon and a big sign, 'The Order of Fantasy'. I took an involuntary step towards them. They were my people. They wouldn't just know Daenerys and Frodo – they'd totally be besties with Kip, Celena, and Rand too.

I couldn't, though. They'd probably read way more than me and had a bazillion inside jokes I'd never catch up on. I'd end up feeling like an idiot, the way I did ninety-nine per cent of the time. Or they'd be awesome and I'd want to hang out with them all the time and I wouldn't be able to get the close-to-perfect marks I needed to transfer to med. I turned my back on the stall. I didn't enter races I couldn't win.

'That's where my bros are at!'

I jumped at Mitra's shout, as she spotted a tent covered in posters of *Top Gear* and *The Fast and the Furious*.

'Kaz!' Mitra grabbed the hand of the guy behind the stall and pulled him forward like she wanted to arm-wrestle him. 'Tara, Kaz is a fellow grease monkey at Amoo Ali's shop.'

Kaz nodded and threw me a casual, 'salam', sunlight glinting on the diamond in his ear. Paired with his tiny ponytail and cropped beard, it gave him a pirate vibe. I wondered if Kaz was his real name, or one he'd taken on because it was supposedly easier to say.

I tuned out their car talk and glanced around. Four guys were wandering through the tents with a quiet confidence and careless cool that made it hard not to notice them. Two of them were blonde, wearing pastel polo shirts and khaki shorts.

Another wore big black-rimmed glasses and a collared blue plaid shirt with denim shorts. And then there was *him*.

You know the type. A jawline they can trace back generations, a swagger you just know will be dressed in a thousand-dollar suit in a few years. He was strolling around the tents like he was some kind of prince, draped in a grey T-shirt and denim shorts, sunnies pushed on top of his dark curls. A brown leather surfer's bracelet on his wrist. He waved as he went, stopped by each stall to chat. I watched people beam after him as he left, like he'd managed to glamour them into thinking he was bestowed on them by the heavens. He oozed that classic private-school alpha vibe – the kind of guy who always knows what to say, which parties to go to, how to wear white shoes.

Sure, he was hot – had a bit of a Peter Kavinsky thing going on – but he would have been much more so if he wasn't so damn aware of his charm. He turned, caught my gaze and winked. Did he expect me to blush, giggle and congratulate myself on that little slip of attention? No way. I held his gaze and did the only thing I could think of that would show him how little I was impressed. I yawned and turned back to Kaz and Mitra.

'Tossers,' Kaz spat.

'Those dudes?' Mitra nodded in their direction. 'What's their deal?'

'Rich brats who pay a fortune to live on campus and make arses of themselves. Last year one of them decided to go for a joyride in the vice-chancellor's BMW and everyone blamed us for it.' Kaz flexed his shoulders and cranked his neck to the left. 'Fuck 'em – when are you heading down for the show?' He looked from Mitra's blank face to mine. 'Wait, don't tell me you don't have tickets.' He pointed to the posters behind him: three dudes with glazed-out eyes and headphones wrapped around their necks, frozen in a dance behind mixing tables.

'The Heat are playing?' Mitra had turned and was leaning so far into the stall that her nose was practically touching the poster. 'I was listening to them on the way over.' She stared up at him with wide eyes. 'No way!' She buried her face in her hands and shook her head. 'I'd give a kidney to see them.'

I deserved a medal for not bringing up the value of pre-reading schedules.

Kaz looked left and right, then wrapped an arm around Mitra's shoulders, pulling her close. 'You didn't hear it from me, but there are ten tickets at the door. First come, first served. I walked past before and there were already a few people lining up.'

Mitra planted her hands on her hips, 'Which way?'

'I'll meet you after, I'm going to the Med Sciences welcome lecture!' I yelled at Mitra's retreating back. I couldn't think of anything worse than paying money to have someone drill techno beats into my skull. Mitra threw up her hands and yelled something indecipherable. I chuckled. There was no way she wasn't going to end up in the front row.

Kaz pointed me in the direction of Eastern Avenue and I wandered through the crowd, watching people dancing, drinking and daydreaming. I was totally focused on them and not at all on the jerk who had winked at me. Really. I bet he was the type of guy who thought handing a girl a condom was romantic. Then all I could do was picture him shirtless on a bed, with tousled hair and that insufferable smirk. I took a swig from my water bottle.

The cascading steel facade of the auditorium caught the

morning sun and shimmered like a waterfall. I shrugged off my bag and rolled my aching shoulder. It was already a hot day, and the sun bouncing off the concrete buildings and floor made me feel like I was roasting in a slow cooker. Between the warm day and impure thoughts, I was a blotchy, sweaty mess.

The air conditioner hit me with gale-force speeds as I walked in, and I sighed happily. I pulled my arms as close to my body as possible and dashed into one of the middle rows, two seats down from a blonde in a white floral dress that I could swear I'd seen on a celebrity's Instagram. Her perfectly manicured fingers typed away at a laptop. She looked like she could school Kate Middleton in etiquette. She looked up, scrunched her face and shifted away from me in her seat.

Shame shivered down my spine and I pulled my arms closer to my sides. Of course, now that I was feeling self-conscious about sweating, my body decided to accelerate the whole process. I rummaged through my bag, hoping there were tissues I could shove under my arms. My phone beeped and the princess next to me glared again. I switched the phone to silent and read Mitra's text.

Emergency. Need my wallet. Stat.

I'm at Eastern Avenue auditorium. Come grab it. I hit reply and went to put my phone away, but it vibrated in my hand.

Can't. Scored the last ticket but will lose it if I leave. Need ID to get in.

I read the text again, swore, and checked the clock. The lecture was starting in two minutes, and the auditorium was packed, with a few people already struggling to find seats. There was no way I could find Mitra and get back without missing some of the session. I ran a finger over the mockingjay symbol on my phone cover. If my fantasy heroes had taught me anything, it's that you don't let your friends down. Besides, helping Mitra wouldn't make me miss the whole thing – ten minutes, tops.

I pulled my bag open, grabbed my wallet and Mitra's, and jumped up as my phone vibrated with a call from Mum. I gazed back at my bag, but someone made a beeline for my chair, so I decided to leave it to save my seat.

'Allo? *Khoobam, mitoonam behet badan zang bezanam?*' I explained that everything was okay and I'd call her back, then I hung up and started running up the stairs. I stopped and threw an anxious look at my bag. The princess stared back at me, her eyes wide. I threw her a greasy and shook my head. Mitra needed me. No one was going to steal a bunch of course notes, and I'd be back in a few minutes. What was the worst that could happen?

Chapter 2

On my way. Where are you?

True to form, Mitra didn't reply straight away. Instead of wasting time blindly looking, I decided to go back to Kaz's tent for directions. Trouble was, all the tents looked the same and most people I asked had never heard of the auto club, or were too tipsy to be helpful. I got close to the tent at the same time as Mitra texted back – *Manning*.

I stopped at a girl with a lip piercing and bright purple hair that jutted up in a weird kind of mohawk pixie-cut. Perched on an awning smoking a ciggie, she had a general *I don't give a damn* vibe.

'Sorry, could you point me to, um, Manning?'

She smooshed her ciggie on the ledge and gave me the once-over.

'I charge a five-dollar finder's fee for first-timers.' I opened my wallet, praying I had a fiver in there. 'Put your money away – I was taking the piss.' My already flushed cheeks hit peak red. 'Turn left, then go straight down, it's the one blastin' music.' I raced off as she finished her sentence, yelling 'thank you!' behind me.

After about five minutes, I realised I was running away from the music, not towards it. I swore, doubled back and ignored my vibrating phone. Mum would have to wait. This was the problem with a campus so big it had its own postcode. It had four or five ovals, two bars and a bunch of coffee stalls, cafeterias and curving roads. I'd thought all this was awesome – until I dashed through a tunnel and hit a dead end. I yelled out in frustration, darted back, ran through another tunnel covered in graffiti. Hot and cranky, I swore I would never try to take a short cut on this maze of a campus again.

Music pulsed and light shone at the end of this second tunnel, where a long queue of tattoo-covered, singlet-wearing, hyped-up revheads was a clear sign that I was in the right place. Victory!

As I turned the corner to get to the front of the line, yells of, *Let us in!* and, *What's going on?* multiplied. I looked around for Mitra as the crowd morphed from bored to angry. Cops appeared at the top of the steps and began nudging the crowd further and further away from the doors. My heart pounded as I edged back. I took out my phone. It was half-past and I had four missed calls from Mitra. I hit callback as I glanced up and down, trying to figure out the quickest way to get back to my lecture.

'Tara!' Mitra grabbed my arm and pulled me back toward her. 'They're not letting people in. Something about a bomb threat.'

'Shouldn't we be evacuating then?'

'They would have kicked us out already if it was a real worry,' Mitra said. 'Where's your stuff?'

'I left it . . .' My stomach sank. No. I was being paranoid. People must leave their bags in classes all the time.

'Alright.' Mitra ran a hand through her hair and shifted her weight from one foot to the other. 'Let's go grab it.' She raised a finger to stop my objection. 'I'll figure it out. Let's go get your bag first.'

The two of us ran down Manning Road and turned towards Eastern Avenue. The students from the auditorium had spilled onto the footpath like cereal on a counter. Cops were lined up around the entrance and two of them headed out of the building with German Shepherds.

Oh God. Oh God. *Oh God.*

My heart pounded against my chest, like someone was slamming a basketball against my ribcage over and over. I was already hot before. Now I had to bend over and put my hands on my knees to catch my breath. I straightened out and rubbed the sweat off my forehead as we moved closer.

A cop wearing thick leather gloves walked out of the lecture theatre, holding a package as far as possible from his body. I leaned forward at the flash of purple and my breath caught. There, wrapped in plastic, was my backpack. He got into a cop car and drove away.

'Shit.' Mitra dipped her face into her hands and inhaled loudly.

I almost didn't hear her. I was staring at the princess I had been sitting next to, who was perched on a ledge, sobbing into some guy's shoulder. One policeman huddled next to her while another stood taking notes. She spotted me, pointed and convulsed into more tears. The cop who had been taking notes closed his pad and strolled toward us.

Mitra grabbed my arm, holding me steady. 'Chill. You haven't done nothing – ' she squared her shoulders and pushed out her chin ' – and I ain't going nowhere.'

A brunette turned, looked me up and down, then shivered as if she was cold. She took a few steps forward, hesitated, then stepped away from us. I glanced to my left. A guy in black square-framed glasses nodded towards me, then whispered something to the dude next to him. I looked around and realised there was a ring of empty space between Mitra and me, and everyone else on the footpath. I took a deep breath in. I felt like I was thirteen again, that time a guy shouted 'Go back to where you came from!' on the street. Breathed out. Was back in Year 11, walking around the playground, overhearing, 'Look it's the winner of Jihadi Top Model . . . What? I hear it's like, totally explosive.' Breathed in. I was okay. Mitra was here. Breathed out. They couldn't hurt me. Breathed in. Could they?

'Tara Lutkari?' The squat cop rolled back on his heels and mangled my name.

'Yes.' I mouthed the word more than spoke it. It wasn't surprising that he knew my name: I had engraved it in three different places on my bag. I didn't correct his pronunciation, though. *Loof-curry*, he had said. In high school, I had always sounded out my name – *Loot-carry* – and told people to remember it by imagining I was a bandit on the run. That didn't seem funny now.

'Should we be calling a lawyer?' Mitra asked.

He ignored Mitra and tipped his head toward me. 'Your bag may have been damaged in the search.'

'Why were you searching her bag in the first place?' Mitra leaned forward and sneered.

'We were notified that the bag was abandoned and, given recent events, the student who notified us was – ' he glanced at me, then Mitra and back again, ' – concerned.'

I tasted bile in my mouth, swallowed it down and looked at the pavement. 'Can I have it – I mean my bag – back now, please?'

The officer took the pad from his pocket, flipped it open and jotted something down. 'Before we get to that, do you mind telling me why you left your bag in the auditorium and ran out crying, *Allah*?'

My body jerked at the word in his mouth. 'What?'

'We were informed that you grabbed two wallets from your bag – ' he leaned slightly forward, narrowing his eyes ' – and answered a phone call where you said *"Allah"* and spoke in Arabic.'

'Farsi,' Mitra spat, fists clenched. I dug my fingers into her arm.

'Excuse me,' the officer replied. It wasn't a question.

'She doesn't speak Arabic.' It turned out I couldn't arm-squeeze Mitra out of being Mitra.

'I was running out to give my friend her wallet.' I nodded towards Mitra, took a breath and tried to steady my hands. 'The call was from my mum. I answer my phone in the French style with an *'allo*.' My voice involuntarily pitched up as I uttered the French word. They had done this because I had spoken French? I chuckled and then swallowed the inappropriate laughter. Mitra was right. This wasn't about what language I spoke, or if I'd said *Allah*. It didn't matter what I wore or how I acted. The princess had taken one look at me, and whatever she imagined was worth more than my dignity. It was bad enough to make people think I could be a killer and real enough to bring in the cops.

'I see.' The officer jotted down a few more notes and flipped his notebook shut. 'The search of your bag didn't find anything untoward. You can pick it up at Newtown Station this afternoon. You'll need ID.' He adjusted his belt and scanned our surroundings before glancing back at me. 'The misunderstanding is unfortunate, but, given the incident at Central, we have to take all potential threats seriously.'

'Misunderstanding? I can think of another word for it.' Mitra was leaning forward, fists clenched at her hips.

The officer leaned back, his hand moving above the radio on his belt. The cops behind him noticed the shift and started closing in on us. I pushed Mitra behind me.

'So I just need to get my bag at the station?' He nodded at my question and I let out the breath I was holding, doing my best to keep calm as the other cops drew in closer. 'Anything else, officer?'

He shook his head. 'No. Good day.' He nodded before turning and swaggering away. He waved at his colleagues, who nodded back and dispersed. He walked past the princess and tilted his head towards her.

I wrapped my arms around myself and glanced around. A blonde with a high ponytail pointed at me before shaking her head and whispering to the person next to her. An older woman, her glasses hanging from a chain around her neck, smiled reassuringly. A dude in a polo shirt sneered at me. Another guy caught my eye and mouthed, *I'm sorry.* They all gawked, like we were rare zoo animals they didn't know how to approach.

'Let's get out of here.' My stomach dipped like I was dropping on a rollercoaster.

Mitra grabbed my upper arm and marched us down the road. I could feel anger radiating from her like a hot oven.

I cracked my knuckles one by one, enjoying the discomfort

and the *thwack, thwack, thwack* that seemed to voice it. His words – *we have to take all potential threats seriously* – played on a loop through my head.

Chapter 3

Mitra snorted, an angry red splotch spreading across her neck. 'Unbelievable,' she muttered, shaking her head.

My thoughts tangled, like they were tumbling in a dryer. Stopping at a coffee stall, I grabbed an iced tea and a muffin, then collapsed into the white patio chairs.

Mitra sat next to me. At first she leaned towards me, elbows on her knees, hands clutching her head. Then she unfurled, leaning back in her chair, her fingers at her lips like she was holding a cigarette. 'What are we even doing here? Why aren't we figuring out where to file a complaint?'

I took a sip of my tea, enjoying the cool liquid running down my throat. My whole body ached, as if I'd just done a super tough workout. But I was okay, wasn't I? I'd had cars pull over and people yell at me over the last few years. Someone had even scrawled that I was a terrorist slut on the bathroom walls of our old school. This wasn't any different, I told myself, willing it to be true.

Besides, the princess had been in tears. She was probably embarrassed at having called the police over nothing. As far as mistakes go, this wasn't a small one, but six years at an all-girls' school had taught me that girls like the princess didn't apologise if you pushed them into a corner. They lashed out again – and harder. I didn't need to do anything because the princess had probably already figured out she was wrong. It was fine. Not a big deal. I just needed to dust myself off and ignore it like I did every other time this kind of thing happened.

Mitra leaned forward and her voice dropped to a whisper. 'You are filing a complaint, right?'

'I'm finishing my tea,' I said, taking another sip and leaning back in my chair.

'But . . .'

I raised my finger, 'I'm not going after some girl who clearly has issues, Mitra.'

Mitra quietened down after that, but you could see the words she wasn't saying whirling within her. She tapped her foot against the table, drummed her fingers on her chair and shook her head like she was having an argument inside it.

I finished the tea, set it down and went to grab my bag, wincing when it wasn't there. 'Alright then.'

'You know, I could come with, if you were thinking about going for a walk in Newtown . . .'

'Okay.'

As we walked down King Street, there was a constant hum of traffic. The main strip of Newtown has a bazaar feel to it. Hundreds of small, brightly coloured shops line the street, posters taped to the windows advertising causes or gigs. The whole suburb is basically flypaper for hippies, hipsters and has-beens. I love it for its books, beatnik fashion and beef pad thai.

I slowed down, pretending I was looking at the shops we were passing. I'd never been inside a police station before and had no idea what to expect. What if this all somehow ended up on a police record and stopped me from getting into med? I grabbed my phone from my pocket, letting my thumb hover over the call button as I wondered if I should call Mum to come and be my lawyer.

I took a deep breath, then another. Then jammed my phone back into my pocket. I was totally overreacting. The knots in my stomach didn't untangle, though.

We turned into the street where the police station was. This was going to be fine: a few signatures on a line and they'd hand back my bag. It would be like picking up a lost wallet. We walked in and were assaulted by fluorescent light. A short hallway was lined with plastic orange chairs. Further out was an open-plan office, where I could see cops typing away in cubicles brimming with manila folders and mugs. The woman behind the reception desk had straw-coloured hair, a pressed police uniform and a tuckshop-mum vibe. 'How can I help?' she said, waving me forward.

'I'm Tara – '

'Oh, of course, the constable told me what happened. Terrible really, hope you haven't been too inconvenienced.' The phone rang. She held up an index finger at me, answered the phone, then continued. 'Do you have some ID on you?'

I took out my driver's license and handed it over. She looked at the photo, scanned it into the machine, then looked back at me. 'Give me a sec, okay love?' she said, disappearing into the back room.

'Thanks.' Behind me, Mitra was tapping her foot loudly on the chequerboard tiles. I turned and scowled at her.

The policewoman came back with my backpack in a clear plastic bag. It wasn't a big deal, but that morning my bag had been Instagrammable. I'd fitted all the books, pens, maps and bits and bobs carefully in compartments, so that the colours were coordinated. It would have made Marie Kondo proud. Now, in the officer's hands, the backpack was scuffed and it looked like everything in it had been jumbled up.

'Alright, just need your signature now, Ms Lutkari, and you can be on your way.'

I wasn't sure what was more unnerving – that she knew my name, or that she pronounced it correctly. She typed for a while and then the printer next to her started humming. She produced a wooden clipboard with a pen tied to the edge, inserted the paper from the printer, and handed it to me.

It was a receipt, with the date, a description of my bag and a place for me and an officer to sign to confirm they'd handed it over. I signed my name and handed back the clipboard in exchange for my bag.

'Have a good day!' She sipped her coffee and resumed typing. The chirpiness in her voice made me clench my jaw. I imagined what it would feel like to swear at her, to yell and push all her perfectly filed folders over.

'Whatever,' Mitra grumbled, shoving her hands in her pockets and marching outside. I followed her silently, thankful she'd saved me from having to fake being okay.

'Let's grab a hot chocolate on the way back to Dee,' she said.

'With extra whipped cream,' I said, gulping in the fresh air. I was so grateful she hadn't asked how I was, I would have fallen apart if she had.

We walked into the first coffee shop we saw. 'I'll order,' Mitra said, pulling out a chair. 'Sit. You look like you're going to pass out.'

All my energy had been wrung from me so I sank into the

chair and rubbed my eyes. I waited for Mitra to come back before I headed to the bathroom to try to wash off the shame of the day.

Thank god no one else was in there. I locked the door and leaned back on it, trembling.

The afternoon kept playing over and over again in my mind. The princess had thought I was capable of hurting hundreds of people. The nausea was too strong to push away this time.

I leaned over the sink and dry heaved.

Tears spilled over my cheeks as I clutched the sink, taking a moment to steady myself. How the hell was I meant to walk back out there, face them all? Was I meant to say, *I know you thought I was a mass murderer, but no big deal, want to share notes*?

I undid the safety pins that held up my hijab, turned on the tap and splashed cold water against my flushed cheeks. The static created flyways all around my face. I pulled out the elastic holding my ponytail and let my black hair fall down. I pulled the hijab off my shoulders and crumpled it in my fist like a rag.

I held it over the bin, pursing my lips. I moved forward. All I had to do was let go. Just like that, I could be like everyone else. Better yet, I could be someone new, someone who they wouldn't think of as *bomb threat girl*.

My hand started shaking. A part of me was screaming, *Drop it, drop it!*

I stepped back and leaned against the cold tiles, shaking my head, thinking of Maman Noosheen, of how she'd taught me to pray. No. I wasn't going to let the princess or anyone else define who I was or what I could believe. This was a test, and though there was no wizard to grant me an amulet for valour, I couldn't fail.

I uncurled the scarf and flapped it like a rug, trying to get the wrinkles out. Wearing the hijab felt like a superpower, giving me X-ray goggles to see into people's souls. I could glimpse people's real selves when they saw me, before social norms closed over their faces, transforming panic into polite smiles, or fear into angry sneers. I wasn't going to give up my superpower – no way.

Pulling the scarf over my head, I tucked my hair into its folds and dried my hands and face. For better or worse, this was part of me. Realising that made it easier.

Two giant iced chocolates sat in front of Mitra. She caught my eye and waved me over.

'I thought they were meant to be hot?' I asked.

She shrugged. 'It's a gazillion degrees. It's so hot, even you're melting. Also, that dip into your whipped cream was totally not my fault.' She said it with a smile that made it abundantly clear that she had in fact stolen a bite.

I had a superpower and a best friend – heroes had conquered galaxies with less.

Chapter 4

'You want me to come in and distract your mum?' Mitra asked, tapping her fingers on the steering wheel. Her body seemed to be moving to music only she could hear. I loved that about her.

I stared out of the car window for a moment. No, it wouldn't work. I shook my head and pushed open the car door. 'Mitra – '

'Don't you dare get all mushy on me.'

I gave her an awkward wave and watched her drive off. I closed my eyes and listened to the faint sound of the ocean, the waves pounding the sand at Bondi Beach, inhaling the salt air. I wanted to run down the block, to Maman Noosheen's house. To run past the brick fence, to see her reading through the stained-glass windows. I wanted to open the doors and be greeted by turquoise walls, to walk on her soft Persian rugs, for her to take me into her courtyard, sit me down on one of the old carpet-covered couches next to the fountain and let me cry on her lap.

Instead, I turned to face our house, its stucco painted the blue that newborn boys are blanketed in, and marched to the door.

My stomach rumbled as I opened the door to the smell of fried onions, garlic and parsley. I could almost taste the Ghormeh

Sabzi, the traditional Iranian stew that Maman Noosheen used to make on special occasions. Mum must have grabbed some from an Iranian restaurant. She had remembered. My chest ached. If only she knew just how 'special' today had ended up being. I closed the door, threw my bag into my room and pulled off my hijab, letting it drape over my shoulders like a scarf.

'*Chetor bood*?' ('How was it?') Mum asked, her voice echoing down the hall.

'Tiring.' I stood by the front door and threw my backpack onto my bed, then moved down the hallway, past the spare room and Mum's bedroom until I reached the living area. Mum was in the kitchen, wrapped in an ivory robe, hair up in a messy bun, looking past the lounge area and dining table to the garden, behind generous French doors.

'*Chaie?*' (Tea?) she asked, turning to look at me. I nodded and sat on one of the barstools tucked against the kitchen island as she put on the kettle. My great grandmother's ruby porcelain tea set was laid out on the counter. A miniature portrait of a mustachioed man etched on the side of the teapot gazed out with a disappointed sneer. I frowned back.

Mum had bought this place when I started high school. Before that, we'd lived with Maman Noosheen, since . . . well, since I was born. There, every room had been a different color. Red, blue and bright yellow. And the whole house – from the pillows printed with whirling dervishes to the swirling lines and angels of Mahmoud Farshchian hanging on the walls – felt like an ode to Iran.

Mum hadn't even decorated with a Persian rug, but a big, shaggy grey one. Our walls were eggshell, our kitchen was white, our accents were grey and the furniture was reclaimed wood with textured cream covers. It was like after living in colour her whole life, she'd gotten nostalgic for black-and-white movies. The brightly painted tea set was the only thing that hinted at Iran.

Mum stood next to the kettle, scrolling her phone. I sighed, but she didn't look up. I stretched, eyes landing on the giant reproduction of Sidney Nolan's *Ned Kelly* on the wall above a cream couch. No, nothing Iranian, just Australian paintings and abstract prints. Even here, Mum had to scream, *I belong!*

Under the painting was the 'slosh' table, where we dumped mail and the occasional car key, always cleared out before we went to bed. I noticed a cardboard box tucked under a bunch of files.

'My DNA pendant is here?' I ran over to the box as the kettle started to sing. I had ordered it months ago. *Khoda ra shokr.* (Thank God.) Something was going right today.

'Wait – ' I looked up. Mum had dashed out of the kitchen, her hand outstretched for me to stop. I plopped the files on the floor and grabbed the box, jiggling it for comic effect.

Then I saw the label. It wasn't from Etsy. The postage mark read *West Hollywood.* I let it thud back to the floor. It was from Dad. Apparently, the universe had decided to go all drill sergeant on me.

'Why don't you open it after dinner?'

I ignored Mum, dug my nails into the edge and yanked. A layer of the cardboard ripped through the stamp. I smiled and wrenched harder, until the box bled packing peanuts. I fished out a black box tied with white ribbon and ran my fingers over the embossed Chanel logo.

'Tara, *azizam* . . .' (Dearest.) Mum's voice softened. She was next to me now, her hand on my shoulder. I leaned into her warmth and flicked the black box open. A blush leather wallet with gold trim was perched next to a card that screamed, *Congratulations!* I swiped the card open without picking it up. A Barbie pink Post-it fell out. *For your girl's first day of college. Don't forget to write a note. The courier will pick up at 3. XOX*

I sniggered and shook my head as I read the note from his secretary. The card underneath was blank. I thought about photographing it all and tweeting it to him with thanks. The idea of the PR team in his swanky plastic-surgery practice seeing it and losing their minds made me smile. I could make it into an Instagram series: Dad's empty seat at graduation, Dad's unfilled-out custody papers, Dad's blank congratulations note.

Mum humphed as she read the note over my shoulder, grabbed it from my hands, then crumpled it in her own. 'Unbelievable,' she said, storming to the counter and grabbing her phone.

'Mum, it's like 1 am there.'

But she was already calling, her back to me, shoulders tense. 'Hadi, Hadi – *Vagheanne?*' What I loved about Farsi was the way it caught the essence of words – the guttural *vagheanne* had so much more bite than the English, *really*.

She kept yelling in Farsi, stormed into her room and slammed the door shut. Like I'd never heard her argue with Dad before. I stretched my neck to the left and right, turned off the stove, grabbed my bag and strolled to my room.

I turned on the twinkle lights that framed the ceiling, and always made me feel like I had a personal collection of stars. When Mum let me decorate my room, she'd expected me to prance around pretentious stores with her. Instead, I'd found random pieces on the street or on Gumtree (the bed we bought at Myer – she drew the line there), and Mitra and I had painted everything over a weekend. We'd sanded down my wooden headboard and painted it bright yellow, my desk was hot pink. My bookshelves were ocean blue and, on top, a sleeping silver dragon guarded my books and my rock and shell collection. The floorboards were covered in a massive rug spotted with rainbow polka dots.

Rumi, my life-sized plastic skeleton, stood next to my window seat. I walked over, straightened his Ravenclaw scarf and held his bony hand. 'At least I can count on you, old friend.' Rumi's skull was at a bit of an angle, his jaw slightly unhinged, so it was possible to imagine he was smiling back at me.

I loved my room, maybe even loved it a little more because Mum would scrunch her nose and complain that all the clashing colors gave her a headache. It felt homey and safe. But tonight, it also made me ache for Maman Noosheen. You hear people joke about grandparents dying, like it's no big deal. I don't think you're meant to pine for them a year after they're gone.

I closed my eyes. I didn't know it was possible to miss someone as much as I missed her. If she'd still been here, I could have walked to her place in five minutes flat. She would have curled up next to me and fed me cake yazdi and tea while I told her what had happened. She would have figured out how to make me laugh about it, then put me to work chopping something.

'Hey – ' I looked up and Mum had snuggled up next to me. 'I'm sorry he . . .'

I sniffled. 'It's not that. I just . . .' I let her wipe a tear that had leaked out onto my cheek. '. . . I've just been thinking about Maman Noosheen today.' It was true. Not the whole truth, but still.

'Me too,' she whispered. She sighed and I looked up at her.

She was looking at a small box in her hands. 'I found this in her bedside drawer. I'm sure she wanted you to have it.' She took my hand and put a small gold gift box in my palm.

The box smelled like Maman Noosheen's jasmine perfume. I held it up to the light, looking for her fingerprints so I could cover them with my own and pretend, just for a moment, that she was holding my hand. But I couldn't see any.

I nudged the box open and pulled out a string of amber prayer beads – her tasbeeh. It was like pulling out my childhood. Maman Noosheen moving each bead between her thumb and index finger. Dangling the beads from one hand as she picked me up and dropped me off at school, her black hair in its signature bob, her eyes rimmed with heavy eyeliner. She'd fervently press the beads through her fingers if I was sick, if she was worried, if I had a test or if she had a house showing.

I clutched the tasbeeh to my chest and let the memories flicker like a slideshow. I let Mum hold me, knew she was remembering too. I didn't have a prayer, so instead I pulled at the beads and asked for the one thing I knew I couldn't have. *Come back, come back, come back.*

I strolled down Eastern Avenue, shoulders back, head high.

I totally had this. Welcome Week was a week ago. I'd done all my assigned readings for the lectures, and so far in both my morning classes, no one had mentioned the incident or even looked at me funny. Wins all round.

Then my breath caught at a flash of blonde hair. Was that her? I twisted like a pretzel to see.

The girl darted out from behind the crowd, threw me a

confused glance and whizzed past. Not her. This was silly. What were the chances that I run into the princess again on a campus of 70,000 people? Except, she had been at the Medical Sciences welcome lecture. I shivered. We'd either be in the same classes or I'd never see her again. *Ya Khoda* (dear God), *I'll do an extra set of prayers for a whole year if I never have to see her again.*

'Who pissed in your coffee?'

I turned towards Mitra's voice and smiled. 'I thought you said you wouldn't be caught dead on the arts side of campus after Welcome Week.'

'I wanted to take one class that wasn't a total sausage fest. Decided I had the best shot staying awake through one with you.'

'I haven't seen you stay awake for a whole hour of class since Year 9,' I said, pushing the heavy wooden door of the auditorium open. The chatter in the room receded into a hush as we walked in. I looked around and saw some people staring, others glancing away, pretending like they hadn't looked. Most of the people here had been in the lecture last week. I stood taller. The air was thick with judgement. I had to concentrate to breathe.

Mitra glided down the stairs and into a seat three rows from the back of the hall. She put her legs up on the chair in front of her and beckoned me over. I pulled my hijab down and scurried into the chair next to her. I scanned the room for the princess. All clear. The universe was finally smiling at me. I opened my notepad, leaned back and wrote the date in my notebook.

A *pat pat* sound echoed through the auditorium. The lecturer, a middle-aged man with the physique of a HB pencil, stood behind a wooden lectern, tapping on the microphone. Satisfied it was on, he pressed a button and the projector blasted the room in turquoise light.

A guy with a blonde ponytail and a bright red top ran onto stage, leaned over the lectern and asked a question of the lecturer, who nodded, stepped aside and made room for the guy to take the podium. 'Listen up,' he began, talking way too loudly into the mic. 'Last week there was a racist bomb threat on campus – '

I looked around. Thankfully, most people were ignoring him. Mitra was nodding vigorously. 'It's time to take a stand against racism – here, on Manus, and everywhere. Tomorrow at lunch, come to the anti-racism rally at the Quad.'

I stared at my notebook, feeling eyes on me, and dug my fingernails into my palms.

'Yes, I think the incident last week merits a mention.'

No. No. *No no no.* Not the lecturer too.

'There's a lot of people trying to convince us that people who look different mean us harm. I never thought that kind of rudimentary thinking would take hold here. Let me make this clear: this class is about curiosity, questions and challenging assumptions.'

'Woooo!'

I jumped at Mitra's support. She framed her mouth with her hands and followed her first *woo!* with a longer, louder one, then broke out into the kind of applause that dares you not to join in. A few did, but the cheering across the auditorium was patchy at best.

I shushed Mitra and chewed my nails. Goosebumps ran down my arms. I pulled down my sleeves and rubbed my arms, telling myself I was just cold from the aircon. The auditorium buzzed as the lecturer leaned back and surveyed us.

A girl at the front of the class stood up and silence fell. I recognised that self-assured posture immediately. Her blonde hair flicked back and forth as she glided from her row and stepped into the aisle. Three girls followed her, like obedient back-up dancers.

My breath hissed when she strutted past me. She didn't pause or glance in my direction. She looked like a model walking a runway: statuesque, confident and accustomed to commanding a thousand eyes.

Mitra leaned over and flipped the bird at the girl's retreating back. I grabbed her hand and pulled it down, shooting her my best *stop it* glare. The door of the auditorium creaked open and slammed closed. Chatter exploded.

The lecturer nodded.

'Time to get to work,' he said, and launched straight into the lecture. A girl in front of us turned and gave me the same look strangers would throw my way when they found out my grandmother had died.

I slammed my pen down. I wasn't going to be 'the bomb-threat girl', someone people looked at like *that*. I grabbed my bag, ran up the stairs two at a time, and pushed open the wooden double doors. They banged shut behind me. I was going to talk to the princess and fix this thing once and for all.

Chapter 5

'Hey!' Mitra called out, shoving through the closed doors behind me. I ignored her as the doors clanged shut again, and stomped towards the circle of girls in the courtyard. It was like they had a uniform: denim short shorts, sparkly flip flops and tank tops. One of the back-up dancers looked up from her phone and pointed, like I was a runaway zoo animal.

I walked up to the princess. I don't know how she made denim short shorts look regal, but she did. She wore them with an understated gold chain around her neck, drop earrings, a white tank and a super slick ponytail. She could have pulled off a tiara, too. Easily. Regina George would have been proud of the way she stared me down.

'I don't know what your deal is, but I think we both want this whole saga to just go away.' I looked her in the eye and made sure I was standing super straight. 'Here's the plan. We go to the rally together, you apologise, people won't have anything to talk about anymore, and this thing will be done.' I pretended that I didn't feel like a frumpy nana, in my long-sleeved white linen shirt and green maxidress.

The princess pursed her lips, made a *hmph* noise and went

back to scrolling on her phone. Her friends just kept gawking. Mitra fidgeted behind me. Fine. I'd tried; the rest was on her. I turned and walked away. Then she scoffed.

'You think *I* need to apologise?' she said, and I turned. She was looking at me like I had told her the sky was pink. 'Over the last week, everywhere I go people keep calling me names, yelling at me and now even a lecturer is clearly biased against me . . .' I could have sworn she teared up for a second. 'You know what? I'm not some sort of racist. I was just scared and I shouldn't have to be worried that I'm not safe all the time . . .'

'Oh, come on . . .' Mitra said. I glared at her, but she just scowled at the princess.

The princess threw her hands up, 'Yeah, I figured. You can't have a real talk about this stuff without the name-calling.' Mitra hadn't called her a name, but that didn't matter. It never did. The princess looked me over from head to toe, sneered and walked away. A minion, the only brunette in their little clique, glared at Mitra for a moment longer before scurrying after the group.

'The hell was that?' Mitra threw out her hands, her voice rising.

'Unbelievable – ' I clenched my fist and let out a frustrated shriek. 'None of this would have happened if they had just kept out of it.' I pointed towards the lecture theatre.

'You're pissed the lecturer and the activist dude said something?' Mitra shot back.

'I was *this close*,' I raised my hand and made a tiny space between my thumb and index finger, 'to this whole thing being forgotten.' I shook my head, ignoring the urge to stamp my feet.

'What, you think those girls were going to be all like, *sorry I was a knob*?' Mitra twirled her wrist and put on a terrible upper-class British accent. 'Nah man – ' she waved her hands like she was trying to stop a plane landing ' – girls like that are never wrong, they're just *scared*'. She made inverted commas with her hands. 'Since bloody Helen of Troy, scared white chicks stir up all kinds of trouble.'

I rubbed my temples. 'And shaming them helps how?'

'Look, if you want to chuck on a *Hug a Muslim* sign and get a shit-ton of YouTube views, go ahead. That girl is still gonna take one look at you and see ISIS. And don't you dare tell me you think that's okay.'

'She's just ignorant.'

'Because she wants to be. Come on, the girl can read, can think. People don't hate each other 'cause they're ignorant. Sure, you're taught that shit, but it only works if you swallow it without asking questions.'

I pressed my forehead into my palm. Mitra had a point. 'Let's get back in there. I'm not missing out on a whole class because of this nonsense.'

We walked back into class and everyone turned towards us. The lecturer even stopped mid-sentence and stared. Was he going to call me out? I sat down as quickly as I could. He just shook his head and kept going. All around me, MacBooks glowed. I stretched my fingers, grabbed a pen and started writing. There's something about putting ink to paper that helps me remember things. Every time I felt eyes on me, I focused more on the lecture – on getting everything down and writing out my questions.

It wasn't until I found myself writing, *that's all for this week*, that I realised the class was over. I looked over at Mitra.

She'd biro'ed incredibly intricate designs all over her hands.

'What have you got next?' I asked as we left the auditorium and started walking.

'I got an hour to kill before my next class.'

A guitar solo reverberated from Manning Bar. I could see a bunch of students already hanging out on the balcony, standing in the sun with schooners of what looked like beer.

'Want to check it out?' Mitra asked, cracking her neck from side to side. 'I could use a cold drink.'

I nodded. I needed to blow off steam. Stuff the princess and stuff the stupid lecturer and activist for deciding they could speak for me. Stuff them all.

We walked through the arched doors and up the sandstone steps to the top floor. The stench of dried alcohol grew with each step. My stomach lurched and I smirked. The awfulness of this place exactly suited my mood.

The *doomph doomph* music was loud enough that the boards under our feet vibrated. It was too early for anyone to be drunk, but the handful of people there were buzzed, leaning into each other, waving their arms around. Some of them were attempting to dance.

Mitra wiggled her singleted shoulders and shimmied her way in. I strolled behind her, scowling.

A few entry rooms led to the main circular space that housed the bar, stage and dance floor. Opposite the stage, glass doors opened to the balcony. A long wooden bar ran on the far end of the wall, staffed by older students, in fluorescent purple shirts, bopping their heads to the rhythm of the music as they passed out drinks.

Mitra turned toward the balcony and I tilted my head back as we walked into the sunlight. The music still pulsed outside, but the open air diffused the beats and made conversation possible.

'What's *she* doing here?'

The words hit me a minute after the sun did. They came from one of two guys lounging by the balcony, both in T-shirts and jeans. One looked like he was drinking water, the other beer.

'I mean, it's one thing when it's an infidel like you.' The guy with the water gestured to the one with the beer and they both laughed. 'But for her? Like, don't wear that shit if you're going to be in a bar.'

Were they deliberately talking loudly so I could hear them? The water guy said something in a language that sounded familiar, even though I didn't understand it. Hypocrites. Why was it fine for water guy to be here, observing but not participating, but not me? Was it because I was a woman or 'cause my hijab meant I had to play by stricter rules? I imagined going up to them, grabbing one of their drinks and chugging it in one go. Instead I caught up to Mitra – I was done with people telling me what I could and couldn't do today.

Oversized wooden picnic tables ran all along the balcony. I shoved down the impulse to flip them over, one by one. A few were full, mostly with two or three groups of friends huddled together. Mitra walked up to a table where four guys we didn't know were hanging out and casually slid in, leaving a good metre between herself and the others. Friendly, but not openly inviting conversation.

'The usual?' Mitra asked as I sat down. I shrugged like it was a silly thing to ask and she slapped the table twice, then boogied her way back inside. I watched her go, smiling. Mitra was always fidgeting, like her body was bursting to dance with music only she could hear, the grooves instinctively pouring out of her.

I pulled out my iPad and sank into a world where dragons lived and assassins roamed. I heard someone sit down on the other side of the table, but who cared when the main character had snuck into the king's bedroom to finally get the key that would unlock the prisoner who could break the curse?

'The thing I hate about those things is that you can't spy on what other people are reading.'

I looked up and it was *him*. The college snob who had wandered around Welcome Week charming the pants off everyone. As much as I hated it, when that smile was turned on me, it was hard not to smile back. But I held back.

'It's so much more fun to *imagine* what they could be reading instead,' I said, putting my device down, trying to roll the tension out of my shoulders. I caught his gaze as I stretched my arms up. His smile turned into an all-out grin, and I couldn't explain why it was so satisfying. He scooched down towards me.

'I'm Alex. Alexander, but everyone calls me Alex,' he said, offering his hand, then abruptly pulling it back and scratching the back of his neck.

Of all the things I'd imagined he'd be, *awkward* wasn't one of them. 'Tara.'

'Tara.' He repeated my name slowly, like he was testing to see how it sounded in his mouth. 'This is my mate Pete . . .' Pete waved at me halfheartedly before turning back to his conversation. 'The others are just drunks who hang out with us.' The *others*, one of whom was wearing bright red suspenders, were too busy laughing at their own shenanigans to notice the dig.

'Okay, I gotta ask.' Alex leaned towards me. 'I didn't think people like you boozed.'

'People like *me*?' I don't know if it came out that way because of how he asked the question, or because I was just pissed off about everything that had happened.

Mitra put the lemon lime and bitters in front of me. It was the perfect chameleon drink. People from high school knew I used to drink, so after I started wearing hijab and stopped drinking, I could hold it at a party and people would assume it was either a cocktail or fancy juice, allowing me to sidestep awkward questions.

Alex leaned closer, his weight on his elbows. His tongue darted out as he moistened his lips. 'You know what I meant.'

I took the lemon wedge from the lip of the glass and squeezed it into my drink. 'What? 'Cause all Muslims are identical? We're turned out by some sort of cookie-cutter?'

Mitra sat next to Alex and put an arm on his shoulder. 'Mate, don't get her started – '

'You don't respect the Quran?' Alex said, cutting Mitra off and raising a finger in objection.

' – about the Quran,' Mitra finished with a toast of her schooner.

I knew I should cut him a little slack, but I had used up my day's quota of patience for well-intentioned misconceptions. He wanted me to give him a gold star for knowing something about the Quran. Nope, no way. Besides, what was this – Everyone Gets To Be An Imam Day? 'Are you going to tell Allah on me?' My breath caught as he ran his finger over the rim of the glass, holding my gaze. I pushed on. 'Do you lecture your Jewish friends if they eat shellfish too?'

My cheeks were warm. I wasn't sure if it was because of him or the sun. I gulped at the schooner in front of me. Mitra laughed and smiled, as if to say, *that's my girl*. I wiped my mouth with my hand.

'Fair point.'

I held his gaze for a moment. At first I thought he was being sarcastic, but his smile and look were sincere.

'Thanks, I guess . . .' I glanced away and shifted in my seat. His concession made me feel more vulnerable than any snappy comeback would have. A part of me wished he'd dug in. It would have been so much more cathartic, made it so much easier to dismiss him as just another overprivileged tosser.

He pushed his beer aside, tapped a fist against his jaw and then leaned in like he was going to make a pitch.

'Who are you?' He whispered the question so softly, I almost didn't hear it. I looked up and made the mistake of catching his eyes. They were deep green, with tiny amber flecks. I wondered if they changed colour with his mood. I turned to look at his friends. They were still talking about some sport thing, but had been watching us every now and then. They weren't the same crowd I'd seen him with at Welcome Week.

I cleared my throat and took another sip of my drink. I was cranky, I wanted to put this dude in his place, and was tired enough that my better judgment had clocked off for the day. So I let him have it.

'Let me guess who *you* are. Given the tan, you probably live close to a beach . . . eastern suburbs probably, so I'm guessing Scots.' His smile didn't falter or change. I paused and put a hand to my lips for dramatic effect, before nodding 'The Bonds T-shirt means your mum still buys your clothes . . .' That got a chuckle out of him. I glanced at his hand, giving him my best *seriously* look when I noticed that brown leather bracelet again. I pointed to it. 'Surfer, but probably not very good.' I heard a few chuckles around me and noticed that his friends had started to tune in to our little game. Okay, I was having fun now. I took another sip of my drink, pursing my lips as I sneaked a glance at the readings in his bag '. . . Philosophy major?'

He held up his hand and pointed to the bracelet. 'Present from my sister, so ouch, and also – swimmer.' He smiled, eyes twinkling. 'Way better than you think.' He held my gaze long enough that I had to look away. When I looked back, he took a sip of his beer and leaned back, taking his elbows off the table.

'Sydney Boys, thank you very much.' A selective public school. I couldn't focus on that because I was distracted by his eyes. Tyra Banks would have been proud of his smizing skills – I could have sworn they were a slightly lighter shade of green than they had been a moment ago. 'Mum wouldn't have dreamed of sending me to a private school.' The chuckles around us turned into laughs. I turned to Mitra, who raised her eyebrows at me like I was missing an obvious punchline.

'But you're in college.'

He tilted his head and I could tell he was wondering how I knew he was part of the elite campus dorms. He frowned, ran a finger over the rim of his beer, but didn't take the bait. I wished I hadn't let what Kaz told me during Welcome Week slip so easily. Would he put together that I had remembered him? Of course he would. I tapped my fingers on the table, irritated.

'Dad's a college alumni. He also picks out my clothes, thinks Mum's taste is godawful.' There was something about the way he was smiling now that made my stomach flutter. It felt like he was enjoying himself too, in a way that he relished. I didn't know why, but I liked that I'd made him smile like that.

'Philosophy major?'

'You got me there.' He rubbed his thumb against the stubble on his jawline.

'I need to drag my arse back to the other side of campus. You staying put?' Mitra was already standing up.

'Nah, I have to hit the library.' I grabbed my bag and stood to join her. For a moment, I thought I saw disappointment flash on Alex's face. 'It was lovely meeting you . . . Alex.'

He nodded and flicked his wrist in what seemed like a goodbye wave, before scooching down to rejoin the conversation with his friends. I looked at him for a second more before I turned and walked out with Mitra.

'So Alex, 'ey?'

'What?' I said. In her head, we were probably a heartbeat away from throwing off our clothes and getting it on right there on the balcony.

She threw her head back and laughed. 'That's hilarious.'

Okay, so maybe something else was going on. 'What?' I said, more forcefully this time.

'You are the only woman alive who would have the balls to just straight-up flirt with Alex Jackson and have no idea you were doing it.'

'Alex Jackson?' That name sounded familiar.

'Oh come on, really? As in, son of Rita and Doug.'

Oh God! Rita Jackson was the Premier of New South Wales and Doug Jackson was the only person who did more shows across more mediums than Hamish & Andy. The whole conversation came back and I winced. No wonder everyone had been laughing when I talked about his mum picking out his clothes. 'Why didn't you say anything, or throw a drink at me to get me to shut up?'

'You kidding me? He was totally into it.'

I gave Mitra a friendly shove and tried to push away the conversation with him that was now playing on a loop in my head. Then my phone vibrated and I glanced at the message from an unknown number.

Insert dazzling smart message here. Also, coffee?

Mitra read the text over my shoulder and smiled. 'Given all the googly eyes, I decided to slip him your number.'

I groaned, 'Mitra!' As I did, I turned and realised that he was leaning over the balcony, watching. He caught my eye and waved. I wanted to die. Mitra gave him a thumbs up and pulled me along.

'I'm not interested.' I said, pulling away from her the minute we were out of eyesight.

'Oh, come on, you're not still hung up on Ryan? What was that, like Year 10?'

'No, I'm hung up on getting into med.' He was like Ryan: that same confidence, that charm that made everyone fall half in love with him. Besides, hadn't he just laughed at me? Wasn't it practically guaranteed that if I let him, he'd break my heart the way Ryan had?

Besides, I didn't want some yuppie with famous parents who lived in fancy private dorms and had it made. I was after a brooding type: someone who asked questions, went on adventures, risked everything to make a difference. Someone who wouldn't freak out camping in the middle of nowhere on a med trip to help vaccinate kids against polio. Preferably, he'd be tall, dark and be totally down to race around the world with me. Alright, so Alex might have the tall, dark thing down . . . but still. The most important thing about my ideal man was that he wouldn't appear until I had transferred into med.

I re-read Alex's message and ignored it. It was better than sending him some silly response, I figured. Besides, he'd probably get distracted in five minutes and wouldn't remember me anyway. Someone like him probably had a whole harem of girls he was flirting with.

'Just to be clear, I've sworn off boys this year,' I said.

Mitra smirked and started making *bawk bawk* noises and flapping her arms like a chicken at me before bouncing off to class. I went to the library. Mitra was right – I was scared. I wasn't going to risk losing study time or worse, losing myself because of some guy. I'd done that with Ryan.

I still couldn't think of the night before the Year 10 formal without cringing. I'd spent forever picking out the perfect dress. I'd gotten it, too: Margery Tyrell inspired, with a gold bodice that cinched at the waist then puffed out into a baby blue tulle skirt that came to my knees. I even liked how *I* looked in it. I was twirling in it the night before the formal. I mean, that had lasted all of two minutes until I realised people, you know, *danced* at formals, and started panic-YouTubing dance tutorials. Because even though I loved to dance, I didn't do it in public. Certainly not in front of a guy I liked. I didn't want to do it wrong. So, I was sitting in my gorgeous dress, freaking out, when he texted.

Hey, I know this is the worst.

Three dots glowed under the message, so I waited. The next one came in a second later.

Fi wants to get back together.

The three dots were there again, but I didn't need to know anymore. I threw my phone on the bed and yanked off the dress, kicking it away. Pulled on my polka dot PJs and an old T-shirt, then shoved the dress back into its box and stuffed it under a bunch of Mum's clothes in the closet next door.

I rolled my shoulders, but couldn't stop all the memories of Ryan rolling through my head like a reel in reverse. All the times he'd kissed me and then reminded me how we were just 'casual', the clothes I'd stopped wearing because he didn't seem to like them, the people who suddenly wanted to be my friends, joking around about how Ryan and I were 'friends with benefits', because it was so impossible that we could be anything else. I'd smiled through it, joked about it, because I hadn't thought I was allowed to really want more.

The way they joked about my frizzy hair, nicknamed me *poodle*, and I'd laughed along like I was totally cool with it. That time I'd drunk beer with him and his crew, because like, it was *no big deal*, right? I'd even cut school a bunch for him, and when I landed in Principal Cartwright's office, she was so surprised that she asked if I was there to give her a message.

I'd pulled a total Bella Swan after he dumped me. Just kind of disconnected: switched off at school, daydreamed at home. That time I'd walked to school, saw Fi and Ryan hand in hand and heard one of Fi's girlfriends look at me and say, *God, she really thought Ryan* like *liked her, how embarrassing.* I broke, ran home and ended up crying on Maman Noosheen's lap.

I'd found her old prayer rug that day, and decided to give it a go. I hadn't expected it to help, to fill a gap that I'd been trying to fill with Ryan – but it had, so I held onto it, hard.

I never wanted to forget who I was, but more importantly, I never wanted to forget that I was worthwhile again.

Did I want to find love some day? Sure, but I wanted the real deal. The kind of connection that drove people to chart unknown oceans, slay dragons . . . or you know, show up with you to a formal.

I found a quiet spot and buried myself in readings, notes and drafting essays. Alex wasn't going to lose any sleep over me. Why would he, when he had plenty of other options? It's not like I was anything special. I stopped, took a breath. *To him*, I added firmly. I was special to others and I had to remember that. I was midway through reading a sentence when a message came over the loudspeakers that it was 9 pm and the library was closing.

Chapter 6

'The fridge is stocked and I left a fifty on the counter in case you want to get pizza.' Mum folded another tailored dress and placed it carefully into her suitcase, 'There's fresh sheets there, you just need to pull out the couch for Mitra.' I sat on the white sofa bed in our spare room, which was really our shared walk-in wardrobe. It had a glass chandelier, a giant full-length mirror and the walls were lined with shelves full of shoes, bags, hats, scarves and clothes that were all sorted by colour, like some kind of weird ombre painting. A big cream velvet pouffe squatted in the middle of the room.

'Are you going to crash with Jonathan?'

Mum's shoulders tensed. She didn't turn around though. She just froze for a moment before grabbing a cream silk blouse from a satin-lined clothes hanger.

'I don't crash with colleagues, Tara.'

I walked over to the bed, reached out to the pile of freshly laundered clothes she was packing and picked up a lacy black g-string with two fingers, 'So you're taking these for comfort?'

Mum inhaled loudly, snatched her underwear back, shuffled to her suitcase and threw them in. 'Get out – ' She pointed her red shellacked fingernails to the door, cheeks flushed.

'For the record, if you stopped the charade for a sec, I could tell you I think you're good together,' I said as I strolled out.

A few minutes later, Mum marched into the living room, rolling her suitcase behind her. 'I expect this house to be spotless when I get back on Tuesday. *Basheh?* [Okay?]' It wasn't really a question.

'*Basheh.*' I folded my arms and glared at her. She obviously knew I was throwing a party. Was she okay with it or being passive aggressive?

'Okay, my cab is here. *Movazeb bash,*' she said. (Take care.) Still scrolling, she wrapped her free arm around me and tapped my shoulder, never taking her eyes off her phone. I watched her walk down the hallway. There was no point stressing over Mum. I had a party to prep for.

I rolled up the fluffy white rugs and stashed them along with breakable knick-knacks in Mum's room, then tossed some old blankets over the couches. An hour later, Mitra unlocked the door and kicked it open, stumbling in with two cases of beer. 'Yo, I think we may have a few extra people coming along tonight.'

'Alright.' I pried open the cardboard and started stacking the beer cans in the fridge.

'I invited this girl, she's super cool man. Walked into our Engo lecture, threw a bunch of condoms into the crowd, told everyone *if it's not on, it's not on* and then just left.' Mitra waved her hands as she re-enacted the scene. 'It was totally rad.' Her smile threatened to split her face. 'I ran into her later and apparently she's like the president of the student union or something – anyway, she said she'd stop by with a few friends.'

'You're such a fangirl.'

Mitra blushed – actually *blushed* – and her shoulders

slumped. 'I don't know, I just don't meet that many people, let alone chicks, with balls bigger than mine, you know?' I nodded. It sounded absurd, but it made sense.

'I'm going to go get changed,' I said.

'Don't touch eyeliner without me – '

I chuckled at Mitra and motioned her to follow me to the spare room.

'God, I love this set-up,' Mitra said, running her hands along the hanging clothes. She grabbed a giant straw hat and put it on.

The next hour could have been part of a *Devil Wears Prada* montage. Mitra chucked on a bright red dress with a fake-fur coat that I called 'the yeti', which *almost* worked. I pulled on a cream silk jumpsuit that dazzled on Mum but looked way too nana on me. By the time we had half the room piled on the floor, we'd figured it out.

Mitra fished out a lavender denim jacket and hugged it, 'Leila had some serious edge back in the day.' She flipped it over a black singlet, teamed with black-and-white checked pants and a black beret.

'She still does,' I said, pulling out some ripped black skinny jeans that Mum sometimes wore if she was strolling around the market. Sure, the rips weren't gaping, and on Mum it always looked expensive, but it was still edgy. Mitra chucked me a white tunic with black polka dots that I tucked in at the front and let hang loose at the back, topped off with a black scarf.

I let Mitra draw crazy-thick eyeliner on me, but stopped her when she reached for the lipstick. The whole get-up felt like a costume since ninety per cent of the stuff in the closet was Mum's – but even in a costume, I drew a line. I looked over at the mirror. I wasn't stunning like Mum, or smoking hot like

Mitra, but maybe at the right angle, I could see how I looked *striking*, or at least memorable, with my mismatched features and bold black-and-white. Maybe that was enough.

There was a knock at the door. Mum would have had a meltdown if she saw the way I shoved silk blouses, fake fur coats and chunky jewellery into a pile on the pouffe and then shut the door on the mess before darting out to the living room. I felt bad for a second, imagining her reaction. I pushed the thought away, rolled my shoulders and did a wiggle to loosen up – after all, I was about to face a gauntlet.

I barely knew anyone at the party. Mitra had been one of those girls who got on with everyone at high school. She could flit between the in-crowd and everyone else like social distinctions were nothing. And to her, they were. She'd already made a ton of friends at uni, whereas I'd just started to work up the courage to say hello to people in tutorials. It might have been my house, but it was Mitra's party. She was the perfect host. She got people drinks, made sure they liked the music, chatted to everyone. Me? Let's just say the popcorn bowl and I were getting super well-acquainted.

Then I spotted them: Jane and Pari – Jane was still rocking a scrunchie, with the same, *I'll wear what I like no matter what you say* pride she had in high school and Pari had shown up wearing a Star Trek pin. They were deep in conversation, occasionally giggling. It was so weird seeing the two of them at a party and not in our high-school library – but since the universe had thrown me a life raft, I wasn't about to start asking questions about why they were here.

'Hey!' I said, trying to sound more excited than I felt. They both waved and smiled, but I guess I had interrupted something, because the three of us just stood in awkward silence for what felt like forever. I couldn't ask them about our assignments, or swap notes – had we really never talked about anything other than homework?

'So, how's uni treating you?' Jane asked, pulling at her mousy brown ponytail.

'I heard about the thing,' Pari said before I could answer, squishing her nose. She kept toying with her too-tight black dress.

'Yeah, I mean, who hasn't pulled in the bomb squad at some point, right?' It sounded funny in my head. But when I said it, they both gave me polite smiles, but didn't laugh. Not so much as a chuckle. Silence descended again. Jane scratched her ear. It was excruciating.

'Um, I just have to – ' I pointed to the kitchen and retreated back to the popcorn bowl, scooping up a handful and shoving it into my mouth.

A group of girls, all with a punk vibe, rolled in around 10 pm. I instantly recognised their alpha: the purple-haired girl who'd tried to charge me for directions before the bomb threat.

'Sam!' Mitra screeched and raced across the room towards her.

There was definitely something about Sam. It wasn't that she oozed confidence – though she did, in spades. It was more that she had a calm about her that somehow set others at ease. 'Hey,' I nodded towards her.

'Tara?'

'I charge a five-dollar confirmation fee for that info,' I said. She laughed, nodding, and patted me on the back. So, she remembered me too.

Sam's crew grabbed some beers and settled down on the couches. I grabbed a Diet Coke and sat on the floor next to a girl with three eyebrow piercings, a see-through top over a black bra and a denim miniskirt.

'So, you going to see *Meow* tomorrow?' she asked a girl who could have passed for Tinker Bell, with her yellow sundress and blonde pixie cut, had it not been for her Doc Martens. I leaned in. Do you just say hi in these moments? Or should you go straight into telling people what your name is? I never knew.

'Meow? Is that the show's name, or are you making random cat noises again?' said Tinker Bell.

'I don't make random cat noises.'

'Meow!' I didn't realise I said it out loud until they stopped and looked at me. 'Ahh . . .' I had to say something. Anything. But now that I had their attention, nothing came out. One of the girls threw a confused look at the other. Was *this* the moment I was meant to introduce myself?

'Heck, no. The last time you dragged me to a SUDS thing, we sat there as a guy said nothing, only to start screaming *Eff you!* as we walked out. I'm good on student theatre.' Yep, I had totally missed my moment. So I laughed. Everyone else was doing it. It seemed right.

'Neanderthal.' That was the eyebrow-ring girl.

'Elitist.'

'Anyone want a drink, or, I'm heading – ?' They shook their heads and went back to trading insults. I chugged my drink, went to my room and settled onto my window seat with a book.

'Hate parties that much?' came a voice. I looked up to see Sam leaning in the doorway, a knowing smile on her face.

'Is it that obvious?' I said, closing my book.

'Nah, mate.' Sam patted me on the back again. 'Retreating to reading after literally meowing at my mates makes you way worse than you think.'

Savage. True, but savage. 'Alright, tell me something embarrassing about you, or else you'll be too cool for us to be friends.' I waved her over.

She sat on my bed, leaning back on her elbows. She looked at me with narrowed eyes, like she was considering her options. Finally, she leaned forward and whispered, 'I'm a Belieber.'

I snorted, the bubbles from my Coke going up my nose. I put a hand over my mouth to stop from spitting it out. My whole body shook with laughter. 'No way!'

Sam wiggled her eyebrows and took a swig of her beer. I tried picturing her, with her piercings and purple hair, headbanging in her car to Justin Bieber.

'Alright, cool – so, friends?' God, I sounded so ridiculously keen.

She laughed and stood up. 'How 'bout we have a drink before you file any paperwork?'

Paperwork? Oh, right. I laughed as she walked me back outside. Her crew were on the couches and had pulled in some chairs to form a tight circle. She marched me to them, held up her drink and said, 'yo, this is Tara, it's her party,' before falling into a couch and pulling me down with her.

'Didya hear that hack Will Dorak is running for Union?' the girl with the eyebrow ring asked.

'Why don't you run?' I asked Sam. They looked at me like I was an idiot. I immediately regretted speaking and wished I had an invisibility cloak to hide under.

Eyebrow Rings snorted. 'You trying to kill her? She can't run the Student Rep Council *and* be on Union. Besides, I love ya Sam, but we need fresh blood.'

'Yeah, that's why they added in a spot for first-years on Union board.' Sam swigged at her beer and looked me up and down. 'Better question is, why don't *you* run?'

I laughed and stopped when I realised she wasn't joking. 'I don't even know what the Union is.'

'You want a first-year who doesn't know what the Union is to run? Does she even have politics?' Eyebrow Rings said, not even looking at me.

'Didn't realise *mean girl* was on the political spectrum.' The words flew out of my mouth before I could think.

'Damn, you need some cream for that burn, Meg?' Tinker Bell said, fist-bumping me in apparent congratulations. I sipped my Coke. *Meg.* The girl with the piercings was Meg.

'Alright, so the SRC is where ratbags like us hang out,' Sam said, waving at her crew. 'We print posters, make chalk – we're the rabble-rousers who get people marching when idiots in Canberra try to hike up our fees, or when, say, some racist shit goes down on campus.' She gave me a knowing look. 'Union is less political. It manages all the restaurants, a bunch of the venues, and the clubs and societies. Elections are a big deal. The candidates have forums, put up posters, get to share their stories . . . this is the first year they've reserved a spot for newbies, so it'll be way easier to actually get elected if you go for it.' Her voice changed at the last comment and she tilted her head, as if she was suddenly looking at me with new eyes.

'Essentially, we print *Honi* and they try to pass off cardboard as pasta,' Meg said, actually looking at me this time. 'You've heard of *Honi*, right?' Of course I'd heard of the student newspaper. I'd read it, too.

'I couldn't. I'm trying to get into med,' I said, ignoring Meg. Besides, if I could barely cope with talking to a bunch of people at my house, how would I manage to talk a whole damn uni into voting for me?

'Girl, if Sam says you should run, then you bloody well should. Besides, faculty loves people who give back. No one, not even them stuffy professors, wants to hang out with straight-up bookworms all the damn time,' Tinker Bell said.

'I'm Tara, by the way.' Introducing myself felt like scoring a goal – I'd finally gotten the timing right. I kinda wanted a medal. I didn't tell her that I *was* a straight-up bookworm, and if Sam had guessed as much, she didn't tell.

'Linda,' Tinker Bell responded, and laughed when I reached to shake her hand. 'Yeah, you're totally the run-for-office type.'

I looked at Sam. She shrugged. 'You'll get used to me being right.'

'I'll think about it,' I said. Linda and Sam started talking about something else to do with the SRC. I leaned back and finished my Coke. I had wondered about things like how staff were treated in campus restaurants, and why we didn't have composting on campus. Maybe if it could help with getting into med, then it wouldn't be so crazy to run for office.

I wanted to test out the idea, so I decided to make a few rounds of the party, catching up with everyone. I managed a whole twenty minutes of *hey, how you doing, how tough is uni?* without saying or doing anything totally embarrassing. When the house was almost full, Mitra turned up the music and turned the living room into a dance floor. When M.I.A.'s 'Bad Girls' came on, I couldn't help but join in.

As I sashayed over, Mitra pointed at me and pretended to reel me in on an imaginary fishing line. She moved from western dance moves to Iranian ones, circling her hips and shimmying her shoulders. I bobbed along next to her, like a bottle floating in the harbour.

Mitra pulled me in close. 'You won't believe who's here!' she shouted into my ear. I followed her gaze. In his black vest and white T-shirt, paired with blue jeans, Alex looked like he'd just walked off the latest Netflix rom-com trailer. He leaned in the doorway, nodding his head to the music. When he caught my eye, he smiled. As if the person he'd been waiting for had finally arrived.

'Mitra, I'm going to murder you!' I hissed.

She threw her arms up in surrender just as Beyoncé started calling us to formation. 'Swear it wasn't me.'

He was staring at me, not even pretending not to. He tipped an imaginary hat in my direction. It made me feel otherworldly, like I was some sort of siren. I kept dancing, trying to ignore the goosebumps lining my skin.

When the song ended, I turned back to the doorway. Alex was gone. I let out a breath. *Good*, I told myself. *It's for the best.* At least I wouldn't have to spend the night figuring out ways to duck him.

'Hey.' Suddenly, he was behind me, so close I could feel his warmth. He smelled of salt water and sunscreen. I wanted to lean back into it, to chase the scent down his neck. I took a breath. *Focus.* I needed to focus, or I'd end up looking like an idiot.

'You didn't reply to my text,' he said.

'I didn't think you'd notice.' I wanted to take the words back when he pressed his lips together and leaned away.

'Of course I did.' He spoke with a certainty that made me look away.

I turned back and was about to ask what he was doing here, when Sam bounced up from behind him and hooked her hand around his neck. He wrapped an arm around her waist, picking her up and lifting her off her feet as he hugged her. He put her down and she mussed his hair. He reached for her head, but she just swatted him away.

Mitra had just geared up her monstrous speakers. It felt like the house was shaking. Even worse, we'd moved off music I recognised to random *doomph doomph*. It took all of my self control not to cover my ears with my hands. Sam pointed to the backyard and practically dragged Alex through the open French doors. She turned, caught my eye and tilted her head to indicate for me to follow. The music was still loud outside, but no longer make-your-ears-bleed, can't-hear-the-person-next-to-you loud. It was crisp outside as the wind rolled off Bondi Beach. Between the concrete tiles, wooden fence and sad-looking shrubs rimming the edges of our courtyard, there was nothing to deflect the chill. For most people it would have been divine, but I usually grab a cardigan when the temperature is anything under 30 degrees. A few people were sitting at the wooden outdoor table and milling about, but we stood a little apart. The breeze on my skin heightened my senses, making the moonlight brighter and the salt air sharper.

'Tara, meet your new campaign manager, Alex.'

'What?' We said it at the same time.

'No, no way,' Alex continued as I fell silent, 'I don't do that.

And if I did – ' he gave me the once-over ' – it would be a total waste of time.'

Who the hell did this guy think he was?

'I'm not running,' I said, wrapping my arms around myself.

'Obviously,' he said. I threw him my best greasy. He shrugged. 'No offence, you don't seem like the go-get-them type.'

'You think I'm a pushover because I wear this?' I said, flicking the end of my hijab.

'I think if you read at bars and ghost texts, then you're probably not going to put yourself out there.'

He was so wrong. I *was* the go-get-them type. Just not with stuff that wasn't going to get me into med. Not wanting to bullshit with strangers didn't make me a coward. 'Some of us don't need people fawning over us every moment of the day to feel special.'

Sam laughed and nudged Alex in the ribs, 'See, she has spunk. Besides, you owe me. Tara, this guy is the best, he ran my campaign. Besides, electioneering is in his blood.'

'Come on, Sam . . .' he said, hands in his pockets.

'I ain't kidding about this,' she shot back, staring him down till he sighed.

'Shame to waste a favour on someone who isn't gonna use it.' He threw me a bored look, but it was obvious that Sam had him on the hook for something.

Screw him. I didn't care what this college-boy snob thought of me. I had a plan and I was going to stick to it. If that meant that I didn't have to spend another minute in his vicinity, then that was just a bonus.

Sam wasn't done. 'Look, don't judge him based on all . . . *this*.' She made a giant circle motion over his face – the dark hair that curled at the ends, hazel eyes, now looking more brown than green, square-looking jawline – and ignored the indignant *hey!* that came out of his mouth. 'I've known this guy since we were little, he's my best mate. And trust me, I ain't the type that says that about anyone who jumps into a selfie with me.' I looked back at Alex, who was shaking his head, rolling on his sneakered heels. Sam looked back, caught him and elbowed him in the ribs. 'Don't let the douchiness get you,' she said to me. 'It's kind of like a bad smell – after a while, you forget it's there.'

I smiled at that. Alex shrugged in surrender. I glanced from Sam, with her piercings and attitude, to Alex, with his designer T-shirt and vest, and pristine jeans – a look that was so mainstream, it looked like the window of the Myer men's department. Unlikely friends, at a glance. But maybe if Sam liked him, there was some hope for him after all?

The balcony door banged open and Mitra tornadoed through, holding up her phone. 'You're not going to believe this!'

I pulled my gaze away and grabbed Mitra's phone from her as if she was a toddler. I glanced at the screen, opened to Facebook, and glared back up at her. She shook her head. It was an online article from *Honi Soit*, titled 'MY SIDE'. I re-read the title of the post, which had already been shared nearly a hundred times. The reposts showing up in Mitra's feed were all headed with comments like, *Unbelievable!* But I bet that there'd be plenty of others who'd shared it in support of the writer. A wave of nausea hit me. I didn't know the name on the article – Jess Wilkey – but I recognised the princess instantly from the accompanying headshot.

The article started with a disclaimer that its contents weren't endorsed by the editorial team. Well that couldn't be good.

I scrolled through, scanning the words. The arguments were old. Muslim women didn't know their own minds because the clouds of patriarchy were thick around them. It wasn't about clothes, but about power. All types of 'coverings' – yes, she used the word 'coverings' – were a symbol of violence, of submitting at all costs. Besides, wherever Muslims showed up, places went to shit. I clenched my jaw and squeezed the phone tighter. She thought she was being original, that her arguments were new – that she was some kind of Voltaire, enlightening us poor, backward masses. How dare she?

'Jess wrote this?' Alex asked, reading over the post on Sam's phone.

I looked up at Alex and nodded. He turned away, closed his eyes and swore.

'You know her?' Mitra stepped between me and him, leaning towards him accusingly.

He shrugged at Mitra, unfazed. 'She's a friend of the family, and I . . . I'm surprised.' I looked at him closely, but his lips were pressed together. I had no idea if he was angry, surprised, or defensive.

'Can we have a moment?' He looked at me and then at Mitra, gesturing a plea for her to leave us alone.

'No!' she snapped back.

I didn't say the words, but tilted my head and raised my eyebrows at her, as if to say *please*. She clicked her tongue, glared at Alex and then walked back into the house with Sam. I knew I was going to get an earful later.

'You okay?' He rubbed the back of his neck and looked at me through what I realised were very long lashes.

'I'll figure it out,' I said, stepping away from him.

He leaned forward, tried to take my hand and then pulled his arm back. 'Tara, Jess is . . .' He paused. The way he chose his words when he talked about her convinced me that the two of them had history. 'She's . . . complicated, and right now, given she's dating Steve . . .'

'Steve?'

'Maddison. He . . .' Alex paused for a second. 'I've known them both for a while and let's just say they don't bring out the best in each other.'

My heart sank. Great, just great. My new nemesis was dating the son of one of the richest men in Australia.

'She was more than that, though,' I said. It was so obvious.

'What are you getting at?' He stared hard at me, his eyes glinting green again.

'Nothing.' My first impression of him had been totally right after all. Was he defending her because he still had feelings for her? No, no way. I wasn't going to compete with the princess. I'd been right to ignore his message, to keep away.

'Bullshit.' He looked at me, opened his mouth, sighed. 'Look we hooked up,' he shrugged, like he'd admitted to them going out for ice cream. 'But it's not like that. She's a mate. It's hard watching a friend make an arse of themselves. That's all.'

I bent to pick a weed from the pavers, taking my time before I stood and looked at him again.

'Do you believe me?' he asked, more of a plea than a question.

'Sure.' I waved my hand like it was nothing. 'It's none of my business anyway.'

He straightened at my words, frowning. 'I'm heading in.'

He didn't look back. I was glad. I couldn't get away from him and the whole idea of running for Union fast enough.

Chapter 7

Mitra pushed her sunglasses up her nose, clamping them firmly over her eyes against the morning light.

'Coffee,' she murmured. We were sitting outside Lorenzo's, one of those hole-in-the-wall Bondi cafes with twenty different blends of coffees, a handful of pastries and two sandwich options. No art on the walls, no furniture aside from a couple of bright yellow barstools and high tables inside, and our tiny table on the footpath, designed as a waystation where you waited for your order. People came here to get their caffeine fix, not to sit around. 'If I see another person walk past with green juice, I'm going to hurl,' Mitra said.

I patted her hand before heading in, getting a flat white for me and a double-shot espresso for her, with an apricot danish to share. When I returned, we sat in companionable silence, watching the street as we inhaled our coffees. It wasn't until Mitra slid her glasses up onto her forehead that I decided it was safe to talk.

'You and Sam seemed to hit it off last night,' I said. They'd danced and spent most of the night glued to each other. Mitra was usually like a butterfly: she flew around befriending everyone. I'd never seen her really focus on one person before, apart from me.

'Yeah, I don't know, she's cool.' She fidgeted and avoided my eyes.

'Come on, we're not twelve. This isn't a *but you're my best friend* thing. I like Sam. I'm glad you two hit it off.'

Mitra sighed and I let it go. This was probably one of those situations where the only way to convince her I didn't have some weird friend jealousy thing going on was to just shut up and *actually* be cool about it. Mitra took a giant bite of the apricot danish and made no move to share. I pulled the plate, used a knife to split off less than half and started nibbling on my portion.

'Sam reckons you should run for Union,' she said through a mouthful.

'Look, I thought about it and it's a bad idea on all sides. Jess's post doesn't need any more oxygen. Besides, I don't care what she says about me.'

'Bollocks.' Mitra pushed her food away and glared at me like I'd just sworn at her. 'Nah, I don't want to hear it, mate. First of all, don't pretend like you're all zen about that chick running around calling you a brainless nit. Then, don't you dare pretend that this is just about you.'

'Mitra . . .'

'Dad saw an article 'bout what happened. He didn't know it was you and even though Roshan ain't covered, he was all like, *maybe Sydney isn't fit for her.* The only reason he isn't trying to pull me out is 'cause he knows *I* can throw a punch.'

'What if he's right?' I couldn't look at her when I said it. Wouldn't Roshan be better off going to a place that was actually open, instead of just somewhere that just *said* it was?

'Oh, sod off. There's a gazillion med programs you could have gotten into like *this*,' Mitra snapped her fingers, 'but instead you're busting your butt trying to get into the Sydney one. 'Cause it's the best. You think others don't deserve that?'

'Of course they do.'

'Then why aren't you doing your bit to make it easier?'

'They called the cops on me, Mitra. Went through my bags, thought it was cool to call me a potential murderer, and you think I'm the one that's responsible?'

'I ain't saying it's fair. I'm saying it's your story and you're the only one who can change it. Look, whatever. You do you. I'm meant to meet up with Sam anyway.'

We didn't talk on the walk home and with a brisk, *bye*, she climbed into Dee and drove off. It was so typical of her to blow up because I didn't want to pick a fight. And to throw a party at my place and leave me with all the cleaning. I pushed open the front door, grabbed a trash bag and started filling it with beer cans, chip bags and Maccas wrappers. She knew how tough the last few weeks had been and had pummelled me anyway.

I wiped my nose on my sleeve as I tied off the bag, threw it into the corner and grabbed another one. Mitra was crazy protective of her brother, Fadi and sister, Roshan. Well, I loved Roshan too. That girl was a total Ravenclaw, but I didn't want her to have to deal with anything like my past few weeks. I wanted her to show up on her first day of uni, have a good time and then fill up that giant brain of hers in peace. Running for Union wasn't going to make anything better. It was just going to stir everything up, make more people pick sides.

I grabbed the bags, wedged the door open with my foot,

stormed to the big bin outside and threw them both in. It's not like I could change how people thought anyway. Even if I *did* run, it wasn't like everything was magically going to change overnight. I walked back to the house, sweaty from lugging the two big rubbish bags to the alley behind the courtyard. I got to the house, went straight to the kitchen and started washing the dishes.

Mitra had burnt two-minute noodles in one of Mum's pans when she was making a late-night snack, so I doused it in scalding water and then attacked it with a scourer. I scrubbed so long and hard, the skin on my hands shrivelled. It wasn't like *I'd* called the police about the 'bomb threat'. I hadn't started it, so why did I have to clean it up? But I couldn't stop thinking about Roshan – about all the other Roshans out there. What did it mean for them if I did nothing? Would ignoring this really make it go away?

The bottom of the pan was still a sooty mess, so I grabbed some baking soda, mixed it with detergent, then scrubbed again. No, ignoring the racism and lazy assumptions wouldn't make them go away. It would make it all fester like an unsterilised wound. Running for Union wouldn't *make* people take sides – they were doing it already, without hearing my side of the story. The idea of letting one entitled princess's ignorance blossom into a full ecosystem of hate was terrifying.

It took ten minutes to get the pan looking brand-new again. I rinsed it off and piled it in the washer with the other dishes. Could I actually make a difference? I grabbed a Coke from the fridge and collapsed on the couch.

I took a blissful sip of the cold, bubbly sugar water. My body ached, but I was smiling as I looked around. It wasn't just the newly pristine house that made me feel good, but knowing that Mitra had had a night off from her parents. She had fun, and made sure I had fun. I had her back and she had mine – even when she was super annoying.

Mum was going to get home in an hour or so, and after the cleaning fest, I'd earned a break. I grabbed a book and curled up on the couch. I'd fallen hard and fast for this book, which I'd picked up on impulse after reading a staff review in one of the cute little boutique bookshops near uni. The book was about a world where a king fought to extinguish magic because he felt threatened by those who had it. I cried as their villages burned, as they fought for their gods, as they marched up to a battlefield that it was clear not all of them would come back from.

The door opened and I checked my phone. I'd spent the last two hours reading and only had twenty pages of the book left. Mum walked into the living room, rolling her suitcase behind her.

'Please tell me you've moved from that spot since I've been gone,' she said. 'Oh, don't give me that look. Like you wouldn't spend a whole weekend reading a trilogy on dragons or something?' She grabbed a San Pellegrino from the fridge and poured it into a glass.

'How was the trip?' I asked.

She took a sip, walked out and leaned against the living-room wall.

'My friend Lisa in Melbourne asked me if you were okay. She wanted to pass on her well wishes after what happened on your first day. It was fun reading about it online.'

Shit.

'I'm sorry, I should have told you, I just . . .' *know how much you hate me wearing the hijab and didn't want to deal with it.*

She put her phone face-down on the counter, pulled her hair up into a ponytail, then picked up her sparkling water again. She sat in the armchair opposite me, holding her glass to the side, eyeing me like she was royalty and had caught me plotting treason.

'Are you okay?'

I pulled my feet up on the couch, staring at the cushions. I'd expected her to go straight into the rage. The care was so much harder.

'Yeah, I'm okay, it was all kind of surreal.'

'I'm so sorry you had to deal with that.' She put her glass on the coffee table, walked over to the couch and pulled me into her arms. I rested my head on her shoulder and nestled into the scent of her Chanel No 5. For a moment, I felt like a little girl again. She kissed my head and pulled away. 'After lunch you can give me all the details. I'll start figuring out the best way to approach the university.'

Here we go again. I folded my arms and arranged my face carefully. I didn't want her to be my lawyer, I just wanted her to be my mum.

'I don't think that's a good idea. I think it might be one of those things that just needs to tire itself out.' It popped out of my mouth sounding way lamer than it had in my head.

Mum stroked my hair and kissed my cheek, 'I understand.'

'What?' Wait – had I said that aloud?

'Look, people behave terribly all the time. I had my fair share of it in my early days of law, believe me. But I kept my head down, kept chipping away and well, now I'm partner.' She stood up and walked over to the mail I'd stacked for her. She picked up an Amnesty International envelope, glanced at it, then ripped it in half and chucked it on the pile she'd take to the recycling bin. 'Changing the world sounds great in a fundraiser, but honestly, the most we can do is look out for ourselves.'

'Right,' I said, though none of what she said felt right.

'Alright, I'm going to pick up food for the week, any requests?' I shook my head. I'd do a grocery run and cook something later. I hated the pre-packaged food Mum bought from the organic store: all superfoods that promised to keep you regular and totally tasted like overcooked oatmeal. She wandered into her bedroom and walked out looking like a Lululemon store had thrown up on her.

I walked down the hall to my room and pulled the white jah-namaz from under my bed. I unfurled the soft baby blue chador, patterned with small pink roses, from around the gold-embroidered white prayer rug. I rolled it out onto my bedroom floor and wrapped the chador around myself. Mitra's mum had given me the rug, after I put on the hijab in Year 11. At first I'd watched YouTube videos to figure out how to pray, until Maman Noosheen saw me doing it, and asked if I wanted to learn the verses in English so I could understand what I was saying to God. She'd laughed when I asked if that was allowed. *No one can tell you how to talk to God.* She had prayed in her own language, Farsi, and not the traditional Arabic. When she told me, it felt like a revelation – that it was okay to do things differently to the way they'd always been done. Even pray differently.

She chopped vegetables as I re-learned the verses in English. I'd asked her why she'd stopped praying and she'd just smiled at me and said, *Khoda midoneh* (God knows), like they'd gotten into a fight and she was waiting for an apology.

Khoda (God). I still remember how my parents had freaked

out in their own ways when I first put the hijab on. Dad called and yelled. Mum had spent months leaving newspapers open to pages profiling all the worst parts of Islam. When Maman Noosheen died last year, they'd backed off, given me space, let me turn to God to grieve. I pushed away the memory. Letting myself in with my key one afternoon, planning to share cake and tea before I did my homework, and finding her on the kitchen floor. Calling triple zero. Not knowing how to help, what to do. Her body strangely still, her face already tinged blue. I probably couldn't have done anything anyway, but I never wanted to feel that helpless again. After that, I was more determined than ever to get into medicine – to know that if someone I loved needed me, I could do something to help.

I tried to clear my head as I arranged the *mohr*, a round piece of hardened clay inscribed with Arabic, at the head of the rug. I always thought of it as fancy dirt, a gentle reminder that no matter what we do, we end up in the earth in the end. I took a breath, feeling the tension ease away from me. There was something about standing in front of God that gave me back a sense of perspective, of the vastness of the world. I adjusted my chador, looked down at the *mohr* resting on my jah-namaz, and began.

In the name of God, the gracious, the compassionate.

I went through the motions of my prayer: standing, bowing, and placing my forehead to the ground. It felt good going through the ritual of devotion. I tried to keep my mind on the words I was reciting, but I had repeated them so often, it felt like repeating my ABCs. Instead, my thoughts kept wandering back to the same questions. I had started wearing hijab because I couldn't change the world without holding on to my own sense of worth. The hijab was a daily reminder that there was more to who I was and what I wanted than other people's approval.

When I was with Ryan, I hadn't asked for respect. I hadn't cared that he hadn't seen me. The hijab was a way of reminding myself that it was okay to want those things, to ask for someone to really *see* me before getting involved.

It wasn't just that though. The hijab, for me, was a redirection, even a second chance and because of that it was a reminder that what made us worthy, special even as humans was our imperfection. That I would make mistakes and still be loved. I needed that reassurance to think about changing the world, to believe that I could do big, bold, scary things – and that even if none of it worked out, I'd still be worthy, still be loved.

And I wanted to change the world. I always figured I'd have to go on an epic quest to do that, Frodo style. But was my battle here? If I did nothing, was I really just looking out for myself, hoping that someone else would take the hit to make things easier for all of us? What were my responsibilities?

You alone we serve, you alone we ask for help. Guide us to the straight way.

I sat on the jah-namaz after I finished my prayers, running my grandma's tasbeeh through my fingers. Was Mitra right – was this fight bigger than me? Of course it was. People had been fighting the hijab since women put it on. Maybe running for office wouldn't change anything. But then again, maybe seeing me campaign to be on the Union board would help a few people to realise they were too quick to judge me? I thought of all the women who were bullied and belittled when they had dared to want an education. Where would I be if they'd all decided to step back and do nothing?

I pressed my head against the mohr, and let my worries about not getting into med, about letting down my mum and Maman Noosheen, about being humiliated if I ran for office, flow into the clay tablet. I surrendered to the power that was so much bigger than me – and remembered that my life was just a moment in eternity, that I was only one soul in billions that God shepherded. My life mattered and there was almost no way for people to remember my name in a thousand years. I couldn't wait until the time was right to do good. I only had the now. I didn't want to be like my parents. I didn't want to make it easier for oil companies to keep polluting, or slice up gorgeous women so they could pretend they weren't ageing. I wanted to do something more. I wanted to be worthy of the life and blessings I had.

I rolled up my jah-namaz, tucked it under my bed and grabbed my phone.

You were right, I texted Mitra. My phone beeped with an instant reply.

Ain't I always?

Chapter 8

I stood outside the lecture hall, holding two coffees. Sam had told me where to find him and that he liked flat whites. He walked out, messenger bag over his shoulder, his cream linen shirt opened one button too many.

Alex spotted me, threw up his hands and shook his head. 'No.' He walked past, but I ran to catch up with him.

'Oh, come on, you know you want to do this with me.'

'Do I now?'

'It's going to be the thing everyone talks about and you know you want to be in on that. Also,' I tilted my head and threw him my best smile, 'you like that I keep you on your toes.' He kept walking, so I stopped and called out, 'you still owe Sam!'

He stopped. For a moment, I was one hundred per cent sure he was going to ignore me and walk away. Instead he turned around, ran a hand through his hair and grabbed one of the coffees from my hand. 'This better be hot.' I did an internal happy dance as he slowed to sip it. I couldn't help but wonder what he had done to owe Sam so definitively.

We reached some picnic tables next to the oval and he

motioned for me to sit. 'Alright, if we're going to do this, I have some ground rules.'

'Okay.' I sat on the edge of the seat, worried that if I did or said the wrong thing, I'd scare him off.

'First of all, you can't go after Jess.' It bugged me that she was the first thing he brought up. Had he been honest the other night, that she was just *a mate*? It didn't matter. I wasn't doing this to get into a mud-fight. So, I nodded yes.

'You gotta be all in.'

He was staring at me so intensely that I wiggled in my seat. I couldn't lie to him. If he was going to do this with me, I wanted us to start out right. 'I can't give it my *all*.'

He stood.

'Wait!' I said, sounding every bit as desperate as I felt. He pursed his lips but sat back down.

'Look, I'm trying to get into med and if I don't get stellar grades, that goes up in smoke. That has to be my main focus. I'll do the work, but I'll still need time to study. I'll make it happen, but I'll need your help to make it work.' I cringed as I said it. 'What do you think?' I wanted to hiss the words back once they were out.

'You'll show up to stuff and you know, be nice?'

'I'm always nice,' I said, crossing my arms and scowling at him.

'You read books at parties, have resting bored face, and talk less than an ice sculpture.'

I shook my head. This guy . . . he went around being effortlessly charming and thought everyone who struggled with small talk was an arse. I didn't have Mitra's X factor. I couldn't turn my day into funny anecdotes or joke around reflexively, so I stayed out of people's way. I couldn't tell him that though, not without him running in the other direction. So instead, I took a deep breath and looked him in the eye.

'I'll be nice.'

'Alright, I'm in.' He sat back down, opened his bag and pulled out his MacBook. 'Let's talk about how we win this.' I took out my notebook and clicked my pen. He gave me a look. 'You need about 700 votes to get one of the five spots. Probably less, given they've put a slot aside for first-years. Given that Jess and Steve are both in colleges, you ain't getting any of that vote. So, we have to go big and hard. We need everyone talking about you. Let's talk about your platform . . .'

'Oh, that I've got covered.' I pulled out a folder from my bag and handed it to him. Finally, one thing I knew I could do. 'I put together some policies I think will benefit the Union and my edits of some of their current standards.'

'You're shitting me, right?' he said, lifting the folder like he was weighing a brick in his hands. 'First of all, you're not going to get the gig if you start off telling people they're not doing their jobs. Sam and I are going to hook you up with a bunch of people and you'll, you know, *listen* to them, and get their input about how things should get better. People aren't going to vote for you because you can write an essay.' He threw the folder on the table between us. 'People are going to vote for you 'cause they *like* you.'

Oh god, what had I signed up for? I wanted people to see that a girl like me could speak up, could be a leader. But getting them to like me? I'd have more luck trying to coax dragon eggs to hatch. The way he'd just schooled me made me realise that I had been thinking of this a bit backwards. He looked at me, waiting for me to continue, 'Can we . . . I mean, I'd love it if we could create a cabal, a cadre – you're right, I don't know much about all this, so if I do win, I don't want to just have a team with me for the vote. I want people who'll be in it for the long haul.'

'You want to join a party? That'll give you an automatic crew,' he said. I shook my head. 'No, of course not.' He put his coffee down when he saw me slump. 'Sorry, that was harsh. Look, let's try it, alright? First, I need some basics, aside from a love of *Hunger Games*.' He picked up my phone and smirked at the mockingjay pin on its cover. 'What else do you care about?' He held up his hand when I opened my mouth. 'Not the essay version, the real version.'

'I care about people feeling welcome, getting to be who they are.' That felt too corny for words. He was probably figuring out a way to back out now. 'I care about us doing right by the staff at the Union. And that, you know, everyone can do their bit to make things better for the next lot that walks through those walls.'

'You weren't one of those perfect, save-the-world types in high school, were you?'

I shook my head. 'Kinda, not really. I just always thought I'd go somewhere and help people through medicine. So, I studied. What? What's that look?'

'You just keep suprising me.' Alex rubbed his eyes and turned back to me, 'We'll figure out the platform later. I'm going to call my mate, Pete. You met him at Manning that time. He's going to take some headshots we can turn into posters, then after you've had a few chats, I'm going to organise a pizza night so we can print T-shirts, test-drive your speech and get people organised for a stall.'

'So, I should get a head start on study tonight?' He nodded and stood. This time, I let him. 'One more thing,' I said. Sure, he was an arse – a rather huge one – but he was doing this and I kind of owed him. Even if he was doing it as a favour to Sam. 'I'm sorry if I . . .' The words got stuck. For a second I just stared at him, then I cleared my throat and seemed to find the words again. 'Well, I heard you the other night and thank you for doing this, it means – '

'That when Sam collects, she *really* collects.' He walked away, then turned and circled back. 'Oh, and one more thing. There will be no funny business while we do this, okay?'

Funny business? Who the hell still said *funny business*? 'Oh, that's awkward. Do you have feelings for me already?'

He laughed. I wanted to do something to make him laugh like that again. 'Alright, I'll text you deets for the photo shoot. Remember, no ghosting, okay?'

'No ghosting,' I said and watched him walk away. For real, this time.

I dragged myself to the library. It was amazing how easy it was to focus on the molecular structure of cells and statistics when I was desperate not to keep picturing a certain someone holding hands with the girl who had made my entry into uni so hard. Then again, Ryan hadn't ever pretended he wasn't into Fi. Hell, he'd *told* me he was still hung up on her, that he wanted to keep things casual. What if the thing Alex and Ryan actually had in common was that they were both telling me the truth? What if I was risking stuffing it up by not really listening, again? I finished an essay and clicked my laptop shut. Had he flirted with me at the end there, maybe? A little? *Khoda*, this was pathetic. I stuffed my computer into my backpack.

It didn't matter anyway. The only guys I was involved with were mages, assassins or fae – and that was how it was going to stay.

Chapter 9

'Should I have put on different make-up?' I asked, fidgeting with the edge of my red hijab as Pete took some test shots.

'Why?' Alex looked up, squinting like he genuinely didn't understand.

You know what? Maybe I didn't need it. I'd worn my hijab differently today, tied it behind my neck with its tail flowing down my shoulder. It was bright red, unmissable, and it popped against my black top and dark jeans. I'd totally channelled assassin vibes when I'd picked it out this morning. I looked fierce, ready to slay.

'Ready,' Pete said, and motioned me to stand in front of him. I *was* ready. A badass who wasn't scared. The camera clicked and clicked and suddenly my bravado crumbled. I didn't know what to do, where to put my hands. I put a hand on my hips, tilted my head. It all felt silly, wrong. Suddenly I had Tyra Banks in my ear shouting, 'smize!' I couldn't stop imagining terrible photos of myself around campus, and the more I did, the more I stiffened. I wished I was watching a photo shoot on *America's Next Top Model* in my PJs with a tub of ice cream, instead of being in front of the camera.

Pete paused and fiddled with his camera. He showed Alex the photos. Alex shook his head, whispering. Then Pete started playing with buttons on the camera. Had they been that bad? Was Pete deleting all the photos?

'Let's grab a few more, okay?' He didn't tell me to relax and I appreciated it. I started posing again. Alex held up a hand, then gestured toward a wrought-iron chair and table. 'Not yet, Pete's going to snap a few shots to get the lighting right.'

I took a breath, rolled my neck and stretched my arms up high. Pete was adjusting the lens and looking into the camera. I reached for my e-reader, but looked up when Alex chuckled. 'What's on that device of yours anyway? I swear I wouldn't be surprised if I saw you reading as the four horsemen charged.'

'I read fantasy,' I said, looking over at Pete.

'So, it's not just a *Hunger Games* thing?' Alex caught my gaze. 'Fantasy, 'ey?' one side of his mouth lifted into a half smile. 'So, you're secretly hot for Jon Snow?'

What? Eww. I scrunched up my face and shook my head. No, my *Game of Thrones* crush was totally Robb Stark – and well, Khal Drogo, but that was less because of the character and more because of Jason Momoa. Alex didn't let up though. 'Come on, tell me about it.'

'People have codes in fantasy: they fight for things, run from things . . . like Celaena in *Throne of Glass*. She's an assassin, but she makes mistakes, you know, comes up with wicked cool plots and . . . well, I don't want to spoil it for you.'

'Right. Spoiler: the people with dragons win!' He moved his hands as if lighting up a billboard.

'There's nothing wrong with wanting a bit of magic.'

'Got it,' Pete said. He gave me a thumbs up. Alex went to

the camera, scrolled through some photos, and nodded before waving me over.

Pete handed me the camera. I was sitting, smiling, my eyes lit up – I wasn't a *Top Model* contender, but the photos looked nice. Good, even.

Pete chuckled, put the camera away. 'Alright, I should dash. Besides,' he looked from Alex to me and back, 'you two probably have a lot of talking to do.'

Alex gave him a friendly shove. 'Alright, man.' Pete smirked and started putting his camera in its case.

'Thanks for doing this, and for making me look photogenic,' I said to him.

'You kidding me? You're a stunner,' Pete said, looking me straight in the eye with a small smile. 'Made my job easy.' It was clearly a polite lie but I beamed up at him anyway.

'Don't you have photos to edit?' Alex said, pursing his lips and gesturing towards the road.

Pete laughed so hard his shoulders shook. 'Right, man – you're welcome, too.' He waved and then walked off, grinning.

'Well that was embarrassing,' Alex said, sitting next to me.

'What?'

'You going all goo-goo eyed at the mention of Jon Snow. So clichéd.' He leaned his head into his palm, his face tipped towards me. Something about his look made me shiver. He was teasing me, sure – but he looked like he was enjoying it. It was unsettling.

'Do you read?' I asked, crossing my arms and tapping my foot under the table.

'Like, the ABCs? Sure, all the time.' He laughed, 'Oh alright, I've always been more of a movie buff. Put away that judgy face!

Like *The Godfather* doesn't suck you into a whole other world, the same way a fantasy book does.'

I'd heard of it, somehow.

'Guys in suits?'

Alex looked at me in disbelief. 'You haven't seen it! Alright, how about this? After the election, we're fixing that.'

'Only if you read a series I pick.'

'Deal.' We nodded to each other. 'I'm heading towards the library too,' he said, slinging his bag over his shoulder.

'You finally realised it wasn't a mirage?'

'Oh, I quite enjoy the library. Tested a few of the windows, too. They renovated it in the seventies, you know. Made sure all the windows were double-paned.'

'Why?'

'It was getting a bit dangerous with all the couples shoving up against them.'

I stared at him for a moment before I got it. Then, I couldn't help but blush. His smile almost made me trip, and just at that moment, my mind decided to filter back to the idea of him shirtless. 'Have fun with the study,' he said, smirking as he left me at the library door.

I stared after him. What had just happened? He kept walking, and just as I was about to head into the library, a stunning girl with wavy brown hair and a gorgeous sunflower-printed dress waved him over. She kissed his cheek, then fiddled with his shirt collar. Judging by the way he was looking at her, she wasn't a stranger. Not by a long shot.

Of course, he had a girlfriend, or *someone*, already. Even if he had been flirting with me, it didn't mean anything. Hell, he looked like he could have his own TV show. And well, I was *me*.

I walked into the library determined to be productive. I grabbed all the books, got set up and then spent an hour reading a paragraph. No, that wasn't quite true. I spent an hour staring at a paragraph and failing to really read a single word of it. Finally, I gave up. I hated that I blushed as I passed the library windows on my way out.

I stopped by the grocer on the way home and left with a bouquet of coriander, parsley and leeks. There was no way I was going to be punching holes into a microwave meal tonight. I put on the podcast *Stuff You Might Have Missed in History Class* and started slicing onions and chopping up the herbs. It felt good running the knife through them, unleashing their aromas. I fried up the onions, mixed my herbs with some eggs, and poured the whole thing into a skillet. Mum would be home soon and would swoon at the food – less because it was Iranian and more because she was convinced that anything green was practically magic.

An hour later, Mum walked in and inhaled the scent with a dreamy look. 'Hope nothing exciting has been happening at uni.'

Ouch. She knew me too well, dammit! 'No. Yes. I mean . . .' This was going real well. 'I've decided to run for the student union.' The plan had been to get some food into her before telling her, but well, here we were.

'Oh?'

'Well, I think hospitals like hiring more well-rounded people, so this would help with that. Besides, I could be helpful and learn a lot.' *Also, I don't want to spend the next four years being bomb-threat girl.* I don't know why I couldn't bring myself to say that.

'Alright then.' Mum grabbed her handbag, sat back at the table with it, and started fumbling through it. 'Aha!' She pulled out her wallet and slid me a credit card. 'Don't you need to copy posters and buy T-shirts? It has a $2000 limit. If I catch wind of you using it for anything else, we'll have to have words. Alright?'

'Really?'

Mum pulled me into a tight hug. 'I'm proud of you. It takes guts to put yourself out there. Now, all you need to do is win so I can brag to my friends.' She hacked off a piece of kokoo from the pan and popped it into her mouth.

I had to focus on what was important: getting into med and doing well enough in the election that I stopped just being the bomb-threat girl. That ache in my chest when I thought of Alex? Well, that was a useful reminder about what happened when I lost my focus. Instead of ignoring it, I held on to it. That ache was going to make sure that my campaign manager stayed just that. Nothing more.

I headed off to my chemistry lecture and from there, biology lab. I felt like Golem by the time I finished four hours of back-to-back classes. Even though it felt like my skin was turning translucent, I dragged myself to the library to read through my notes and get a head start on the next round of assessments. My head felt like it was going to explode from holding in all the information I'd consumed: the course materials, and everything I'd been told by the organisers of Welcome Week, Radical Sex and Consent Week, Pop Fest volunteers, and the club and society coordinators. Alex had warned me that the next two weeks were going to be brutal. It was hard to imagine it getting more intense, but still, since I wasn't going to let my grades go down, every minute counted.

By the time I got out of the library, it was late in the afternoon. I grabbed a bus down King Street to Sam's place. A gorgeous old terrace, it had beautiful wrought-iron details on the gate and the balcony. The windows and door were painted bright purple, and a menacing crack crept halfway up the outside wall. I heard laughter and running after I knocked. Mitra threw open the door.

'You're here! Finally.' She grabbed my hand and pulled me through the house. We squeezed past the bikes in the hallway, through to the living room, with its mismatched furniture and milk crates, then into a lime-green kitchen, and finally out into the backyard. Fairy lights were strung along the fence, candles sprouted from the necks of wine bottles, and a little herb garden grew next to a wooden deck area where everyone was either painting banners or screen-printing T-shirts. Pizza and beer were scattered around and angsty indie music blasted from a Bluetooth speaker.

Sam paused in chowing down her pizza and threw me a salute. 'I can't believe you did this,' I said.

'The crew needs stuff to do, or else we all just start pecking at each other.' She shrugged and wandered off. I looked around the yard. Linda (aka Tinker Bell) was painting a banner. Alex was talking to a few people I didn't know. I took a step closer.

'Look, everyone will send you to the Thai joints, but no one ever talks about how good The Italian Bowl is. I mean, the way they cook up that pasta in the pan, it's gotta be some kind of alchemy.' Alex. The two girls he was talking to looked like they were eating it up. Sure, he was always charming, but this sounded different, almost deliberate. It subtly sounded like he'd switched to some sort of campaign mode.

I looked away from him and spotted Mitra with . . . was that Meg? I looked closer and yeah, the girl who'd scoffed at the idea of me running for Union was here, arguing with Mitra over a machine that looked like it belonged in a museum. I thought of Sam with even more respect. The people close to her were loyal as hell. The two of them were elbowing each other out of the way to swing down its arm, making faces at each other when it made a snapping noise.

'It's a badge-maker.' I jumped at Alex's voice. Was I imagining it, or had his campaign voice disappeared? 'Could be worse, at least they're not arm wrestling.'

'Give them five minutes and they'll get there,' I whispered, refusing to look up at him.

'You promised to be nice,' he said.

'I am. Or do you have some sort of internalised bloodsucker hate?'

I couldn't help but sneak a peek at his face. His lips had curled up just a bit, like he was smiling despite himself.

'Glowering at people across the room doesn't count as socialising,' he said. 'Go – talk.'

I pursed my lips at him. Sure, walk up to strangers and just say, 'hi'. Like that wasn't the scariest thing ever. My mind swiped through all the ways I could make a fool of myself again as I walked towards Linda and the girls who were painting the banner. They looked up and smiled as I crouched next to them.

'Hey, Linda,' I said, nodding at her. 'I'm Tara,' I continued, directing it at the others. Win! I got in the whole intro thing right off the bat. I didn't knock over any paint or trip over them, which was a great start.

'This is Anaya and Kate,' Linda said.

'Thanks so much for being here.' If there was an award for being super uncool, I would have won it.

'Sure, yeah, the whole bomb threat thing was ridic,' said Anaya, beaming a smile any anime character would envy. 'Besides, we need a bit more colour up in the Union.' Her round face was browner than mine.

I grabbed a paintbrush. 'That's awesome.' I nodded at her T-shirt, which was printed with a cartoonised photo of Buffy, over the words, *I SLAY*.

'Isn't it? The Order of Fantasy stall was giving them out at Welcome Week. Apparently, it was controversial, 'cause, like, Buffy isn't technically fantasy.'

'I wish Joss Whedon had written all my comebacks in high school. They would have been so much better than the *ahh*s and *umm*s that I came up with.'

They laughed – all three of them laughed at my joke – like I was actually *funny*.

Kate leaned forward as she laughed, and her strawberry blonde hair fell over her face. She pushed it away with a freckled hand.

'So, did you all, like, go to school together?' Not original, I know, but lightning striking in the same place twice was more likely than me making two funny jokes in a row. And I was curious.

'God, I wish. I'm old . . . third-year,' Linda said, smiling up at me. 'I know these two 'cause they're women's collective newbies.'

'Women's collective?'

'You know, just a bunch of femme-identifying people hanging out, brewing potions, eating babies,' Kate said. And we all giggled. She looked up at the three of us conspiratorially, then in Alex's direction, and whispered, 'So, is it super weird that I used to love watching his parents on the *Today Show*?'

'Remember that time Doug teased Rita about how slow the light rail is? It was hilarious,' Anaya added. I nodded. That segment had gone viral.

It must have been weird, having your parents flirt with each other on breakfast TV every week. For it to become a thing – a politician who talked in plain English, who joked around with her hot comedian husband. God, I was insecure enough about living up to Mum, who has it so together all the time. I couldn't imagine how much more acute that would feel if she was on TV, and famous.

'Is it true that he hooked up with Kendall Jenner while she was in town?' Kate whispered.

'Alex has always had game. Good for him. You don't get reviews like that without doing something right,' said Linda.

A supermodel. He'd kissed an actual supermodel. *Reviews like that?* What the hell did that mean? I dabbed my paintbrush into a blob of acrylic a little too enthusiastically and managed to splatter blue paint all over myself. Great. A supermodel and a smurf. I sighed.

'Look, we did it!' I said, waving at the banner. Sure, there was a bunch of paint splatter next to the 'A', but who cared? It said TARA FOR UNION, and I'd painted while interacting semi-normally with people I'd just met. 'Pizza?' I asked. I wanted to refocus on the race. Nothing good could come from daydreaming about the person who was running my campaign.

'Wait, let me get some shots first,' Anaya said, getting us to pose next to the banner. 'Who's running your socials for this?'

'Ahh, I'm not sure. I think Alex?'

Anaya harumphed, then Kate cut in. 'Oh, she's totally going to be your socials person.'

'Brilliant,' I said, and meant it. Sure, I'd known Anaya for all of two seconds, but a shared love of Buffy and that she laughed at my jokes was enough for me to like her already.

We walked over to the table where the pizzas were stacked. Alex was hanging there too, so I hung back, pretending to check something on my phone. From the corner of my eye, I caught Sam and Mitra huddled next to each other, whispering. I smiled.

'Told you it wouldn't be that bad,' Alex said. I scowled at him. 'Come on, I have something to show you.'

I followed him, cursing supermodels and the whole stupid beauty industry. He took me to the pile of white T-shirts in the corner and held one out. 'Ever printed a shirt before?'

I shook my head.

Alex lay down a piece of newspaper, then lay a T-shirt on top. Then he handed me a big screen that looked like a frame, a cloth stencil stretched over it. He pushed the frame onto the shirt. 'Grab some paint,' he said. I squeezed some blue fabric paint onto the screen. 'Now, pull the squeegee down.' I grabbed what looked like a long window cleaner, kneeled opposite Alex, and tried to ignore the way his arm muscles pulled taut as he pushed down on the screen, and pulled the squeegee down it. I stared at the shirt he'd made, then at him.

Hermione. Katniss. Buffy. Arya. Tara.

The names ran down the shirt. I looked from the words to

him, 'You'll love the back.' He turned it around so I could see. *Bring some rebel vibes to Union. Vote for Tara.*

'I . . .' I looked up at him.

'Look, I should have cleared it with you first, but everyone will know one of these characters and like them. You can't exactly campaign on parties and booze, so I figured we'd set up a rebel alliance instead. This is you – and people are going to like it.'

Well, that might have been the nicest thing anyone had ever said to me. Dammit, he'd *seen* me. I had been going to tell him that I didn't want anything about diversity on the slogan, but he'd gotten that – and found something that made me *me*, and wasn't just about my hijab. I grabbed a towel and tried to wipe off some of the paint on my hands. It didn't matter that I was wearing a bunch of layers – I suddenly felt naked.

'I thought you said you didn't like reading fantasy,' I said.

'You know they made TV shows and movies from all of those books, right?'

'Don't get me started on the last season of *Game of Thrones* . . .'

He smiled, reached over and looked like he was about to wipe some paint from my cheek, but pulled his hand back and handed me the towel I'd just put down. 'You have a little something.' He tapped his own cheek with his finger. 'Anyway, you'll get the hang of it. I'll send Anaya over to help. I'm just going to check in with Sam.' Then he bolted.

'Hey,' Mitra said, appearing next to me. She'd been plastered to Sam's side for the last little bit. The two of them had been giggling – actually *giggling*, together – not to mention hooting, hollering and generally carrying on. It was good. I hadn't seen her so darn happy in a while. 'What happened there?'

I shrugged. Damned if I knew. 'Probably had to check in with his girlfriend or something.' I was going for nonchalant and instead landed on totally sarcastic with a hint of bitter.

'Nah, Sam said he's not the girlfriend type.' Mitra took a swig of the beer she was holding. 'Besides, he totally has the hots for you.'

'Sure, and he's about to sprout wings and summon a warlock,' I said, motioning for her to pass me the printing screen.

Mitra raised her eyebrows. 'Huh, so you're into him too.'

I took the only rational course of action available to me. I squirted her with paint and then ran.

'Tara, this is war!' Mitra screeched behind me. I ducked behind a tree and saw a spray of blue paint fly past. I ducked my head out, but couldn't spot Mitra so made a beeline for the food. She wouldn't risk getting paint on the food, would she? Just as my shoulders relaxed, I saw her, grinning, paint bottles in each hand, advancing on me like a cowboy in a western. I started getting up, but before I got to my feet, Sam raced up behind Mitra and shoved the paper plate we'd been using as a palette right onto Mitra's face.

I laughed so hard I was worried I was going to wet myself. Mitra squirted the two bottles she was holding right onto Sam's hair. The two of them were soon covered in white and blue paint. They looked ridiculous.

'Oh. You think we're done?' Mitra said, pointing at me and stalking in my direction.

She was too close for me to escape, so I closed my eyes and braced for impact. But something warm encircled me – and when I opened my eyes, I was standing in Alex's arms, as Anaya and Kate ran at Mitra wielding paintbrushes and tubes.

'That was close,' I said, turning to look at him. Our eyes locked and his grip tightened. He looked like he was about to say something, but instead, he let me go and threw me an empty pizza box. He held up another like a shield. 'Back to back!' he shouted, and I scooted behind him to obey, feeling like we were gladiators. Sam pointed in our direction from across the yard and Anaya and Kate, who were chasing her and Mitra, changed direction and charged at us. Within seconds, Alex and I were surrounded.

'Truce! Truce!' I called out, waving my pizza box shield, my body streaked blue and white. Kate and Anaya were the first to stop, and when Sam said 'alright', Mitra turned to her with a furious look and tackled her. They fell onto the grass together, laughing.

'Drink?' Kate asked, puffing as she reached for a water.

'Coke, please.' Kate threw me a can, while Alex grabbed a handful of paper towels and handed them out. We sat in a circle, dabbing uselessly at ourselves. I gave up and scrunched my paper towel to the side, leaning back to watch the others. There was no way the paint was going to come off unless I jumped into a shower.

'Oh my God, I jump on a call and it's like *Lord of the Flies* out here,' Meg said, opening the back door and looking around the yard in horror.

I laughed with the others and for the first time realised that maybe, just maybe, Alex was right about socialising. If afternoons like this were possible when I let new people in . . . well, suddenly the idea of opening up to a whole campus didn't feel scary, so much as exciting. Or even . . . fun.

Chapter 10

Wednesdays were my late-start days. I went into the kitchen in my periodic table PJs, took out a frying pan and broke an egg into a saucepan. I planned to take my breakfast into the backyard and go over my readings before heading into uni.

Buzz. Buzz. Buzz.

I groaned and flailed around for my phone. *Mitra work* flashed on the screen. Why on earth would the garage be calling me? 'Hello?'

'Tah-rah.' I knew that masculine, Iranian-accented voice. It was Mitra's uncle, Amoo Ali. I got ready to tell him about uni and that Mum was doing fine. But instead of asking how I was, he just said: *'Beyah-vareshdar.'* ('Come get her.') Then hung up.

I stared at the phone in shock. In the decade I'd known him, he had never once talked to me without spending ten minutes asking after my health and family. For him to be so curt meant something was very wrong. I got dressed, then grabbed my keys and ran out to the car. Mitra worshipped Amoo Ali. He was the only person she listened to. What the hell had happened?

When I pulled up next to the garage, Amoo Ali was sitting on his usual stool in the corner, sipping a cup of tea from a traditional Iranian glass that curved inward like an hourglass. As always, he was surrounded by other old men. They listened to the ABC on radio and talked their days away.

Usually a smile tugged at the edges of his lips, but today they were pressed together. The group wasn't chattering away, but sitting in silence and listening to a weather report like it was a war announcement. Dread crawled up my spine as he caught my eye and tipped his head towards the left garage.

I walked over. Mitra was in navy coveralls splattered in oil stains, angrily polishing the boot of a car. I tiptoed up to her and almost gagged as I got closer. She stank of booze and weed. If she was sober, which I doubted, she couldn't have been for long.

'Hey,' I said.

Mitra looked back, then turned and grabbed a towel to wipe her hands. 'You stalkin' me or somethin'?'

'Amoo Ali wanted me to pick you up.'

Her face fell, and she shuddered. For a second it looked like she was going to crumble. Then she straightened her shoulders, clenched her jaw, hurled the towel into a bin and stormed past me, towards my car. She threw open the driver's door and got in. 'You comin' or what?'

I ran behind her and paused when I saw Amoo Ali, standing red-faced a few metres from the car. Shaking, he raised a hand, index finger pointing in a clear warning. 'Mitra.' He barely had to raise his voice to be sure she heard him, 'Agar Roshan shod [If it turns on], don't come back.'

My heart pounded at the gauntlet he'd thrown down. If she started my car, he'd fire her. She'd been working here since Year 7, despite her dad's disapproval. Her dad tried to ban her from going, but it did no good. Then he'd asked Amoo Ali to fire her, and he refused. The two brothers had stopped speaking after that. I looked from Mitra to Amoo Ali and back, hoping she wouldn't let her ego win. She sat there, but didn't start the engine. She just looked at the dashboard. I turned away. I couldn't watch her drive away from the man she loved more than her own father – and the workplace that was the very heart of who she was.

Then the car door flew open and she stalked over to the passenger seat, slamming the door behind her.

Amoo Ali motioned me over and I obliged him. '*Havast hast*?' he asked. ('Are you paying attention?') It was the way his eyebrow rose, the way he held my gaze, that let me know he was disappointed in me too, for somehow not seeing whatever it was that had caused Mitra to snap. I nodded without looking at him.

He sat down and one of his friends put a hand on his shoulder. He turned away and ran his thumb against his eye. I stared. He hadn't cried when Mitra's dad had disowned him for letting her work in the garage, or even when the news had come that his mother had died. I was going to throttle Mitra for coming so close to breaking the old man's heart.

Khoda, give me strength. I opened the door and pulled back as a wave of smoke hit me. Mitra rolled down the passenger window and blew out a mouthful of pungent smoke. I glowered at the joint in her hand. 'You're such a goody-goody,' she said as she butted it on my dashboard and chucked it from the window to the gutter below. I took a deep breath of fresh air before I got into the driver's seat. We drove back to my place in silence. She was still simmering with rage, and I didn't want to hear about whatever had happened while I was driving.

As we pulled up to the driveway, I pressed the power lock so she had to stay and listen to me. 'Well?'

'Dunno.' She yawned deliberately and turned to look out the window.

'The act's piss weak, Mitra. What the hell is going on?'

She shrugged and rolled her eyes, trying to pretend like she was bored. I reached out and took her hand, squeezing it. She moved away from me and pressed her palm against her forehead.

'I . . .' She coughed up a sob, then unravelled into tears.

I stared at her for a moment, dumbstruck. I'd never seen her cry before, either. She and Amoo Ali could totally beat the British royals in a stiff-upper-lip contest. Except today. The sight of her so vulnerable twisted my stomach. I grabbed her hand and held onto it. 'Mitra . . .'

'I'm gay.' She sniffled and looked up at me, 'I . . . I had sex with her. I had sex with Sam.'

Oh. I held her tighter. I thought of the posters in her bedroom: cars with bikini-clad girls draped over them. How she had never been interested in guys in high school, I just always thought she was too cool for any of the boys around or didn't want to piss off her parents but no, she was gay. I had known that, didn't I? On some level maybe. I mean, it seemed so obvious now – and yet, we'd never talked about it before. I pushed it aside. I'd analyse it later. For now, I just needed to make sure she knew she was still my best friend, that nothing was going to change that.

'Was it . . .' I paused, trying to find the right word '. . . fun?'

'Yeah.' The word was so soft, I had to lean in to hear it. She smiled and a wistful look passed over her face, as if remembering what happened. I felt myself blush.

'We went at it in Dee's back seat. A girl like that in the car I built . . . it was pretty perfect.'

Of course Mitra's dream first time was going at it in the back of her car. 'I love you. Okay? Always.' I said, and her face crumpled.

'I can't go home.'

'Are you sure?'

'Yeah. The old man's still feuding with Amoo Ali over me working in the garage. Mum looks at me like a stubborn stain she can't scrub away. Now this? Dad lost it when Roshan watched five minutes of *Queer Eye* and went around putting up *Vote no* signs for the gay marriage plebiscite.' She turned away, her voice cracking. 'If they find out, they won't ever let me see Roshan or Fadi again.'

'They might surprise you.' At least, I hoped they would.

Mitra shook her head and her shoulders trembled. I squeezed her hand. 'We'll figure it out together, okay? For starters, you can stay with us as long as you want. Mum won't mind.'

'Really?'

'Well, under one condition.'

'What?'

'You have to tell me all about you and Sam. All the details.' Her smile let me know we had a deal.

Chapter 11

I zapped the herbs through the food processor again, before pouring them into a pan, drizzling them with olive oil. The smell of crisping coriander and parsley swirled through the kitchen.

'Let me help. I could do the rice.'

I pointed my wooden spoon at Mitra like it was a sword. 'Don't you touch anything. The last time you put the kettle on, you almost set the place on fire.'

She smiled and leaned back on the counter stool. 'I owe you one.'

I waved her off, stirred the lamb and kidney beans and poured the herbs over them. Big, lazy bubbles pricked the surface of the stew. I squeezed a lemon over it, then turned the heat down. I licked the lemon juice off my palm and turned to Mitra. 'It's going to be okay. Mum's really cool about stuff like this.'

'I just hate having to ask her, is all,' she said, fiddling with her phone.

The door rattled open. 'It smells amazing!' Mum called down the hallway. She walked into the kitchen, her hair smooth, her black pencil skirt, oversized belt and white sleveless blouse as crisp as they were this morning. She let her satchel bag thump on the floor, and looked from me to Mitra before stepping out of her heels. 'What happened?'

'Salam, Leila,' Mitra said, before ducking off to the bathroom, like we'd planned.

'Hi,' I said, walking over and giving Mum a hug. She hugged me back, but when I pulled away, she was frowning.

'It's that bad?' She gave me her *don't pretend* look and a wave of guilt washed over me.

'Is it okay if Mitra stays here for a bit?'

'Sure,' Mum said, her shoulders descending from her ears and her posture relaxing. She moved towards the pot on the stove, stirred the ghormeh and licked the spoon.

'I mean, for like, a few weeks,' I said. Mum arched an eyebrow. 'She . . . she's realised she's gay and wants a bit of space.'

'Do her parents know she's staying with us?' Mum asked, putting down the spoon, moving to the cabinets and taking out a wine glass.

'Hey.' Mitra walked into the living room, ignoring my glare, clearly not caring that she was thwarting our game plan. 'Look, I'm going to find a hotel or somethin'. Dad went a bit mental on the phone when I said I'd be staying here and threatened to come get me, and there's no way I'm dragging you into this.'

Mum sighed and shook her head. She uncorked a bottle of wine and poured generously into her glass. 'Don't be silly, you're here and staying here. I'll deal with Mehdi.' She took a sip, then gestured for Mitra to come closer. She did. 'We love you, okay, for who you are.' Mitra nodded slowly, looking at the floor. Mum took another gulp of her wine. 'Stay as long as you like.'

'Leila, I – '

'Stop! *Khoneyeh kohdeteh.* [This is your home],' Mum said. I'd heard that line a hundred times. It was part of the tradition of *taroof*: of saying something to be polite, prioritising the comfort of others and occasionally saving face. Only this time she wasn't pretending. It wasn't just a line.

She opened a cupboard, pulled out three plates and set them on the counter. 'You both look horrible. Let's get you both some food and sleep.'

I walked up behind her, wrapped my arms around her and held them there. She leaned into me and squeezed my arm.

'Come on, let's eat.'

Chapter 12

'Not bad,' Sam said, placing a splayed hand under her ribcage. 'But next time, really talk from your diaphragm.'

I wanted to scream. Did she not see what I just did?

My legs were so wobbly that I almost stumbled as we walked out of the lecture. I could still see their faces, all hundred of them. Some had watched me with curiosity, others with mocking or boredom. But I hadn't thrown up, which had been the measure of success for the first speech. I'd remembered my lines. And shockingly, a few people had even clapped – *clapped* – when I was done. I'd walked out of the lecture feeling like I'd slayed a dragon. Like maybe, *maybe* this was going to work. That I could show everyone that people like me could lead, could speak for ourselves.

I pushed down my indignation, and practically bounced over to the campaign stall, powered by adrenaline. Mitra and Alex were waiting for us behind a trestle table strewn with clipboards, posters, giant staple guns and calico bags. I cringed at all the leaflets with my face on them.

'Hey you,' Mitra smiled, moving out from behind the table and kissing Sam on the neck. It would be gross if the two of them weren't so darn cute.

Alex made gagging noises, then picked up a cup of chamomile tea and handed it to me. 'Drink. We can't have you losing your voice.' He paused, shuffling through several sheets of paper. 'Now, you have three more lectures today, then I think we should do a couple of poster runs on the hour. Oh, and you're off to the debater's party tomorrow night.'

'Okay.' I fiddled with the handle of my bag, my insides twisting. 'Alright then, see you. I'm heading over to the next one.'

'That's the spirit!' Sam slapped my back.

I looked at the leaflets with my face one more time before walking away. It was only the first day of the campaign, but already people were starting to look at me curiously as I walked the campus. Curiosity instead of pity was a nice change.

I got to the lecture, sat in the front row of the empty auditorium, and picked at my nails. Did I really want to get up and do my Union pitch in front of my own class? I couldn't pretend that I wouldn't see them again, but it wasn't like they wouldn't find out I was running. Eff it. I had already jumped. The only way this would work was if I committed.

By the time I finished my chamomile tea, the room was pretty full. It was a minute past the hour and the lecturer hadn't showed up, so I stood up, went to the lectern and checked the mic. The loud *thump* caught most people's attention. I was about to start when I saw her standing in the far corner, blonde hair hanging down her back, dressed in a grey tulle skirt and white singlet. The princess. *Jess.* She looked at me almost gleefully, like she was glad I would speak, because of course I would embarrass myself. I didn't feel like a nana this time. In my campaign shirt over a black tunic and ripped jeans, I felt hip. I was totally going to show her what I was made of.

My toes twitched and my whole body seemed to want to fly out the door. *I won't run.* The thought anchored me. I cleared my throat and began.

'Hi, I'm Tara,' I said, my voice shaky. I glanced away from Jess and scanned the crowd. 'I'll be honest, I never thought I'd be standing here running for Union. Then I realised that's part of the problem. We all love clubs and societies, love the festivals and revues. And at the same time, so many of us just don't take the next step. I'm not going to stand here and pretend I have all the answers. I'm a first-year, I don't.' People were nodding. A few even smiled encouragingly. Suddenly my voice was clearer – confident, even.

'Here's what I *do* know. I want to help shape a Union that helps us be us. For some of us, that's swooning over Buffy. For others, it's debating. Everyone should be able to find a crew who loves what they do. I also think that we should take care of the staff who help make our uni experiences so special and, of course, that we push each other to be better – with more spaces to learn. That'll take lots of doing: from supporting Radical Sex and Consent Week, to creating a Wellness Week, committing to a zero emissions Union and making sure that we have space to celebrate our traditions, whatever they may be.'

I heard a cheer, looked up and saw Badal clapping. He was also running for Union, on a platform that focused on international students. The back of his shirt read *VOTE FOR BADAL* in lots of different languages.

I wasn't sure if it was because they knew me or because I was less nervous, but there was a lot more nodding and a lot less looking bored in this lecture.

'I'll be honest, I'm not going to be able to do this alone. I'm asking you for more than a vote – I'm asking for you to get involved, so that together we can build a Union that's strong and really gives all of us what we need.'

There wasn't just a *smattering* of applause as I finished this time. Most people actually cheered. I felt invincible, like if I closed my eyes and concentrated, I could fly. Was this how people felt when they took drugs? I sat down, not sure that my skin would be able to hold the excitement that felt like it was sizzling through my blood.

Badal went to the front of the lecture. 'If you don't vote for me, you should totally vote for her.' I mouthed *thank you* to him as others clapped and then he started his pitch. A girl behind me leaned over, her messy copper ponytail falling from one side of her head to the other. 'Great speech,' she said. 'I'm totally going to vote for you.'

I couldn't help but beam. 'Thanks,' I said, before sneaking a glance at Jess. She was tapping a pen against the little foldaway desk chairs in the lecture hall. Her jaw was set, her eyes staring straight ahead. She looked determined.

You know what? I didn't care what she was planning. I was telling my story, showing people who I was, and people *got it*. It wasn't just that they saw me – it was that they wanted to help, to work together to make things easier, kinder and fairer for all of us. That mattered no matter what Jess did.

I walked out of class feeling lighter than I had in forever.

'Tara!'

I turned at my name and froze. Jess was running towards me. I squeezed my phone, trying to channel some fierce energy from its mockingjay cover. I braced myself.

'Let's agree to keep this civil, alright?' she said, pulling herself up to her full height pouting like a Kardashian. What on earth was she talking about? 'Since you've decided to run for Union board too . . .'

I stared at her for a second, and then scoffed. 'Yeah, sure.' A few days ago, the idea of running against Jess would have totally freaked me out. Now, with Alex, Sam, Mitra and a growing team in my corner, I almost felt sorry for her. If she was going to try to screw me over . . . well, bring it on.

'Look, I don't have anything against you, okay?' Jess folded her arms and glared at me like I was wasting her time.

'Alright,' I said checking the time on my phone. Of course she didn't have anything against me *personally*. I was just a representation to her. It wasn't even that we all *looked the same*, it was that we all *were* the same in her mind.

'I just think we should be able to talk about tough issues without being called names.' She tilted her head and smiled tightly, like I was somehow making it hard for her to be polite.

Because obviously, behaving like a racist wasn't nearly as bad as being called a racist. I wasn't going to be able to change her mind any more than I could make Voldemort a model citizen. I'd given her plenty of chances to make amends. And I was fresh out of damns to give.

So, I smiled back at her, and in my brightest, airiest voice said, 'Good luck with that!'. I could feel her staring at my back as I walked away.

'You know, Alex has a thing for lost causes,' she called out after me.

I laughed. Bullies always play dirty when you're getting too strong for their liking. I couldn't help but turn around and call back, 'Is *that* why he had a thing with you?'

I'll admit, I enjoyed the outraged look on her face as she stormed off.

The next few days of the campaign felt like running a marathon. Meet Alex for coffee at 7:45. Speak in front of as many lectures as I could. Go to class. Stop by the stall and judge whoever Alex was flirting with, then feel super guilty for being so judgemental. Talk to people hanging out at the cafeteria at lunch. Go to class, speak in front of more lectures, check in with Alex. Hit the library. Go home, collapse into bed and then do it all over again.

When Thursday night rolled around, Alex handed me a coffee and said, 'You look like hell.'

'Well, aren't you just a gentleman?' I said.

'When was the last time you ate?'

Lunch? No. I'd been running from speaking at a lecture to my own class. I had breakfast, right? Well, no, I'd slept in that morning. But I probably had dinner the night before. I was at least fifty per cent sure I'd burnt my mouth on something at around that point.

'Well, eat this.' He extended a warm paper bag. I opened it to find a cheese and tomato toastie. I bit into it and then practically inhaled the rest.

'I'm taking you out.'

'I'm okay,' I said, but then my tummy gave a very loud rumble. I clamped a hand to my stomach, like I could somehow shush it.

'Come on,' Alex said, grabbing my backpack and slinging it on his shoulder. We walked to the college carpark and got into his car. He opened the door for me. I chuckled and curtsied. 'Why thank you, kind sir.'

He threw his hands up and laughed as I got in. My feet hit a pile of books scattered in front of the passenger seat. I looked back. The back seat was covered in towels, gym bags and sand. I wondered for a second if his room was as messy as his car. I could almost see him apologising to me for the mess as we sat down on his bed . . .

'Want me to turn up the air con?'

'No, I'm okay.' Shit, he had totally caught me blushing. And judging by that smug smile on his face, I bet he somehow knew I'd been thinking about his bedroom. I grabbed a book and did what any self-respecting girl would do. I deflected. 'Aristotle? Well that's just a cliché for a philosophy major.' I waved the book around like it was my lifeline. 'What made you study philosophy anyway?'

He started the car and reversed out of the spot before looking over at me. 'I guess I wanted to learn how to think,' he shrugged. He rubbed his chin with one hand and steered with his other. 'I didn't want to be one of those guys who wakes up at forty thinking the same way I have my whole life, never questioning it.'

'Your parents are cool with that?' We were driving through the city, surrounded by buses and traffic. I glanced out the window, watching the lights of Sydney's skyline flicker between the steel beams as we drove across the Harbour Bridge.

'Mum thought it was clichéd really, and Dad, well he's convinced it's a sign that he's failed and I'm going to somehow end up as a lawyer.' He smiled, and I realised how rare it was that his whole face lit up like that.

'It must be nice to have them back you up like that,' I said.

'Yeah.' But it hardly sounded definitive. He checked his blind spot and switched lanes.

'What?'

We stopped at a red light and he rubbed his eyes with one hand. The campaign was probably getting to him too.

'Sorry, I didn't mean to pry.'

'It's not that, it's just, everyone thinks Dad's so chill and that Mum's grooming me to follow in her footsteps, but it's not like that. I'd get dragged to shoots and events, and as long as I smiled, nothing else really mattered. It was never like, *here's the ropes*, only, *there's the camera*.' Another red light. He tapped his fingers on the steering wheel. 'I busted my butt in high school, did a bunch of stuff on my own – but it was always *Rita's son* this, *Doug's boy* that. They're both happy to drag me to their events, but neither one actually sees me as someone who could do what they do.'

'That sucks.' I just blurted it out, then looked over, worried he thought I was kidding around. He glanced over at me and nodded as he watched the road.

I closed my eyes and stretched. It was nice to know that he had issues with his folks too – that his parents might be super famous, but they weren't some kind of perfect sit-com family. He pulled over and I looked around. We were near a park, right by the harbour. He opened the door to waves lapping the rocks and the smell of salt.

There were no rings under his eyes – if anything, he looked well rested. Over and over during the campaign, I'd seen him walk up to people, say exactly the right thing and leave smiles and glowing eyes behind him. After doing it ten gazillion times, I was getting better at it. But didn't each one of those conversations erode him? Was it something he was born good at, or something he'd gotten good at?

'How do you do it?' I asked, looking up at him. 'How do you get people to like you so easily?'

I cringed. It sounded so much worse aloud than it had in my head. I turned and opened my mouth, determined to blurt out something, *anything* to smudge away my words.

'People don't see me, they just like the idea of me,' he said. I thought about that. I knew what it felt like for people only to see an *idea* of you. What they imagine you represent, rather than who you are.

It took all of my self control, but I didn't say anything. I just waited. He walked over to the green iron railings, and leaned over, staring out at the harbour. 'I'm Rita's son, or people stop me to ask if I know how much I look like Dad. You'd be surprised how many people hang out with me trying to get into their good graces.' It might have been the first time I'd seen him so raw. 'If people don't know who I am, they tend to hand me my arse.' He looked up at me then, a gleam in his eye.

Wait, did he mean me? 'I did not . . .'

'You totally did.' His smile got cheekier. 'I liked it. Still do.'

I bumped my shoulder against his and shivered despite the warmth of the evening. *If his shoulder touching mine could make me shiver like that . . .* Nope. Wasn't going to go there.

'Did you really hook up with Kendall Jenner?' Okay, I was deflecting again. I couldn't help it.

He burst out laughing. 'No, it was one of Dad's set-ups.'

'*What*?'

'He was interviewing her, he told her I was super picky and

since she was like, the ideal woman, would she agree to go out with me? She said yes, so he called me and put me on speaker. He didn't say a word about who was on the other end of the line with him. He just said, *I got the perfect woman to agree to go out with you.*'

'What happened then?'

'I laughed and asked if he had Kylie on the show. Everyone was so mortified that it thankfully never made it to air. And no, we never actually went out. It was an on-air stunt.'

We walked together in silence for a bit. Our footsteps echoed on the gravel and harmonised with the waves. He kept turning to me, like he was trying to work up the guts to say something. It was the first time we'd been quiet together, and the air was heavy between us. I kicked a pebble off the path.

'Why do you wear it?' he asked.

My first instinct was to say something silly, but I didn't. He'd been real with me. 'Because thinking about God – *Khoda* – helps me remember what matters.' He looked over at me, but didn't say anything. I took a breath and looked away. At the ground, at the harbour. At anything but him.

'I don't know. Dad left me and Mum before my first birthday. He lives overseas, barely communicates with us – with me. And when he does, it's like he's talking to the daughter he wants to have, not who I am. He doesn't care who I am. It just makes me feel like I'll never be good enough.' But that wasn't it, not really. 'I don't feel like people see me. From when I was little. They tell me how good my English is, or how pretty I am – and the thing I can always hear them saying is, *for someone like you.*'

His sigh made me look up. He was shaking his head, his forehead wrinkled. I had to get this out before I lost my nerve.

'Then I let this guy walk all over me, and I kind of fell apart. I started meditating, I found my grandma's old prayer mat and figured, why not? YouTubed to learn how to use it. Then my grandma found me praying, and it became something we shared. The idea that there's a God out there, or something in the universe that we don't really understand, that's infinite, but still cares, that will always care? I don't know, I wanted to hold onto that feeling, so I started wearing hijab, to shut out the noise, so that I could just be me.'

For once I was too exhausted to overthink, to worry about him running the other way, so I just kept talking, 'My grandma passed last year.' I paused, pushing away the memory of her on her kitchen floor, of calling 000. 'Heart attack. It was like someone tore away a chunk of me. All of it – the praying, the hijab – made it bearable.'

'I'm sorry,' he whispered, so quietly that I almost didn't hear him.

I wiped away a tear, sniffled. 'She used to love telling me about her and my grandfather. About how they'd fallen in love, how they'd plotted to get her dad to say yes to them getting married. She turned me into a romantic.' I smiled, holding onto that feeling of warmth, using it as a foothold to climb back out of my grief. 'I know we're all meant to hook up, swipe left or whatever, but I'm not cut out for it. I want someone to really *see* me. And even if it doesn't last forever, I want to know that if I'm with someone, it matters.' I laughed, trying to lighten the mood. 'Besides, I figured, the hijab was probably a better filter than some algorithm no one understands.'

'Oh.'

'What?'

'I just never thought of it that way,' he said.

'No one assumes that I had to sneak around to pray, or that my parents both hate that I wear it. You know, saying I believe in magic is cool, but that I believe in God? That crosses a line.'

'I'm sorry.' He stopped and I turned to face him. The muscles on his jaw clenched and then relaxed. 'I just . . . I never got how relentless all that crap is until the past few days, watching you cop all the questions and the looks. It would have done my head in if it had been me.'

'You get used to it.'

'You don't though, do you?' He gave me a look and a part of me knew he got it. 'Besides, you shouldn't have to,' he said. We started walking again. The silence between us was different this time. It felt like we were in it together. I revelled in it as we meandered along the water.

'We're here,' he said.

I looked over and saw that we were standing by the huge laughing gates of Luna Park. 'I know it's a bit corny, but between the election and everything else, I figured it would be nice to just have some old-fashioned fun,' he said, his hands in his pockets, an eyebrow raised a little, like he was nervous maybe?

'It's perfect.'

Chapter 13

We pushed plastic balls down the mouths of porcelain clowns, shot darts at balloons and smashed into each other in bumper cars. We strolled through the park, the ocean breeze mingling with the sizzle of sausages and popcorn and the bright lights and carnival music. I wanted to twirl around, throw my head back and squeal with joy. Instead, I smiled at Alex and said, 'I'm having so much fun.'

'Pirate ship before dinner?' He squinted and *arr*-ed like a pirate.

'Alex!' came a nearby voice.

His whole body tensed as he moved towards it, away from me.

'What happened to the pub crawl?' Alex had an edge to his voice. I pretended I was looking at a souvenir stand, while checking out the group he'd drifted to talk to.

The guys were all in polo shirts with jeans. Sunglasses that probably cost more than my car were perched on their heads or dangling from their collars. The girls were in short skirts, sparkly tops and fancy flats, their hair hanging down their backs. I looked closer at one of the blondes. One of the taller guys had an arm wrapped around her shoulder. Her head was down, intent on her phone. She looked up at him and I got a clear look at her face. Jess.

'One of the guys at Dad's firm scored a big deal,' the guy said, the breeze catching his artfully messy blonde hair. I assumed he must be Steve. 'So they're having a little get-together here. These tossers can't turn down free booze or a side of fireworks, so here we are.' He flicked his arms proprietorially, like we were in his living room. It made me want to grind my teeth.

'I texted you like twenty minutes ago, you said you were hitting the books tonight. Please don't tell me you have some creepy fetish for clowns . . .' one of the guys said, swigging his Corona and smiling. The others laughed. Twenty minutes ago we were getting into a car together, I thought, but kept my face as neutral as I could.

Alex threw me an apologetic glance before turning back to the group. 'I'm here with someone, actually.' He didn't get any points for that, since he made no move to point out he was with me or to introduce me to his mates.

'Why don't you both join us?' Steve asked, glancing at his Rolex.

'Nah man, he's here with *her*.'

My stomach sank like I was free-falling on a rollercoaster. The guy who had spoken was pointing at me, a sneer curling his lip. Jess stared too, her face blank.

Alex stepped in front of me. 'Don't be a dick,' he said, folding his arms in front of him.

'Or what, she'll get her cousins to blow me up?'

Alex lunged forward, but Jess stepped in front of the guy who'd made the comment. Alex stopped, took a breath and glared at her.

'Oh, come on,' Jess said, twirling her hair and tilting her face up at him. 'Can't you take a joke anymore?'

'Didn't see you laughing,' he said, pulling himself to his full height and looking down his nose at her.

Jess shrugged and walked back to Steve. 'Let's go already.' The guy who had first called out to him stared Alex down for another few moments before following the rest of the group. I clenched and unclenched my hands as I waited for Alex to face me. Everything – the ocean air, the music, the lights, the sweet, salty food aromas – made my stomach turn now.

It took Alex a good minute or so to turn around. His brows were furrowed, his body tense. I worried he might snap. 'You okay?' he asked. It sounded more annoyed than concerned.

I shrugged. 'I've been through worse.'

He shook his head and ran a hand through his hair. He looked back at me and held my gaze. Then he seemed to unfurl. 'I can't believe Drew. I'm sorry . . . for all of it.'

I didn't know what was worse. The smug look on Jess's face, the contempt from his mate, or that Alex had lied about hanging out with me.

'Whatever.'

He flinched like I'd hit him. 'Tara – ' he said.

'Don't. We should go, since you're apparently studying. Wouldn't want anyone else to catch you out here with me.' In my head it sounded like a joke, but the words cracked from my mouth like a whip. I couldn't pretend I wasn't hurt.

I expected him to tense back up, but he shook his head and sighed heavily. 'You think I'm ashamed of you?'

'Why else would you lie to them?' It was one thing to run my campaign and totally another for us to just hang out.

'You know, at some point you're going to have to stop assuming the worst about me.' He rubbed his eyes and then looked at me. 'I'll explain over dinner and I promise you can throw the drink in my face if you're still mad by the end of it.'

I was still pissed off, but it didn't feel fair to walk out now. Besides, I was hungry. He nodded, his shoulders relaxing when I didn't say anything. For a moment I'd been relieved that he was ashamed of me. It would make it so much easier to draw neat lines around our friendship.

He led me over to one of the hot food stands and got us some chips and falafel, before hiding the food in a souvenir bag and walking us over to the line for the ferris wheel. 'Might as well have dinner with a view,' he smiled sheepishly. Within five minutes, we had a whole cabin to ourselves.

He leaned back against the circular walls of the cabin. 'I'm going to tell you something about the colleges. But you have to promise not to share what I'm about to tell you, okay?'

I nodded.

'During Welcome Week, there's always piss-ups and well, let's say the freshers have to prove themselves. Last year we had to take a mate to hospital for alcohol poisoning, but that wasn't the worst of it. I did a bunch of stuff last year that I'm not proud of. There's this game called King's Haul, where you're meant to nick embarrassing stuff from other people's rooms – they wanted me to steal undies from a girl's dorm. I knocked on her door and asked for them and she gave me a pair. It felt gross, even though she was okay with it. It still feels gross, and I've kept my head down since. We all live together, but I try to keep my distance.'

His voice was so soft that I had to edge closer just to hear him.

I was practically leaning against him. It was as much to comfort him as to steady myself. I still felt rancid after spending just a few minutes with that lot. I couldn't imagine what it would be like to share a dorm with them. 'Why don't you leave?'

He moved his arm, and for a second I thought he was going to pull away. Instead, he moved his arm just behind me, poised above my shoulders.

'It would break Dad's heart. He loved it there, told me it was the best time of his life.' He leaned his face against my head and I turned to look at him. His green eyes darkened, his eyelids lowered and he moved his face closer.

'Alex . . .'

The cabin swayed, pushing us away from each other as the ferris wheel started to turn. He chuckled. And, well, I was superstitious enough to take that as a sign of the universe waving its finger in my face. *No, he's not for you.*

'We should probably eat before it gets cold.' I now clearly held the new record for the least suave thing anyone had ever said. He gave me an odd look. Goosebumps prickled my arms. I looked away.

How had I been so wrong about him? He might not have a cape, or a magic amulet, but he was brave, he was honourable – and, most of all, he had my back. A voice in the back of my head whispered *careful,* but it felt like it was already too late.

As we tore the foil from the falafel wraps, a sharp whine tore the air and exploded into a fizzing red shower over the harbour. We ate in silence, watching the lights dazzle and dance, stealing glances at each other between mouthfuls.

Chapter 14

I noticed the lights on as Alex pulled up by the house. Mum had waited up?

I unbuckled my seatbelt. If we were in a movie, this would be when we kissed. But I wasn't ready for that. I had no idea what I was meant to say. *Thanks*? Why did that feel totally insufficient?

'That was fun,' Alex said.

What if, for him, the whole night had just been two mates hanging out?

'Ahh, thanks,' I said, groaning inwardly about how childish I sounded. I pushed the car door open, desperate to escape the awkwardness.

'Tara, I . . .' He stopped, staring at me, then shook his head, 'I . . . I'll see you tomorrow.'

I nodded. That was clearly not what he had wanted to say. Was it going to be this weird through the rest of the campaign? I waved as he drove away.

'You fucking held out on me!' My whole body relaxed at the sound of Mitra's voice. 'I have to hear from *Leila* that you're going on dates now?' I'd texted Mum that I was having dinner with Alex. An accelerating car boomed from whichever *Fast and the Furious* movie Mitra was watching. 'Spill, spill – how'd it go?'

I fell onto the couch next to her. 'It wasn't a date,' I said.

'*Riiight*, 'cause that's like, *banned*, by the Union bylaws?'

'It is?' I said. Mitra pinched me. Okay, I deserved that. 'It doesn't matter, I can't date.' It wasn't about med, or about God. It was more that I didn't do things like that. I didn't understand how people dated for a few weeks, or even months, to test someone out. When I fell for someone, I *fell* for them, and I couldn't risk that with Alex.

'Yeah, 'cause if you touch the Quran after holding hands with a man, that's haram. I hear you can burst right into flame just like *that*.' She finished the sentence with a click of her fingers.

'Be serious,' I said, grabbing a punnet of chocolate ice cream from the freezer, and two spoons. As I pushed the cutlery drawer shut with my hip, Mum emerged from her bedroom.

'You're back.' She looked me over and smiled. 'You should wear eyeliner more often, it suits you.' Okay, yes, I'd started wearing eyeliner, since campaigning made me look like a zombie . . . and, yes, because I was spending so much time with Alex. But there was something about the way Mum smiled when she said it that made me want to rub it off. But I didn't, because I wasn't five. Instead, I walked back to the couch and handed Mitra a spoon. She grabbed the punnet from my hands and managed to scoop out a third of the carton for her first bite.

'Don't stay up too late, you two. And *vaveyla* [God help you] if you spill ice cream on my couch.'

'I'm voting for you!' a girl yelled as I walked out of the library. I gave her my best *thank you* smile. It was still weird walking by posters with my name on them. I couldn't believe the elections were next week. I had to head by the stall to get tomorrow's schedule of my lecture talks, or Sam would murder me. It was so weird. Anaya, Linda, Kate and Meg had all become regulars at the stall and every day, new people joined them. They'd all signed up to put up posters and stickers, and hand out leaflets.

Alex schooled them all in his campaign hacks. 1) Poster ten minutes before the hour, so you get the most foot traffic, 2) Don't forget to put a poster under the clocks in lecture theatres (yes, that's where most of us look), and 3) If someone asks you more than two questions, bring them back here for a free T-shirt. Two weeks ago, those little tips had blown my mind, but now, they felt routine.

I turned the corner and froze. On the pavement in big, bold letters, someone had chalked the words MUSLIMS OUT. I pulled my thin cardigan closer to my body. I rounded a corner and – oh god – there was another one. SAY NO TO ISLAM was spray-painted on the wall.

It felt like a gut punch. I ran back into the stall. Alex was there, yelling into his phone. He looked up, saw me and ran over.

'You okay?' he asked, putting a hand over his phone.

I nodded. He shook his head, swore and put the phone back to his ear.

'Look, if it's not cleaned up in the next few hours, I swear I'll get news crews down here.' He hung up and looked back at me. 'Sorry, it was campus security. They're going to wash it off.'

'No.' I didn't want to wash it away – I wanted to respond. I thought back to Katniss, and how she'd used her costumes to help overthrow an empire. I had to be creative. I had an idea, but I didn't know if it would work.

'Do we have chalk?' I asked. Alex nodded. 'Good. I'll grab

that, and the others. Can you see if there's anyone from *Honi Soit* who can come by and take a photo in an hour?'

'Tara . . .'

'I got this, okay?' I said. He nodded and started texting everyone he knew on the campus newspaper.

I bounded towards the stall. Four volunteers were hanging out there: Anaya, Mohammad, and Nick and Jane, climate activists who were volunteering because they really wanted to see an emission-free campus. I got them to huddle in close and talked them through the plan, which they enthusiastically agreed to. We all grabbed some chalk, walking towards the graffiti with the swagger of an eighties rock band.

We started on SAY NO TO ISLAM. Anaya filmed and took photos while the rest of us attacked the writing on the wall, adding in more letters, drawing in hearts and flowers. After twenty minutes we stepped back, muscles sore, breathing hard, like we'd just been out for a group run. It was worth it. The wall now cried out SAY NO TO ISLAMOPHOBIA and was covered in rainbow swirls and hearts.

We moved on to the other slur. MUSLIMS OUT. The words made me shiver: they reminded me of angry crowds in the Reclaim Australia marches that had played on the news, and made me look over my shoulder whenever I walked home. We huddled on our hands and knees, applying chalk to concrete. It felt cathartic, blotting out the hate with a new message. When we finished, we stood up. I pulled out my phone, snapped a photo and texted it to Mitra. *This is for you.*

The chalk now spelled, MUSLIMS OUT AND PROUD!, adorned with rainbow flags and hearts. Anaya wasn't done, though. She wanted to get footage of us dancing, so she could add music and cut it with before-and-after shots of the graffiti. I was so proud of what we'd done that I not only said *yes*, but really went for it, shaking my hips and hands to the beat.

Alex appeared and I stepped towards him. 'The *Honi* photographer is going to be here in a minute. One of the editors wants to interview you, if you're keen. Will you tell me the . . .' I pointed to what we'd done. Alex looked at the new mural, shook his head and fist-bumped me.

I wanted to tell him that I was only brave because of everyone who was doing this with me. That for the first time I felt like I belonged, that I fit in – that I wasn't just some awkward nerd, but was actually *doing* something. I didn't know how to say it though, and before I could get something out, Sam bounded towards us, slapped us on the back and said, 'This is fucking awesome!'

Anaya edited the video on her phone and then showed me the clip before she posted. Taylor Swift started singing *haters gonna hate, hate, hate,* and the footage was of all of us dancing. Then as the words changed to *shake it off, shake it off,* the footage turned to us shaking chalk over our new graffiti. 'This is sooo good Anaya!' I said, looking up at her.

'I know,' she said, winking at me and posting the video.

Then, between the photographers, the interviews, the comments online (including a few people who didn't like that I was dancing in hijab) and just the sheer number of people who stopped by to take selfies with our team and the mural, we all decided to go grab some Thai food to celebrate.

Alex sat next to me at the restaurant. We barely said two words to each other the whole night: there were volunteers to chat to, and we were pretty much co-hosting this impromptu shindig. At some point, his knee tapped mine under the table. I didn't pull away. For the rest of the meal, his leg stayed pressed against mine.

If there was a perfect Saturday, this was it. Mitra, Mum and I had gone out for fancy brunch at Mum's favourite cafe, which had six-dollar watered-down coffees and three different haloumi options on the menu. I'd had one of those study days where it feels like you smash every hurdle. Weekly online exam? Nailed it. Essay due in two weeks? Drafted. Exam notes? On top of it.

Weirdly, running for student union had made my grades better, since I'd replaced stretches of day-dreaming – and yes, okay, stolen chunks of time fantasy reading – with just doing the work. So even though I was spending less time studying, I was getting as much, if not more, done when I *was* doing it.

My phone beeped and I looked at the message from Alex:

Any chance I can pop by?

Mitra was with Sam and Mum was at the gym, so I had the place to myself. I couldn't just say yes to having a boy over, could I? Apparently I could.

Sure.

I stared at the message, surprised I'd had the nerve to send it. Then I made a mad dash around the house, clearing away all the embarrassing baby photos I was aware of.

Twenty minutes later, Alex was at the door, hiding something behind him as he walked up the driveway. 'Hey.' He pulled a box from behind his back. I couldn't help but melt as I looked at the worn cardboard box reading *Operation*. 'Since you're transferring into med soon, I figured you might as well start practising being a doctor.'

'Come in,' I said. Mum had found some jasmine on her morning run and brought back a handful, so the house smelled of it.

'Do you want some tea?' I asked, feeling jittery. He nodded and followed me to the kitchen. My neck tingled and I pressed my fingernails into my palms. I was alone. In my house. With a boy.

I wanted to think of something clever to say, but between that smirk and the way his hair curled above his eye, I could barely think at all. The whistling kettle saved me. I reached up for the mason jars where I kept my special blends of tea. I grabbed one of my favourites, Earl Grey mixed with lavender and jasmine. It had taken me months to get the blend just right. I twisted the jar open, taking a moment to enjoy its pungent, sweet scent before holding it out to Alex.

He sniffed the jar and looked up at me. 'Wonderful.'

I turned and spooned some of the tea into a pot, then slowly poured the steaming water over the leaves. There was something magical about the process, the way it conjured a soothing scent.

I lifted myself on the tips of my toes to grab the purple mugs painted with little flowers from the cabinet, but before I could, Alex reached up and took out two easily. For a second I could feel him against my back. I turned and our bodies brushed against each other. I could have sworn that he took a sharper breath before taking a step back.

'I have to warn you, I'm very good at this game,' he said as he walked into the living room and started to unpack the game on the coffee table. The way he smiled told me that he was more than a little bit proud of it.

'I've never played before.'

'Okay. So all you need to do is try to help this poor dude.' He gestured to the nude man with cut-outs for body parts on the board. 'You grab a card.' Alex grabbed one from the pile on the table and turned it over for me to see. 'I need to get a butterfly out of his stomach for one hundred dollars.' I looked down. There was a plastic butterfly in the man's stomach cavity.

'They're not kidding when they say surgery is expensive in the States.'

Alex chuckled, but held up a finger. 'Now don't go trying to distract me.' He grabbed a pair of tweezers and scrunched his lips to the left with concentration. 'All you need to do is – '

BEZZZZ

'Wait, it's like . . .' He prodded the tweezer back into the toy.

BEZZZZ

'Dammit!'

I hadn't laughed this hard in forever. The board buzzed an alarm whenever the tweezers touched the edges of a cavity. It was the first time I'd ever seen Alex sulk.

'Maybe he likes the butterfly?' I said, leaning over and giving his shoulder a squeeze. He brushed his fingers over mine, before pulling away to reach for his cup.

'This is really good tea.' He looked at me without a hint of sarcasm.

'It's my secret blend.'

'You have your own blend?' he asked, eyebrows raised.

'Yeah, I spent a whole weekend playing around with different tea and spice combinations. This one turned out the best – well, it's the one I liked the best. I put chilli powder in one blend as a joke and Mum loved it. She said it was about time that tea got some backbone.' Eep, I'd started babbling. I twisted the edge of my hijab around a finger before pulling up my sleeves and reaching for the deck of cards.

'Wishbone for three hundred dollars. That looks hard! Okay, I'm going in.' I bit my lip, trying to keep my hands still. I grabbed the white plastic wishbone. I pressed the tweezers. I was going to do it – get it out on the first go. I was almost ready to celebrate when . . .

BEZZZZ

'Show off,' Alex said, eyes bright. He reached out, the tips of his fingers grazing my left temple as he tucked a stray hair under my hijab. I looked up at his eyes and he leaned closer. My eyelids fluttered closed and my heart pounded. He was going to kiss me and I wanted him to do it.

'Tara!' Mitra called, slamming the front door behind her. Her voice had sucker-punched Alex all the way to the other side of the coffee table. 'Oh, hi – '

'Hi,' I snapped. Alex gave her a quick wave, pulling himself up to sit on the couch.

'There's a queer Arab dance party happening tonight, and you're coming!'

'What?' I looked over at Alex and threw him my best apologetic look.

'Your insides are gonna grow mould if you drink any more tea. Besides, it's Saturday.'

'Do you want to come?' I asked Alex. He opened his mouth –

'What am I, the straight brigade? You don't understand the cred hit I'm taking just bringing you. No offence, Alex. Besides,

I'll spew if I have to watch the two of you making googly eyes at each other all night.'

'Mitra!'

She had the audacity to wink at me.

Alex chuckled, shaking his head. 'No worries. Tara, I'll text you? Mitra, impeccable timing as always.'

I stood and waved awkwardly as he walked to the door. He gently punched Mitra on the shoulder as he made his way to the hallway and whispered something in her ear that made her laugh and punch him back.

'You're alright mate,' Mitra said, before shutting the door behind him. 'You know the whole Elizabeth Bennett thing got passé with the third Bridget Jones movie, right?'

'You're the worst. The literal worst, you know that?' I said, packing up the game and trying not to pout. 'And no,' I held up a hand and looked her straight in the eyes, 'there's no way you're dragging me to a dance party.'

'You gotta come.' Mitra fell on the couch beside me and ran a hand through her hair. 'Look, Sam wants to go, and I need back-up. I'll go berserk if I walk into a party that's a bunch of white girls pretending to be belly dancers. How 'bout it – save me from being the only pigeon in a pack of doves?'

I pouted at her for a moment, then sighed, 'What would I wear?'

'Oh . . .' The gleam in Mitra's eyes gave me instant regret. 'I got you covered.' She grabbed my hand and pulled me to the closet room.

Chapter 15

Mitra rummaged through a suitcase in the corner. 'Uh-*huh*!' She threw a sparkly red thing at me. I just caught it, and was surprised by how soft the chiffon was. I unfurled a long skirt, sparkling as if someone had dusted it with glitter.

'I bought it for a few bucks at Newtown Vinnie's. It's too nice to chuck, but too princessy for me. Pair it with that tight black blouse and wear your black scarf turban-style.'

'Yes ma'am,' I said, giving her a general's salute as I stepped out of my jeans.

Mitra switched her black jeans for harem pants, and her signature black singlet for a black blouse with a plunging V-neck, worn with giant hoop earrings and a chunky gold necklace. Cleopatra probably would have told her to tone it down a bit.

'Ooh, that looks good – it needs something though.' She looked me over. 'Oh, I know.' She reached under the bed and pulled out a necklace: giant fake rubies mounted in gold. With my hijab tied so it looked like a turban, people would actually be able to see my neck.

'Isn't that a bit much?' I asked.

'You look hot,' Mitra said as I kept toying with the necklace. 'Trust me, take a risk and live a little. It's just one outfit, one night.' She was right. It would be fun to see how people reacted to me in this ensemble. Well, it would be nice to see how one particular person reacted. Though of course, he wouldn't be there. Mitra nodded, satisfied.

She pulled on some gold sandals and re-applied her bright red lipstick. She rubbed her lips together and blew a kiss at the mirror. Then she handed me the lipstick. I put it on her bedside table.

'What are you doing? Put it on.' It took me a second to understand. I had worn strawberry chapstick once in Year 10, but red lipstick? There's no way I could pull it off. 'Forget it, sit,' Mitra said. I pushed off some clothes from the unfurled couch bed. Mitra grabbed two bags the size of clutches from the floor, then sat down next to me.

'Don't look so scared, it's not gonna hurt.'

'To be clear. This is a one-time thing. This doesn't mean you can empty out a Myer beauty counter's worth of make-up on my face.'

'You've seen my daytime look. I can do subtle.' Was she joking? I must have looked horrified, because she burst out laughing. Mitra got out a make-up brush. She dashed some liquid on my face and then pulled back, like an artist examining her work. Her brows pulled together, unsatisfied. She got out another tube and mixed some foundation on the back of her hand. Once she had a base layer she was happy with, she moved to my lips. She inspected four different lipsticks, then moved to the corner, where she started rummaging through one handbag after the next. After she tipped out the third handbag, she gave out a victorious *a-ha!* and came back to the bed.

'Open up,' Mitra instructed, tapping her finger to my mouth. I obeyed. She smudged the lipstick across my lips and grabbed a tissue from a box on the floor. 'Dab,' she said. I did. 'Have a look.'

I was impressed. Mitra had more skill with that make-up brush than I gave her credit for. Red lipstick suited me after all – but I never would have worn it without her prod. She hadn't given me winged eyelids, but a subtle, smoky eye that brought out the amber flecks in my irises. It felt like I was wearing a pretty-girl disguise. It was like a Cinderella deal, except that the illusion would disappear with my next shower, instead of midnight.

We headed out, climbed into Dee and drove to Marrickville. It was Saturday night and the streets were filled with the after-work crowd and uni students looking for a good time.

'So, are you and Alex a thing?' Mitra asked.

'I don't know, are you and Sam a *thing*?' I made quote marks with my fingers.

'The drawer I have at her place seems to point to *yes*. You and Alex looked like you were ready to suck face as I walked in.'

I rested my head against my palm. 'I don't know. You know me, I don't do anything casually.'

'What makes you think he does? Wait, don't tell me you've internalised that sexist bullshit that all guys just want to bang and run?' She gave me a wicked side-eye as she turned past the giant Coca-Cola sign.

'Of course not.' I said. Of course, I one hundred per cent had. 'I mean you know what they say about him.' Hadn't Mitra herself told me he didn't do girlfriends?

'Have you heard what they say about *you*? I mean come on. People assume you're a nun in that thing.'

Well, she had a point. I had totally bought the Kendall Jenner hook-up and that hadn't been true. I'd seen him flirting with a bunch of people, but that was also him just being . . . him. Since we'd met, I hadn't seen or heard of him hooking up with anyone.

We drove down to Marrickville and Mitra parked the car into a tight space with the smooth confidence of a race-car driver. We got out and I was glad for the chill in the air. It made my face tingle and anchored me in the moment.

We walked for a few moments before Mitra abruptly stopped in front of the black door of a run-down-looking warehouse. The block was deserted and there was no sign that anyone had passed here in days, let alone that a party was going on inside.

'Are you sure?' I asked, ashamed that it came out as a whisper. Mitra threw me a wicked grin and slammed her body against the door, which creaked open in response. The man inside would have scared a demon back to Hades, with his shaved head, leather vest, ripped jeans and solid glare.

'What are you doing here?' he said, arms folded across his massive chest. He was standing in a small corridor. Behind him there were stairs. No music, no other people, nothing. I pulled at Mitra's arm. There was no way this place was safe.

'Fairydust,' Mitra said. The man unfolded his arms and sat down on a stool next to the door.

'Head down. The knob is dodgy, you have to give it a good shove to get in,' he said, waving us forward. I jumped when the door banged closed behind us. 'Don't worry love, we don't bite. Unless you'd like us to.'

'Don't scare her, Rob,' Mitra said, before grabbing my hand and heading down the stairs.

'Rob?'

'Sam loves it here. You'll think of Rob differently after he starts twerkin' on the dance floor.'

The image calmed me down. As we moved down the stairs, the faint music escalated to full-blown thudding. The door at the end of the stairs was white, with a small rainbow sticker. Mitra turned the knob, the door swung open and music erupted out.

It had the soul and head-bobbing feel of boy-band-style pop, but instead of synthesised violins, it was seasoned with sitars and percussion. The singing was as smooth as a Britney or Mariah, but the lyrics were in Arabic. I started swaying with the music – it felt familiar. I could catch some of the words – enough to feel kinship, but not enough to understand. It teased me the way French does with some English speakers who eat *croissants* and drink *champagne*.

The place was the size of your average corner pub. It was hot. It wasn't mosh-pit packed – you could move, dance – but it was brimming. The walls and ceilings were black. Rainbow lights bounced off a mirror ball in the middle of the ceiling. There was a bar in the corner and a slightly elevated area for the DJ. Right next to the door was a woman with khaki pants and a striped collared shirt. Next to her a sign screamed: NO PHOTOS.

'Phones, please!' she yelled over the music, opening a bright orange tub with the number 587 plastered on the side. Mitra chucked her phone in the tub and I hesitated, before a glare from the counter woman made me drop my device. Mitra grabbed the number and winked at the phone snatcher.

'So people don't get outed on Insta!' Mitra yelled, as she shimmied into the party.

I nodded. The music wouldn't let me process the idea, though. It hammered on, demanding my attention, and my hips yielded to its command. Mitra led us into the crowd, no doubt looking for Sam. She was in no danger of being a pigeon among doves. There were brown bodies everywhere. Swaying, dancing, kissing. We walked around two guys, who I would have described as wog bros, passionately making out. An Adonis walked by, bare-chested, the tree of Lebanon tattooed on his neck. He nodded amiably.

A guy with a cap on backwards and a Sex Pistols T-shirt had wrapped a belly dancer's shawl around his waist and was shimmying his hips and singing his heart out. Then there were the belly-dancing drag queens, who moved with the grace of cobras. Watching them made me realise how much of what we think of as gender was a performance. It made me cringe about how casually I had walked in and decided who was a 'he' and who was a 'she.'

I almost fell headlong into Mitra when she suddenly stopped. Sam's purple hair was pink under the light. She was wearing skater-boy pants and a white singlet. The piercings in her lip popped like fireworks under the spray of the mirror ball. Sam grabbed Mitra's hand and pulled her close, saying something in her ear before kissing her. A few people spotted them and started doing ululations. Hearing that *kou looo looo* sound reminded me of every Iranian wedding I had been to. I joined in, though my *kou loo*s weren't nearly as good.

Sam and Mitra started laughing mid-kiss from the attention. Mitra turned towards me. Sam dipped her head backwards in greeting. I waved. Mitra motioned for a drink, then pointed to the bar. I shook my head and she rolled her eyes at me and disappeared towards it. I was about to make my way towards Sam when someone grabbed my wrist and twirled me around.

'Dance!' one of the drag queens demanded. I obliged. We swayed our hips together. I hadn't even noticed that people had formed a circle around us to watch until the dance was done. I laughed and wrapped my arms around my new belly-dancing friend.

It felt like we'd found a portal into a magical world where you could be whoever you wanted to be. Fear meandered below the surface, lurking in little glances, in the pauses between the music, in the empty glasses. There were so many people who would object to everything this party stood for, who would lash out, or try to wipe out what was here. I closed my eyes, marinating in the music. Yes, this world was fragile and there was no part of me that believed God punished people for love. I thought about all the people who believed that events like this meant the end of civilisation. That people like us just wanted to burn it all down. You know what? Maybe we *would* burn down their world. Maybe it was about damn time.

The bar was packed. Even though there was a water station on the corner, the jug was empty. While I was waiting for the bartender to refill it, Mitra appeared by my side. She mimed walking away. I nodded, ready to leave. She grabbed my hand and pushed into the crowd. Sam was standing at the counter by the door, our phones in her hand.

I turned on my phone as we walked up the stairs, waving to Rob the bouncer. He nodded back like we had known each other for years. I glanced back at my phone to see I had a message from Alex.

How's the dance party going?

'Ooooooh!' Mitra cooed behind me, her voice a slightly higher pitch than normal. She was gently swaying too, Sam's hand around her waist holding her steady.

'What?' Sam said, stumbling and almost taking them both down.

'Tara and Alex sitting in a tree. F – U – C . . .' Mitra made lewd hand gestures as she sang.

Sam swatted Mitra's hands and pulled her in for another kiss. The two of them were so fierce. I wanted that too. So I started typing.

Awesome. Haven't danced like that in forever. I paused, biting my lip and then typed out: *Fancy a nightcap?* My thumb hovered over the backspace button, but I took a breath and pressed send instead.

Yep, I'm at the Courthouse, meet me here?

We were only a 15-minute walk away, but seeing how intertwined Mitra and Sam were, I ordered an Uber and waved goodbye. I pulled out my phone once I was in the car.

See you in five.

Chapter 16

He was waiting for me outside the pub, wearing a red plaid shirt over a loose white tank, leaning against the sandstone wall. His head tilted towards the stars. The glow of the streetlight caught his hair, accentuated the curl. Then he looked up and smiled. It wasn't a big, toothy grin, just a curve of his lips – but that look, the way he took me in, the way his eyes shone, made me want to giggle with glee.

'You look . . .' He stopped, took a breath. 'Hi.'

Now that I was closer, I could see it wasn't the light that made his hair curlier. It was damp. I fidgeted with my phone to keep my fingers from itching towards his head.

'Run here in a hurry, did you?' I said, trying to keep it light, like the sparks between us were no big deal.

He brushed one of the curls behind his ear with his fingers.

'Nah, ducked in at Redleaf for a quick swim. Needed to cool down.' He said the last two words slowly, holding my gaze.

'Oh,' I said, unable to keep a ridiculously big smile from spreading across my face.

There was so much I wanted to say to him. That I couldn't stop thinking about him, that I wanted to throttle Mitra for interrupting this afternoon when I was sure he was about to kiss me.

'A bunch of my mates are inside. They'd disown me if I disappeared without buying my round.' He shifted on his feet. 'Is it okay with you if we hang out here for a bit?'

He wanted me to meet his friends. Butterflies danced in my stomach as I nodded. I could still feel the energy of the dance party, that freedom and fragility. It pushed me to stay in the moment. He offered me his hand. I took it.

Bodies were sardined into the pub. We had to push through friends and conversations to get through the crowd. I almost tripped when my foot caught a hole in the carpet, which was still a dull emerald beneath the grime. The whole place still smelt of smoke, the odour somehow lingering, though smoking inside had been banned for a decade. Alex helped me weave through the crowd and push out to the courtyard. I breathed in the fresh air. Fairy lights were garlanded through tree branches and over picnic benches and pop beats played above the chatter of the tables.

Alex's friends waved us over, their faces flushed and decorated with big alcohol-fuelled grins.

I spotted Pete and smiled. He smiled back, nodding. Alex nudged one of his friends aside as he slid onto a bench at the table and made room for me to join him. He introduced me to Scott and Ben, who with their glasses and vintage-print shirts, had the whole laid-back librarian chic look down. I realised they were the same guys who'd been hanging out with him that first day, at Manning.

'This is Tara.'

'Hey,' I beamed. Alex didn't let go of my hand.

'So what are your intentions for our boy Alex here?' Pete said, giving me a deadpan look.

'I, well . . .' I watched them all stare at me and panicked. What was I meant to say? A smile cracked through the serious mask Pete had plastered on. He looked like he was about to say something to save me. I licked my lips, pulled myself up straighter and said, 'Downright dishonourable.'

Scott almost coughed up his drink, but the others laughed, and Alex winked at me. I felt like I'd passed a test.

'I'm going to get another round, be right back.' Alex squeezed my hand before he dove into the crowd.

I almost ran after him, but reminded myself that this wasn't Jess's crew. These were his real friends and they didn't seem fazed by me at all. I reached out for the cardboard coaster in front of me and twirled it in my hands,

'Don't take this the wrong way, but did you get glitter bombed?' Ben asked, trying to brush the glitter from his pants and fingers.

'Sorry! Yeah, I was at this underground party and got doused in the stuff.'

'Underground, 'ey?' Scott said, leaning forward. I told them about the party, about its spirit – and how sad I was that it felt so fragile.

I finished the story and the four of us sat in silence for a moment before I rallied my courage and asked, 'Did you all go to high school together?'

'Yeah,' Paul said, raising his pint glass to his lips.

'Come on, what was he like?'

'Alex? Total wallflower – like, no one ever noticed him,' Pete said with such obvious sarcasm that we all chuckled.

'When he wasn't at some event for his mum or dad, he was a walking school newsletter reel,' Ben said, scratching his chin. 'School captain, made the national swim team, helped take the debating team to the state finals.'

'Okay, but what about the embarrassing stuff?' I pressed, pouting. The three of them threw glances at each other, obviously trying to figure out if they were going to share.

'I mean, there was the time he had to walk home from Rose Bay naked after his clothes got nicked,' Pete said. I rubbed my hands together – now we were getting somewhere.

'Or that time we got kicked out of the French Ambassador's house,' Scott said

Ben was already pounding on the table, laughing. 'I forgot about that – his face when he saw Alex pissing on his fence . . .'

'What did I miss?' Alex said, plopping down a tray with two jugs onto the table and handing me a glass of lemon lime with bitters before sitting down next to me. He threw me an *everything okay?* look, and it took all my control to not burst out laughing.

'They were just telling me about a party with the French Ambassador.'

I swear he paled a little at my words, then turned to his friends. 'Seriously, I was gone for like, what, five minutes!'

'Mate, you should bring her to drinks next week too,' Paul said, looking from me to Alex.

'I think I'd like that,' I said.

'I bet you would,' he replied, still shaking his head in fake outrage. But under the table he reached out for my hand, laying his pinky on my thumb.

We settled into easy conversation after that, and before I knew it, two hours had passed and our little group was outside the pub waving goodbye to each other and heading our separate ways. There was a park opposite the pub, and I had a sudden urge to run over to the swings. That's when it hit me. I was happy – really happy.

'Feel like a walk?' Alex asked.

'Sure.' I said, rubbing my hands together and blowing hot air on them.

'You're cold?' he asked, incredulous.

'What can I say? 25 degrees feels arctic to me. Maman Noosheen used to say I had desert wind in my veins.'

He pulled off his plaid shirt and draped it over my shoulders. Then he held on to the lapels, pulling me slightly closer to him, leaning down to whisper in my ear, 'You look incredible tonight.'

I shivered and said, 'Thanks.' *Kiss me.*

His eyes narrowed for a moment and I could have sworn he leaned in before he straightened up, pressing his hands into his pockets. I looked away, trying not to be disappointed. He wanted to kiss me, didn't he?

We walked in silence for a few minutes, down the back streets of Newtown. I touched my face and flinched when my hand came away covered in glitter. The stories about the ambassador's house, about getting caught naked at Rose Bay – they were funny, but seemed more like one-off random stories than anything more telling.

'So you were a total goody-goody two shoes in high school?' I said, looking up at him. I couldn't help it, I wanted to figure him out.

'I kept trying to show people that I could do something on my own, and the more I did, the more people would say, *well, there's something in that family!* Like no matter how hard I worked, it was pre-ordained or something.' He paused for a moment, looked away, then stared at the ground as we walked. 'Did Sam ever tell you why I owed her?'

I shook my head.

He tensed beside me.

'I tagged along to a lot of Mum's stuff. In Year 12, when Young Labor had a chair position open, I was going to put my hand up. Mum had a friend over for a drink that night, and he asked if she thought I'd get into politics. She laughed and said, *Hope not, he's not cut out for it.* If it had been a public conversation, or if she was talking to someone in the party, I would've assumed she said it because of the whole nepotism thing. But to Carl, her mate . . .' He sighed and cracked a knuckle. 'I was pissed. Went to a party, let people pass me weed before we headed out to a concert. I bet they called the cops too, 'cause all of a sudden they were there with sniffer dogs.' He smirked. 'It was stupid, I think a part of me wanted to get caught, to see if people would say screw-ups ran in the family too.'

He stopped, turning to me, raising his hand. 'I've known Sam since we were in nappies, and she doesn't let me get away with shit. When the sniffer dogs showed, I was all blasé, but she wasn't having it. She took my jacket and took the fall. Wouldn't let me get a word in about it, either. She made sure it didn't end up in the papers. I got Mum to pay for her to have the best lawyer, made sure she didn't get a record, but still. Sam was the one who pulled my arse into line.'

'She's special, that one,' I said, and he nodded.

I glimpsed a new vulnerability. He opened his mouth, then rubbed his chin before trying again. 'My dorm is only five minutes away. Any chance, you want to . . .' He paused, looking at his feet before looking back up. 'Feel like a movie or something?'

'Yeah, I'd like that.' For once, I said something that didn't feel awkward at all.

After ten minutes, we got to the wrought-iron gates of the college and my breath caught as we walked through them. I had walked past the giant sandstone building and its sprawling lawns a dozen times, but had never really taken them in as a place where people lived. The whole thing screamed 'old money' in a way that did exactly what it was designed to – make me feel inadequate.

Alex veered left from the main walkway. 'We're not going through the front?' I asked.

'Trust me.'

He took us through a narrow path around the building till we got to a tiny door at the back. He pushed it open to reveal a spiral staircase that looked like something out of *Harry Potter*. Halfway up the second series of stairs, it hit me that he was taking me to his room. That we were going to be alone: *really* alone. I realised the heat racing through me wasn't nerves, but excitement. There were lines I wasn't ready to cross yet. All I could think about was how close we could dance to them.

Alex pushed open a door, put a finger to his mouth and peered into the hallway.

'What, no girls allowed?' I whispered. He just chuckled.

His room was pretty bare: a double bed with a navy quilt, a broken lamp held together with duct tape on his desk. The floor was covered in books, shoes, and a handful of clothes. A surfboard leaned against the wall next to a small bar fridge and the floor was covered in sand. The only decoration was a poster of a beach sunset.

'Can I get you a drink?' he asked, taking a bottle of sparkling water from the fridge.

I nodded. I took off my shoes, walked over to his desk and cringed. There were cups so mouldy they were supporting whole ecosystems, books piled on top of notes, and a random array of coins, cash, gum and receipts. 'You *really* weren't expecting me.'

He turned and glanced around the room like he was seeing it for the first time, and looked a bit sheepish. 'Ah, yeah, I mean, no. Would you believe me if I said it wasn't normally this bad?'

'I guess this is your superpower.'

'What?'

'Finding clean, unrumpled clothes daily.'

He chuckled, the tension seeping out of him.

'Marvel, eat your heart out.' He handed me a bottle, then pushed a pile of clothes off his bed. He sat down on the mattress, pulling his laptop on his lap. 'In the mood for anything in particular?'

I plopped down next to him, peeking at the screen over his shoulder.

His Netflix recommendations were a mix of subtitled movies, documentaries and trashy teen dramas like *Gossip Girl*. I raised an eyebrow at him.

'What? I'm complicated.' He threw his arms up and smirked. 'And . . . my sister has my password.'

'*The Godfather*?'

'Nah, too heavy for tonight. Ever seen *Casablanca*?'

I shook my head. I knew it was a classic – one of the most

romantic movies of all time, according to Mum – but I'd never gotten around to watching it.

He nodded towards the bed and I sat down, pulling my feet under me. He pulled out his chair so it was in front of the bed and put the computer on it, then turned off the lights and settled in next to me. After he pressed play, his hand drifted behind me. I leaned into him and a second later, his arm was around my shoulders. I rested my head in the crook of his neck as the movie started playing.

A few minutes in, he took my hand into his, interlocking our fingers and drawing casual, mindless circles along my palm. I practically purred. He kissed my temple. I couldn't think. The movie in the background made it all the more intense.

I could feel his eyes on me. I turned. His face was dim in the light from the computer screen. He lifted our entwined hands and kissed my knuckles, one by one, his eyes never leaving mine. I bit my lip. He paused the movie.

'Tara, I . . .' His voice was low, husky. He pressed my hand against his chest. 'You know I'm totally falling for you, right?'

Oh.

'I . . .'

He ran his fingers up my arm. Well, he couldn't expect a response when he was doing that.

'I've been thinking about kissing you all day,' he said, as he ran his thumb across my bottom lip.

I looked him in the eye, tilted my head and said, 'Maybe you should stop *just* thinking about it.'

Something sparked in his eyes. His hand creased my cheek as he leaned down and softly kissed me. I wrapped my arms around his neck and kissed him back, just as tentatively. Something like a growl rumbled from his chest, and I felt another surge of adrenaline go through me.

Alex wrapped his arm around my waist and kissed me again, harder this time. He pulled me to him as he nudged my lips open. I ran my fingers through his hair and a small moan escaped me as his hands slid from my back to stroke the sides of my body. He pulled back, but didn't let me go.

I loved feeling his chest against mine. I held my hands on his shoulders, keeping him close. 'About time,' I whispered in his ear.

In response, he pulled me into his lap. I let out a startled gasp.

Something twitched under my thighs . . . *was that . . .?* Oh God, it was. It felt like crashing into an electric fence. 'Wait – ' I said, cringing at the panic in my voice.

Alex lifted me off his lap and shuffled away from me on the bed. 'You okay?' His voice was soft. He leaned forward from his new distance, just over a metre away, looking at me carefully.

'I just need to slow things down a little . . .'

'Yeah? Of course. Whatever you want.' The softness in his eyes, the way his voice almost broke on the *of course* signalled that he was being sincere. He had stopped and moved away the minute I said I wasn't sure.

I shuffled towards him and laid my head against his shoulder again. 'Is it okay if we finish the movie? I want to see what happens.'

'Totally,' he said. I nestled into him. It was a long few minutes before he wrapped his arm around me and leaned his chin against my forehead.

I woke up because my neck felt like someone had stabbed a dagger through it. I stretched it out and rolled my shoulders, only to hit a body beside me. *What the hell?* I opened my eyes. Alex? I saw navy bedclothes beneath us and a sunset beach on the wall. I shook my head, memories of last night flooding back. Alex groaned and opened an eye.

'We dozed off?' he asked. That sleepy, husky voice and his half-open eyes made me want to curl back into him. But I pushed those thoughts aside and nodded back.

It was dark outside. We couldn't have drifted off for more than a few minutes, surely. I stood up and my stiff and sore body protested. I reached out for my phone and . . . nothing. The battery was dead.

'What time is it?'

Alex ran a hand through his hair, as he reached out for his phone. He cringed as he said, 'Five am.'

My stomach dropped. 'I have to go,' I said, scrambling around to find my bag and shoes. I'd sent Mum a text saying that I'd be out with Mitra. She probably thought I'd be out late, but not *this* late.

'Everything okay?'

'Yeah, I just need to get home. Mum's probably worried sick.'

'I'll call you an Uber and walk you out,' he said, noticing my dead phone. We walked down the spiral staircases and through the labyrinthine halls together. He was still on his guard, checking that the halls were empty before we walked through.

The air outside was warm. The car was waiting for me already. I turned back to Alex, not really sure what to say.

He took my hand, opened his mouth and then closed it. At

least I wasn't the only one who was struggling with words. I squeezed his hand. 'I had a great time.'

'I did too . . .' He looked me in the eye and hesitated, before shaking his head and saying, 'I always have a great time when I'm with you.'

I stared at him for a moment. Was that what he meant to say? Or was he holding something else in? The Uber driver beeped. I stepped closer and kissed him on the cheek, lingering a second too long, hoping he understood how I felt.

As the car drove away, the night flashed before my eyes: the dance party, meeting Alex's friends, kissing Alex. His smiles, his eyes, the feel of his arms around me. By the time we pulled up to the house, I was smiling dreamily, and maybe even humming as I walked through the front door.

'Where the hell have you been?' Mum's hair was a mess. The landline, her mobile and an empty bottle of wine were on the coffee table in front of her.

'I'm so sorry, my phone died – '

'Are you okay?'

'Yes.'

Mum nodded before leaning back into the couch. She rubbed her eyes and turned back to me. 'You were with the same boy you had dinner with the other night?'

I opened my mouth to argue, but couldn't. She was right. 'Yes . . .'

'Okay, we're getting you a portable charger so this won't happen again.'

I nodded, wishing that she'd yell at me, or lash out. I had clearly screwed up. 'You're not mad I was with him?'

She looked at me for a long moment and sighed. 'I worry, yes,' she shrugged, 'but you have a better head on your shoulders than I did at your age – I hope you're being safe, that you're setting the bar high for how he treats you.'

'Thanks, Mum,' I said and pushed myself to give her a hug. She hugged me back and I didn't pull away.

'Don't thank me until after I meet him.' I looked at her in disbelief. 'No buts Tara – you're going to bring him over.'

Chapter 17

I couldn't stop smiling on my way to uni and through the coffee-cart line. By the time I saw Alex at the campaign stall, I might have been glowing like some sort of drunk supernova.

'Hey,' I said, handing him a flat white.

'Hi.' He sipped the coffee, put it down and grabbed his clipboard. 'First-year psych lecture, then head over to first-year philosophy – and I've blocked out all of this afternoon for debate prep.'

A few hours ago, I was in his room, in his arms. Now, he was talking to me in his campaign voice, like nothing had happened. What the hell?

'Mum was okay, by the way. She does want to meet you, though,' I said.

He looked at me like I'd asked him to storm an army of White Walkers by himself, then shook his head. 'Maybe after the election.' I reached to take his hand, but he moved away and shoved it in his pocket. 'Look, I think we need to keep things professional in public, okay?'

That hurt. 'Okay,' I said, taking a sip of coffee and looking away so he wouldn't see the sting. 'I . . .' I shut my mouth before I could ask what was going on. I didn't want to fight with him now, in front of the team. I took a step back, took a breath. 'Okay. Tell me about the debate prep.'

'Sam is going to meet you at her place at three. She'll take you through the drills.'

Oh. Okay. I nodded. 'Great,' I said. For a second, I thought I saw him flinch, so slightly that I wasn't sure if I imagined it. I had no idea what was going on and didn't want to stick around to find out. 'I'll see you round.' I grabbed my stuff and headed over to my first lecture.

He had to be exhausted. Something real had happened between us. Hadn't it? I pushed my doubt away. He'd probably call in a bit to apologise. I was just overthinking the whole thing. I had to be. The possibility that this was history repeating was too awful to think about.

Give me strength, I whispered as I ran the beads of Maman Noosheen's tasbeeh through my fingers. There must have been a thousand people packed into the bar.

'Chill,' Sam said, catching my eye and holding my gaze. 'You got this.' Her eyes flickered for a moment, as if she sensed that I was still wavering, then she stood taller and whispered lethally, 'I made sure of it.'

I remembered the prep session. She'd spent three hours throwing questions at me, heckling me and generally trying to provoke me. I wanted to push her and tell her she was crazy, but she wasn't. Sam was level-headed, smart and the most competent human I'd ever met – her confidence shoved some steel down my spine.

'Don't let Jess get under your skin,' Alex said. He was trying to play it cool, but I could tell he was nervous too. 'Remember: ignore Taylor. He's only here to troll everyone.'

'Round up folks, in a few moments we're going to bring up the fools who want to govern this place and let you unleash your questions on them.' I looked up at Luke, the MC. He'd climbed the stage now, and his voice – much louder than you'd expect from his short stature – boomed through the room. He was one of the most recognised faces on campus, as part of the all-star improv team who performed twice a week here.

I looked around and tried not to think about throwing up. In the back corner was a group in bright red caps that shouted *MAKE USYD GREAT AGAIN* and matching red T-shirts that said *TICK TYLOR*. Even the shirt was a troll: if you ticked the ballot, your vote was nullified. Next to them were the bright orange *Just Jess* group. I recognised some of them from the Luna Park trip.

I swallowed and looked away. I wouldn't let them get to me. The candidates' entourages were scattered around the room. I looked up and spotted Alex in the centre of the crowd. He nodded as if to say, *you got this*. I nodded back and looked away. He hadn't called. But I couldn't go down that rabbit hole right now.

Next to him was Anaya, already snapping photos on her phone for social media. I saw two others who'd been hanging around the Order of Fantasy stall at Welcome Week. Had she recruited them? Sima, vice-president of the Muslim Society, smiled proudly next to Anaya. She'd been at the stall handing out leaflets every other day for the past few weeks, always in an immaculate outfit and hijab. My crew had taken over two tables and seeing Meg, Linda, Kate, Mohammad and a bunch

153

of fantasy nerds all huddled together gave me a surge of confidence. I wouldn't let them down.

Half of the room didn't seem to have picked a candidate yet. *They* were why I was here. I had to make sure I got through to the people who had come out of curiosity. I wanted them to vote for me, sure. But more than that, I wanted them to see me as a person. As a leader.

'Tara!' Luke called me to the stage. We were going to get started. I did my best not to roll my eyes at Jess, who was taking a selfie by the stage with one of her back-up dancers, as I passed them. Eight of us were huddled in the corner, vying for five spots.

There was Taylor and Jess, then Will, Lee, Maya, Badal, Hannah and me.

Will, the guy who'd crashed my second psych lecture to announce an anti-racism rally, was the official Labor Left candidate and was running on experience. Anaya had shown me his TikTok account when we were talking social media strategy: in one post, he'd switched through all the shirts he'd collected from being involved in Union for the last two years, flicking his blonde ponytail.

Lee, an art student with an indie vibe, was running as an independent, like me. His crew, spread across five tables, were men with facial hair and girls in purple bowler hats and too-cute outfits, all of them in matching purple shirts they'd found ways to customise – presumably to preserve their individuality.

Maya was wearing a bright blue blazer with matching blue hoop-earrings over her white campaign shirt. She looked like she'd stopped here on her way to work at some glam start-up. The Labor Right candidate, she was running on a platform of revitalising the union.

Badal and I had gotten to know each other well by now. He was wearing his green campaign T-shirt again, with its *Vote for Badal* in seven different languages. His campaign message of support and advocacy for international students had only grown tighter since we first started campaigning. His Instagram feed was now full of students from different countries endorsing him in their own languages. Now, we nodded to each other. His lips moved slightly, practising his lines.

Hannah wasn't affiliated with anyone, didn't have a campaign T-shirt – I hadn't seen anything from her so far yet. She was the wildcard. She stood to the side of the stage, fiddling with a strand of brown hair that had escaped from her messy bun.

'Nervous?' asked Will from beside me. I gave him a tight smile. Did he just assume I always needed his help? He took my silence as confirmation. Because, of course he did. 'You'll be fine,' he smiled.

'Good luck,' I said, using all my self control to be deliberately casual. Maybe after this was all over, we could have a coffee and I could tell him that asking how to help was key to actually *helping*.

I walked up to the stage feeling eyes on me, sizing me up, trying to understand why I was here. I sat on one of the black fold-out seats on the stage. We each had been given a hand-held mic. Thankfully, I was sitting in the middle, with Luke and Will either side of me. Taylor and Jess were at opposite edges of the stage.

'Before we begin, I just want to acknowledge and pay our respects to the traditional owners of the land, the Gadigal people of the Eora Nation,' Luke said.

'God save the Queen!' A hiss went through the room as the

heckle echoed. A few people chimed in with shouts of *shut up!* in the direction of Taylor's supporters.

'A bit of respect, alright?' Luke held up his hands and managed to quiet everyone down. He shook his head, like he was trying to forget what had just happened. 'None of you want to sit through an hour of hearing this lot read out their CVs, right? So let's make this interesting. We're going to dive in. There are two people wandering around with mics. I'm going to hand over to you all to ask them questions.'

One hand shot up immediately, above a smug smile. He wasn't wearing a T-shirt connected to any of the candidates. *Breathe in. How bad could it be? Breathe out.* One of the volunteers ran to him with the microphone and he said, 'Who do you think shouldn't win and why?'

The question hit me like a cricket bat to the face. This was how we were getting started? Surely no one would be silly enough to take the bait.

'Taylor,' Will said from next to me. I turned to stare at him, as he looked to Taylor. 'The union stands for diversity, and you've made it clear you don't uphold that.' There was a round of applause.

I wanted to kick him in the shins for giving Taylor an opening. Jess jumped in.

'So, anyone who disagrees with you shouldn't run? I thought we were at a university, not an indoctrination camp where we need to pass a political test to be involved. Independent thought should be encouraged. Isn't that what diversity is meant to be about?' She glanced over at Will and gave him a sickly-sweet smile. She leaned back into a smattering of applause. Some of it seemed reluctant, but it was there. I shoved down my frustration.

Lee was next. 'You know what? The union should be about students, not politics. I don't care if you're from the Libs, the ALP or the Greens, but the minute you're part of a party, you have a conflict of interest.' There were equal parts cheering and hisses from the crowd at that.

I turned my mic on. 'If you don't think someone is going to show up for you, then don't vote for them. They shouldn't win.'

I smiled when my table applauded. But my heart leapt when there were murmurs and nods from the crowd. I caught Sam's eye. She gave me the slightest nod, which was her equivalent of dancing on a table with joy. Maybe this wouldn't be so bad after all. I reached into my pocket and squeezed Maman Nosheen's tasbeeh, to make sure I didn't somehow jinx it.

'Alright, we're going to try to take as many questions as we can, so, who's next?' Luke asked. This time a dozen hands shot in the air.

Luke looked around and pointed to a woman with a tight black ponytail and dark glasses. She took the mic from the volunteer and said, 'If you're elected, would you shut down the union in solidarity with striking university staff?'

'No.' Taylor was first to answer this time. 'The union is meant to make students' lives easier, and shutting down services is a really expensive way of not doing that.'

'As odd as it is, I agree with Taylor. The union is a service provider, not a hub for activism,' said Lee. A few others jumped in to agree.

I shook my head and turned on my mic. Alex told me to deflect this one, but I couldn't. I knew Sofia, who worked the lunch shift downstairs, and Alastair, who swept the library when I was there late. They worked hard and I couldn't let them down. 'Well, I would. We'd have no experience here as students without university staff. Staff being forced to work under bad conditions doesn't make our lives any better.'

'Me too,' Will said, 'Unions like the NTEU have always been there when we needed them. They were marching with us students when the government talked about hiking up student fees. We should remember that. If I'm elected, I won't leave them alone when they need our support back.'

The next question came from a woolly-bearded guy who could have doubled as a young Hagrid. He took the mic and asked, 'What do you reckon sucks about the union?'

'Easy – the food,' Jess said with a shrug. 'If you all elect me, I promise we'll have a Subway on campus next year.' There were groans through most of the hall and hollering cheers from her and Taylor's tables of supporters.

'We need more art. Pop Fest is great, but there's so much more we could be doing. From supporting poetry, to theatre, to Buffy re-enactments,' Lee said. He basked in the thunderous applause, and I cringed as I saw the Order of Fantasy kids at my table join the cheers.

'Oh, we clearly need more programming to help us with what we do when we get out of here: more mentorship programs, accreditation programs. That's what we need.' Maya said.

'Pretending that international students are some kind of unworthy side project,' said Badal, to one of the biggest rounds of applause so far.

I pulled my microphone closer and jumped in. 'I agree with Badal, the union sometimes pretends we're all the same when we're not. The Club and Socs program is so amazing because it gives us all space to be who we are. Events like Pride do that too. Not everything needs to be for everyone – but we need everyone to have something that makes them feel seen.'

There were nods and murmurs. I looked at one guy who had been passing through, and now hovered at the edge of the crowd. I could see him thinking, considering. It was working.

'Alright, last question folks.' Luke pointed to a woman in a floral summer dress, standing on the sides of the crowd.

'Who do you look up to as role models when it comes to leadership?' There were a few groans and exaggerated eye rolls. This was a softball question, but I was lost. Victor Chang, Fiona Wood, Nicola Roxon, all of them were people I looked up to . . . but none of them felt right.

'Gough Whitlam,' Will said from next to me. 'He made education free, helped create universal healthcare – he took care of people, made sure no one was left behind, and that's real leadership to me.' I smiled. It was so predictable, and yet it was also genuine, honest and inspiring.

'Joss Whedon,' Lee said, to another huge round of applause.

'Hillary Clinton,' Jess said. 'She did so much to help women around the world.'

'Lee Lin Chin,' Badal said, getting another huge roar of cheers.

I took a breath, my mind blank. I couldn't afford to panic. I reached into my pocket again and held the tasbeeh as I turned on my mic.

'My grandparents,' I took a breath – this was a bad idea, but it was too late to stop now. 'They were revolutionaries in Iran . . .' It was suddenly so quiet. I wanted to take it back, to go with Victor Chang instead of sharing something so precious with a group of strangers. 'There's a photo of them at a rally, they'd painted *Azadi* (*Freedom*) on a sign.' I lost my voice for a second, pushed back tears. I took a breath. 'They just wanted to have a say.' I could barely see, my eyes rimmed. 'My grandfather didn't come home after that protest.' The tears spilled, I sniffled. 'Things obviously didn't turn out how they wanted, but they taught me that you have to show up, stand up for what's important, even if you're not sure how it'll turn out.' I fidgeted after I finished talking. Manning was never that quiet. I heard a few claps and sighed, dabbing away tears with my fingers. I'd blown it. This was way too heavy for a forum like this.

'Any final words from the candidates?' Luke said, breaking the silence.

'If you want an experienced candidate and a union that's strong, progressive and student-centred, then *Give Will a Go*,' Will smiled.

The other candidates gave the short version of their stump speeches, too. But I decided to go off script. Again.

'The promise of this place is that when you walk in the gates, this community will help you become the best you can be. I want the union to be a place that helps us do that – through the arts, through clubs, or through providing a space where we can grow, learn and make mistakes. If that's what you want too, then come see us over there.' I pointed to the tables with my team. 'Sign up, vote, but also – keep active after the elections, so we can figure out what we want this place to look like together.'

There was a moment of silence as everyone waited, but no one jumped in. Luke finally cleared his throat and declared, 'Alright, everyone give it up for the candidates! And thanks for showing up to our liveliest soapbox yet!'

There was half-hearted applause as people dispersed, talking among themselves. Will smiled at me. 'You did great,' he said.

'You too,' I said. My cheeks were going to get seriously sore if I kept having to hang out around him and his patronising. I deliberately walked off the opposite end of the stage to Jess, towards my team.

Sam saw me and walked over. 'You went off script,' she said. I braced myself. She was going to chew me out for getting so heavy, for making everyone's work harder. She grabbed my shoulders and leaned closer. 'That was next-level.' She moved back, patting my shoulder. 'Really,' she said, her eyes twinkling now. 'I thought my instincts were good, but damn, I didn't realise they were that good.' She winked.

I looked away. 'You don't think it was too much?'

'It was real. It was you. That's the whole reason you did this right?' she said, looking at me like it was the most obvious thing in the world. 'Come on, it ain't over yet.'

She swung an arm around my shoulder and led me towards our crew. I couldn't believe it, there were at least twenty people huddled around our tables. Some of them were grabbing T-shirts, pulling them on. Others were filling out their details on their phones so they could volunteer.

Had it actually worked? I felt someone take my hand and looked up to see Mitra.

'Don't let it get to your head,' she said. 'They're mostly here because you happen to have the hottest supporters.'

It didn't matter what would happen on Tuesday. I got through to people. In every way that mattered, I had already won.

Chapter 18

'You know, for someone who wants to be a doctor, you really haven't grasped the concept of how important food is to being able to do things like stand upright,' Alex said, pressing a Twix bar into my hand. 'You look like you're going to faint.'

My head was swimming, but not because I hadn't eaten. Talking about my grandparents and then meeting a bunch of new people had sucked the energy out of me. I felt like I could sleep for days.

'Thanks,' I said, looking up at him. I unwrapped the chocolate bar and bit into it.

He sat down next to me, pulling his chair out so he could face me more easily. He laced his fingers and leaned his chin against them. 'That must have been hard to share, I know how much your grandmother meant to you.'

He remembered the conversation we had at Luna Park. It killed me that he was bringing it up, after his seeming selective amnesia.

'I wish . . .' He stopped, cleared his throat. 'You did great out there.' And just like that, he was back to using his campaign voice, back to pretending nothing had happened between us.

'I should get back out there,' I said, getting up. I could feel the anger rising in me. If I didn't get away, I wouldn't be able to trap it in.

'Let's catch up over the schedule later,' he called after me.

I raised a thumb to say *yes*, but didn't turn around.

I walked away. It wasn't just the debate prep, or planning volunteer rosters for election day. It wasn't a coincidence that we hadn't had two minutes alone since he kissed me. And apparently, he wasn't going to just snap out of it.

I was such a fool. He had said from the beginning that he didn't want us to get involved. I'd been silly enough to think that I could be like one of the heroines from my fantasy books – and that he'd be there when I triumphed. He'd have my back. The worst part of it was that technically, he *did* have my back. He'd stand by his word – he was going to get me elected – but he didn't want me. I wasn't enough. I was so naïve to think I ever could have been. No. I shook my head and stopped the train of thought. Whatever was going on was about him, not me. Even though I had no idea what was going on, I wasn't going to doubt my own worth. Not again.

I straightened my back, plastered on a smile, and returned to the crowd.

I went from the debate into a chemistry lecture, then a lab and then a psychology tutorial. By the time I walked out of my last class, it was dark, cold and I was completely spent. I headed to the bathroom, locked the stall and leaned against the wall. I hadn't had a quiet moment since that morning.

I heard the bathroom door swing open – and a familiar voice.

'Hey, it's me,' said Jess. I closed my eyes and tried to stay as still as possible. Surely hiding in the bathroom and waiting for her to leave was not just polite, but the right thing to do?

'Look, I'm in the bathroom at the old teacher's college. Can you come get me? No, I'm not okay. I'm tired of having people hiss at me and tell me to go back to Cronulla. I just . . . can you walk me back to college?'

I knew how that felt. Shit. What we went through wasn't the same, and yet, she was hiding in a bathroom, scared. What had happened in her life that made it so easy for her to jump to the worst conclusions about someone like me, without even realising she was doing it? Most people on TV, especially Australian TV, looked like her. On the rare occasion there was someone who looked like me, they were usually either in trouble and needed help, or they were a threat. And at school, sure, we learned about Mabo and the White Australia policy – but it all always felt so far away, like history that wasn't relevant anymore. We were taught that the country had moved on from those days, that things were better now. We got to eat other people's food – but when it came to understanding what it was like to be different? Why people might be angry or frustrated, how they might be disadvantaged? That didn't really happen – which made it so much easier for Jess and people like her to have totally screwed-up opinions.

'Twenty minutes?' Jess's voice broke on the words. I tried to steel myself against her anguish. 'Nah, look don't worry about it, I'll be fine. Sure, sure.'

She didn't need me to be a hero. She just needed me to be human. I opened the stall door and walked out. She was standing by the sink, her face in her hands. I opened my mouth and closed it, unsure what to say. But staring at her like some freak from a horror movie was hardly the best option.

'Hey.' Yep, that's all I had.

She looked up and stared at my reflection. I braced myself for whatever sarcastic comment she was going to throw at me. After a few seconds of silence, she turned on the tap and washed her face.

I almost walked away, but I couldn't. I sighed and said, 'I'm heading towards the colleges if you want to walk near each other.'

'Don't.' She tore off a paper towel with an angry tug.

I washed my hands slowly, thoroughly, scrubbing between my fingers, my palms, my thumb. I wasn't going to run out of the bathroom because of her, not a chance. I dried my hands on a paper towel, crumpled it, then pulled some hand cream from my bag. I'd give her another minute to change her mind and then I'd be gone. She leaned against the wall, scrolling through her phone. Fine.

'There's a security guard on the first level, I'll tell him to keep an eye out for you.' Nothing. No response. She didn't even look up. I stalked to the other end of the bathroom and yanked the door open.

'I'm sorry.'

I stopped at her words, but didn't turn around.

'I didn't realise . . . about your grandparents.'

I turned back and looked at her. She fidgeted under my gaze. I nodded, just enough that she'd see I'd heard her – so she'd understand that I'd forgive, but I wasn't ready to forget. Not by a long shot.

Then I walked out and let the door shut behind me.

I sipped a cup of tea and clenched and unclenched my fist, trying to stretch my cramping muscles. I had spent the morning chained to my desk: reading, taking notes, highlighting readings and sketching arguments for my essays. I closed my eyes and rolled my shoulders. My phone buzzed and I flipped it over.

Free to go over the game plan for Tuesday?

Maybe he was trying to say *sorry*. Or maybe he really did want to go through the game plan. The idea of the two of us spending an hour talking about the campaign as if nothing had happened between us was unbearable. He'd already gone through the plan for election day: *Meet up at 7 am, do chalking, make the rounds to all the polling places, talk at the biggest lecture theatres to remind people to vote.* Hell, I was more prepared for election day than I was for exams.

Can't. Need to study. Let me know if anything's changed?

I put my cup down, picked up my highlighter and flipped a page. I didn't want to think about him, or the elections. All I wanted to imagine was a stethoscope around my neck and a chart in my hands.

'Right, I'm taking you out.'

I jumped at Mitra's voice and turned to glare at her.

'I have to study.'

Mitra walked over to my desk, grabbed a stack of papers I'd sorted, and started going through them. 'This essay is done and due next week,' she said throwing it back on the desk. 'Exam notes you'll need next month, finished essay due in two weeks, more exam notes . . .' She picked up an old assignment that I had just gotten back. 'Are you fucking serious? You got pretty much one hundred per cent and a note saying *let's talk about your future* and you're trying to pull the *I'm behind* routine?'

'I'm trying to get into med!'

'Get up. We're leaving. Now.'

'No.' I grabbed my highlighter and turned away from her. She would yell, throw a tantrum and then burn herself out and leave me alone. I just had to weather the storm.

'I miss you.' The words were so quiet, I almost didn't hear them. I turned towards her. Her hands were covered in black marks from the garage and there were circles under her eyes. She looked deflated. 'You had so much shit going on that I didn't want to bug you with my stuff. I . . .' her voice hitched. 'I need you, mate.'

Never had words pushed me into action so quickly. I jumped up. 'Give me five.'

Mitra nodded and walked out. I pulled on my jeans. How could I have not noticed Mitra was struggling until now? I was a terrible friend, I didn't deserve . . . No, I didn't get to do that now. Mitra needed me.

I walked outside. Mum smiled and threw what looked like a grateful glance at Mitra, who was leaning against the door, twirling her car keys.

'So where are we going?' I asked, knotting my hijab.

Mitra looked at me like I had asked her the question a million times. 'Around. Let's just go.' She opened the door and tapped her foot.

Mitra revved the engine as I got into the car. Dee was stuffed with leaflets and posters from the campaign. Electro beats burst through the stereo, but Mitra didn't tap her fingers along. She didn't swerve or pull any crazy moves while we drove either.

I stared out the window and waited for her to be ready to share whatever was on her mind. She was quiet until we pulled up in Marrickville, on what seemed like a random street.

Marrickville is another suburb where students hang out. It's cool, hip and young, but sleepier, more residential than Newtown. Fewer terraces, more apartments and brick federation houses. More parents, less hippies. Even though it's sleepy, it's spotted with industrial pockets and giant warehouses that give the place a gritty feel.

Mitra parked outside an older apartment block with a giant *For Lease* sign outside. I raised an eyebrow, but she ignored me and got out of the car. The footpath was crowded with murmuring couples and students, whispering excitedly to each other. I opened my mouth to ask what was going on, but decided against it. Whatever this was, I would let it be a surprise.

Mitra led the way. We walked up stairs carpeted in a bright yellowish-brown that surely would have been considered hideous even when someone laid it back in the seventies. The building smelled like curry and mould. We walked up two flights of stairs before we reached what was apparently our destination: an open apartment door.

A woman in a blazer and heels stood in the doorway with a clipboard, and handed us a photocopied flyer of rental properties. The apartment's address was on it, with a price attached. It was reasonably priced for the location, but reasonable was still a lot. The living room was small but bright, with plastic venetian blinds open to show a view of a carpark. The kitchen had chipped, lemon-yellow counters that slanted slightly crooked. The lime-green bathroom was tiny. The bedrooms were fine but *meh*: a bit on the small side, but enough space for a double bed and desk, and there were built-in robes. I walked out of the bedroom and spotted Mitra standing on the balcony that opened out through the living room. I slipped outside next to her.

'What is this?'

'I can't keep bouncing from the couch in your closet to Sam's.'

'Sam makes you sleep on the couch?' She didn't laugh at my joke.

'I can't afford a place on my own, and I can't go home.'

I reached out and squeezed her hand. She finally turned and looked at me. 'I met Fadi for our usual catch-up. He took me home, said it would be fine. It was a disaster. Dad kicked me out, said I wasn't to come anywhere near Fadi again. Said I wasn't his daughter.' She stopped and shrugged, 'I mean, I knew he was hella mad since I left. I haven't even told him I'm gay, but I thought that maybe . . . anyway, what do you think?'

I wanted to give her a hug and say her dad didn't deserve her. That I didn't get her parents. That she'd be able to see her brother and sister soon. But that wasn't what she needed, not right now. I turned back to face the house, taking in the room, the space, and nodded.

'Okay, let's do it,' I said. I'd worked as a receptionist at a walk-in medical centre over the summer, so I had a bit saved up. And they were always looking for more people, so I could pick up weekend and evening shifts. Maybe ask Mum for help. There wasn't anything I wouldn't do for Mitra.

So we walked back into the living room.

'Can we please have two application forms?' I asked the agent.

Chapter 19

My back ached and my wrist was sore enough that I felt like I could snap it off. I plastered a smile on my face and kept talking to the volunteers around me as we kneeled on the concrete, chalking massive colourful billboards on the floor together. This was it. I dusted my hands off on my jeans. I was wearing my campaign shirt over a white blouse. I'd also tied a deep blue scarf, back behind my neck, because somehow that made my hijab feel more like armour. And if I was going to channel warrior vibes, well, today was the day to do it.

Remember to vote today! Tara for Union.

I still couldn't believe half a dozen people were already out here with me at 7 am. More than sixty people had signed up to help today, to staff polling stations, put up posters, or leaflet at busy intersections on campus. I was a general, a badass, a fae warrior. When Anaya told me it was time to do a video update reminding people today was the day, I called on that energy.

'Ready?' Anaya angled her phone towards me. I nodded.

'Today is it, polling stations are open till 5 pm – so come on down, vote and then let's work together to make our Union everything it can be.'

'That's lit!' Anaya said. She waved me over and played me back the video. I didn't recognise the girl who was talking: her confidence, her swagger.

I looked up at her. 'You're a wizard with that thing, you know?'

'Yeah, transfiguration, potions and motion capture are my specialty,' she winked.

Of course she'd get it and make a *Harry Potter* reference back – she was part of the Order of Fantasy 'Ravenclaw pride?'

'Absolutely,' she replied, as she posted the video. Then she looked up at me, and shook her head. 'You're a total Gryffindor, though.'

Maybe she was right. Maybe this whole time I'd wanted Hermione to be a Ravenclaw because I'd been hiding behind books and wanted her there with me. Either way, I couldn't keep the goofy smile off my face. Anaya got me. We loved the same things. I was totally going to join the Order of Fantasy after the election. Getting to know Anaya proved that I'd been right – they were my people. I'd been silly to worry that they'd be a closed clique, that I wouldn't be cool enough, or nerdy enough, for them. Maybe, sometimes, I judged myself more than others did. Or before they could.

'Have you seen the posters Alex made for today?' Anaya asked. When I shook my head, she passed me her phone with our latest Instagram post. I flicked through its images of four different posters, each of them featuring a character: Hermione, Princess Leia, Katniss and Buffy. All four were emblazoned with, *Rebels vote early. Vote Tara for Union today!* The Instagram text read, *Who's your favourite?* and there were already a bunch of comments. My heart twisted at the thought of Alex up late on his computer making these, then I pushed it aside. I couldn't let boy trouble distract me – not today.

I checked my watch. It was 7:25 am. The first big round of pedestrian traffic was going to hit in a few minutes. 'Alright folks, we should head back to the stall.'

There was a huddle of people already there. Some were pulling on our blue campaign T-shirts, most of them well-worn. I stopped and took it all in. Anaya, Sima, Linda, Mohammad, Meg, Kate, Pete – so many of them had showed up for the campaign, and together we'd made it about more than just me, we'd made it about the campus we wanted.

I spotted Alex at the same time he saw me. He grabbed a coffee from the stall and walked over. I thought about going after a volunteer in the other direction, but I didn't. We couldn't avoid each other completely, or people would start to notice. *One more day.* I could do that.

'I have a good feeling about today,' he said, handing me the cup.

Don't talk to me like that. If you don't feel that way about me, just say it. Stop pretending like nothing happened. 'Fingers crossed,' I said.

Then we just stood there. Silently. It was that horrible, awkward quiet when you can almost hear your relationship tearing at the threads.

'Hey!' I don't think I'd ever been happier to hear Mitra's voice. 'Sam needs you at the stall.' Mitra said, nodding toward Alex.

'Right, text me if you need me okay?' he said and walked off.

'You look like shit,' Mitra said the moment he was out of earshot. 'I spend one day at Sam's and you fucking fall apart?'

'I missed you too,' I said. It was meant to be sarcastic, but didn't come out that way. It was the truth. I could just *be* around her. The good, the bad, and the ugly sides of me – Mitra had seen it all, laughed at it all (or most of it) and always came back for more.

'I'm going to throw up if you keep that shit up.' She rolled her eyes at me. 'Come on, we need to get you to your first lecture or else Sam will have my arse.'

'I would've thought she'd well and truly covered that area by now.'

Mitra roared with laughter and somehow, everything felt manageable again.

We walked towards the Eastern Avenue auditorium and I ran through what I was going to say in my head. I wasn't making new speeches today, just reminding people to vote and giving them the quick highlights of my platform. I had stood in front of so many lectures that I wasn't nervous anymore. I'd even started responding to the occasional heckler. Once or twice I'd landed a joke.

I went in, did my thing and came out. Whatever happened tonight, at least the campaign was going to be over.

'You're still here?' I was genuinely surprised to see Mitra waiting for me outside the lecture.

'I've been assigned to be your body woman for the day,' she shrugged.

'Alex wants you to get me coffee and keep me on time?' It seemed like a colossal waste of Mitra's day.

'He said something about you eating or fainting.' She smiled at me then shrugged, 'I offered to bring him an apron if he wanted to fuss, and he got all worked up about that, pretended like I wasn't being helpful.' I could see her watching for my reaction. She knew something was up. I just chuckled and gave her a friendly shove.

I was glad that she'd be the one to hang out with me today. She was the one person who could make me smile no matter what.

The next few hours were a blur of leafleting, speaking in front of lectures and talking to people. A bunch of people shouted encouragement as they passed, telling me they'd voted for me, or hoped I'd win. I didn't realise I was running on pure adrenaline until Mitra shoved a sandwich in my hand.

'Scoff that down before we head to the polls.' I nodded. The campus looked like a rainbow had thrown up over it, with practically every metre of the footpaths chalked with competing campaign messages, and the bulletin boards covered in overlapping posters. The energy felt different too. Everyone seemed to be either campaigning, talking about the election, or grumpy that they had to move around campus like they were playing tag. Nearing a polling station was like being hit by a wave of confetti, with volunteers from every campaign shoving leaflets into people's hands, grabbing at them like a tidal rip. They'd push, pull – do anything – to walk a student to the line on the ground that marked the spot where you couldn't campaign anymore, giving people a second to think before casting their vote.

It was easy to spot Sam's bright purple hair from where we stood. She was expertly walking people to the line. I couldn't hear what she was saying, but whatever it was, anyone by her side didn't so much as look at any of the other campaigners. Between the hair, the boots, the tattoo on her shoulder and that swagger, she looked like some kind of badass pixie.

For the millionth time since we started the campaign, I thanked Khoda that Sam was on my side. I didn't ask where Alex was, didn't wonder how he had somehow managed not to cross my path.

Mitra shoved a handful of leaflets at me and we stepped into the fray. Around thirty campaigners were crammed into the courtyard outside the library. Thankfully, only two of them were part of Jess's crew. How bad could this be?

I walked up to the first person I saw walking towards the library, a guy with big glasses and a bunch of books under his arm. Surely the books were a good sign? I squared my shoulders and walked up to him. 'Hi, I'm Tara, I'm running for Union,' I said.

He stopped and said hello, but glanced away, starting to shift his weight from one foot to the other as campaigners started circling us. Stopping him had been a rookie error. I should have kept him moving, kept him talking until he crossed the campaign line. He took a step and I tried to keep up, but one of Lee's people stepped right in front of me, essentially cutting me off. They disappeared into the crowd together.

'Alright, I'll take the other side of them from now on, and we move together, that should help' Mitra said. If two of us approached one voter together, it was much harder for other campaigners to be able to cut us off. The strategy was essentially giving me training wheels. I nodded. I was tired – exhausted even – but I wasn't going to give up.

Mitra pushed a Red Bull down the table towards me. 'Thanks,' I said, taking a giant gulp. She wrapped an arm around my shoulder. Campaigns usually ended up huddled in an off-campus pub, but I wanted all of my volunteers to be comfortable. So instead, we'd hired out a room at a kebab joint on King Street. Amr Diab's 'Habibi' was playing as I walked through the door. It was one of the only Arabic songs that I knew some of the words to and its familiar beat helped soften the tensions in my shoulders. We moved back through the restaurant, and into a room covered in murals. One panel featured a peacock, all deep turquoises with gold leaf highlights that caught the light. Another featured a mosque, its domes and mosaics proudly glittering under a setting sun. And another showed houses in a desert, so vibrant that you could almost feel the heat radiating from the painted sand. Instead of chairs, the room was filled with cushions – on the floor and leaning against the wall, next to low tables – so everyone would be sitting on the floor together.

A bunch of people were already there, eating hummus and biting into dolmas. The tables were littered with soft drinks, fancy mocktails and beers. Anaya spotted me at the edge of the room and started cheering – and I almost started crying right there. I wedged myself between Meg and Mitra.

Meg waved at the drinks, and when I nodded towards a jug of Coke, she poured me a glass. 'Gotta say, I didn't think you had it in you,' she said. I wondered if the piercings hurt when she lifted her eyebrow.

'I know,' I smiled. She'd hardly been subtle that first night at the party.

'For damn good reason – you looked like you were gonna pass

out just talking to us. Besides, you had that goody-goody *I just want something on my resume* vibe.'

'And then?' Okay, I was totally fishing for compliments.

'People comparing you to Katniss gave you a big head,' Mitra said, cutting Meg off. The three of us laughed. I grabbed some lavash off a plate, slathered it with feta and plopped on a walnut. I was about to take a bite when the next wave of people came through. They cheered as they walked in, smiling and dancing to the music. Pete sat down next to us. I took a bite of my snack. Then I spotted Alex, and the lavash suddenly tasted like sand in my mouth.

He was sitting on the other side of the room, cosied up next to a girl I didn't know. Blonde hair hung down her back, over a T-shirt with my name on it. He always flirted with everyone – I was used to that. But this felt different. She whispered something in his ear and he laughed. She inched closer to him. He leaned into her and whispered back. She giggled and playfully punched his shoulder and even this far away, I could see him pat her knee. I put my food down, my appetite gone.

'Let's go order,' Mitra said, grabbing my hand and pushing the others out of the way as she dragged me out. We got to the counter and she turned on me, 'What the hell is going on with you two?' She asked the question like she'd been holding it in with everything she had.

'Nothing.' It was true. How could anything be going on between us if he was over there carrying on with *her*?

'I'm sorry, does my breath smell like milk to you? Is that why you're acting like I was born yesterday?' Mitra waved her hands around as she talked.

'I can't get into it tonight, okay?'

Mitra tapped her knuckles against the counter. 'Fine, get some food for the team.' She nodded towards the two waiters who were chatting by the cashier. I leaned on the counter for a second, taking a breath.

The waiters were both young, probably uni students. The one facing towards me had a Drake vibe. I caught his eye and threw him a polite smile. He nodded, grabbed the dishtowel he'd shoved in the back pocket of his black jeans and walked over.

'What can I get you, sister?' he asked. I ordered three plates of kebabs, falafels, salads – way more food than we could possibly eat, but it didn't matter. I wanted to do something nice for everyone who'd done so much for the campaign. Even after the waiter nodded and disappeared into the kitchen, translating my order into Arabic, I dawdled, pulled out my phone and mindlessly scrolled through Instagram.

'If the kebabs are like their dolmas, I'm going to use this place to cater our big Iftar this year,' Sima said, leaning next to me at the counter. Her cream hijab complemented her skin beautifully. She looked great in her campaign T-shirt worn over a long white shirt-dress that skimmed her knees, and jeans. I knew she was only two years older than me – a third-year – but she had this presence, this kind of perpetual calm, that always made me feel much younger in comparison.

'You're holding a big Iftar?' I put away my phone, turned so I was facing her.

'You'd know that if you'd joined the Muslim Society.'

I cringed. 'I just . . . wasn't sure I'd fit in.'

'Ahhh.' she stood up straighter, hand at her hip now. I winced at the disappointment in her eyes. She had pushed back against the people who'd made comments about the videos of me dancing, when people had questioned my faith. I looked away. I couldn't imagine her ever sneaking around with a boy like I had done. Even though the thought of Alex made me want to throw things now, I didn't feel bad for kissing him. Maybe it was because I inherited my love of God from Maman Noosheen, who'd never felt bad for sneaking around with my grandfather. I knew it was a big deal for so many in the community, but that just wasn't the faith I had grown up with.

'It's just, my parents never wanted me to wear hijab, I didn't grow up with a lot of the same rules. You know?'

Sima's lips dipped in a frown. 'Yeah, you're not one of *those* Muslims, right?' The look she gave me could have silenced a classroom in a second flat. I ran a hand over my face. She was right, there was no way round it. Realising it made me want to hide under the counter away from her gaze. I had assumed that everyone in the Muslim Society would have a particular way of thinking, would be the same.

'I'd love to join and help with Iftar,' I said.

Sima nodded, giving me a knowing smile, like she'd known I'd pass her surprise test. She moved closer, rubbed my shoulder. 'What you did here mattered. You know that, right?'

'Yeah.' It came out as a whisper. I leaned into her and together, we headed back to the room where everyone was hanging out. Even though Sima had pulled me up on my ridiculous hang-ups, I felt better rather than worse for it. I was growing, learning – and that was good.

When we walked in, I didn't look at Alex. Didn't need to. Instead, I took a deep breath and held on to my feeling of strength.

I sat back down next to Mitra and piled kebabs and tabbouleh on my plate. I was exhausted, but sitting around, talking to the people who'd worked on the campaign, seeing so many brown faces around me – sharing stories, making jokes in Urdu, Farsi and Arabic – made my heart swell. No one could take this away from me: from us.

'Can I borrow you for a sec?' Alex was squatting between Anaya and Kate, peering through them. I nudged Mitra aside and didn't miss her glare at him as I pulled away, following him to the curved entryway. We stepped just to the other side, so we were away from the noise of the party, but close enough to see everyone. 'Results should be out in a few minutes,' he said, leaning against the wall.

'Alright,' I said, folding my arms across my chest.

He took a step towards me and I stepped back, feeling the wall behind me. 'Tara – ' he started, but his phone beeped. It was Sam, our scrutineer, who was huddled in with the officials counting the ballots to make sure everything was legit. This was it.

Alex put his fingers in his mouth and whistled. Everyone turned to him instantly. 'Results are about to come in.' Drinks were grabbed, breaths were held and fingers were crossed.

He read the text and threw me a look I couldn't read. 'In first place is Lee, and in second place is Tara!' Applause exploded all around me. I was assailed with hugs. Before I knew it, I was standing on the chair, looking out at a little crowd of people, most of them wearing my name on their T-shirts.

'Umm . . .' This really wasn't a great start. I pulled myself together. 'Look, this campaign was so much bigger than me. I'm really proud of what we did. The change we already created.

Thank you. For all the chalking, leafleting and poster runs. This is our win and I can't wait for us all to get started.' It was short, but I think I got the general point across.

Alex cleared his throat and I looked up at him. He leaned forward, lowered his voice. 'Will, Badal and . . .' he stopped, sighed, '. . . and Jess, all got up too.' Fine. Whatever. I'd deal with that later. For now, I was going to enjoy this moment.

I pushed away thoughts of Jess and sat back down. Upbeat Arabic pop beats played around us, the table laid out with a feast. The skewers of lamb kebabs, and plates of basmati rice, tabbouleh, hummus and baba ganoush reminded me of Maman Noosheen. I reached into my pocket and squeezed her tasbeeh. If she was watching, I was sure she'd be smiling, if not straight-up bragging to all her friends in the afterlife.

Just then, Sam bounced in and all of us started cheering again. Linda shuffled down so Sam could sit next to Mitra. Sam leaned to bite Mitra's shoulder as she squeezed in next to her. I looked away and glanced over at Alex, who was still sitting next to the blonde girl. She was so close to him, she was practically on his lap.

'If I lean back just enough, I can tip the table and throw his drink into his lap,' Anaya said. I looked up at her. She knew?

'Ahh, what?' I said, trying to look nonchalant and certain I was failing.

'Oh, puh-lease,' Anaya said, letting her fork fall to the table before tearing a piece of lavash from her plate, 'there was less soppy staring in *Twilight* than between you two.'

I shrugged. 'He has that effect on a lot of people.'

Anaya pursed her lips and sipped her beer.

I didn't want her to feel like I was trying to push her away. 'You mentioned there's an Order of Fantasy trivia night on Tuesday?' I asked.

'Oh, it's so good! I think this Tuesday is *Game of Thrones* themed.'

'Will you take me?' I didn't realise how nervous I was until I asked.

'Duh,' she said, smiling again. 'Everyone wants to be on my team because I drink and know things.' I chuckled at the *Game of Thrones* reference and raised my Coke glass to her schooner.

Then she turned to Pete, whispered something to him and laughed. He put an arm around her chair, but kept debating something about sports with Ben on his other side. I looked from Pete to Anaya and wondered.

'What you think you're the only one on the campaign with any game?' Mitra whispered, elbowing me in the ribs. I laughed, relaxing back into my chair, and listened to the hum of chatter of my friends. I looked around to Anaya, Sam, Pete, Meg, Linda, Kate, Sima, Mitra and the others. I knew that the bond we'd formed over staple guns and chalking was going to last for a long while yet.

The next hour – or was it two? – disappeared in a haze of food, stories and cheers. By the time the last of the team left, the resturant was closing and we were being gently shepherded outside. Just four of us were left: me, Mitra, Sam and Alex. I wasn't going to panic. But I wondered where the blonde had gone, and if Alex was meeting up with her later. The four of us had spent almost every other hour together over the last few weeks, but now it felt weird (awkward, even) with Sam and

Mitra pawing at each other and Alex and I standing as far apart as possible.

Mitra squeezed the air out of me in a chokehold.

'I'm so fucking proud of you,' she said. I nudged far enough away so that I could breathe, but pulled her into a tight hug, holding onto her for a good two heartbeats longer than the norm. We pulled away and she glanced from me to Alex. 'You gonna be okay?' she said, loud enough that he would hear. I nodded and she stepped back, but didn't stop glaring at him.

Sam took Mitra's hand in hers and then pointed at me like she was some sort of game show host.

'I told you so! I told you so! I told you so!' Her face was so bright it could have lit up a stadium.

I laughed and bowed down to her brilliance. 'You did,' I admitted. 'Thank you for that. For everything. This wouldn't have happened without you.'

'I know,' she said, and I laughed even harder.

Hands in each other's pockets, they strolled away, stumbling into kisses as they meandered down the road in the direction of Sam's house. I watched them go, knowing Alex was behind me. The adrenaline of the night had worn off. Every time I thought about taking a moment to celebrate what we'd pulled off together, I would just see him with that girl. Was he dating her? Had he kissed her? Had he done *more* than kiss her?

'Tara . . .' The way he said my name made my heart ache. He wasn't using his campaign voice anymore.

'Thank you.' I turned around. 'I know how much time and effort you put in, and I really appreciate it.' I reached out to shake his hand.

'Seriously?' He pushed my hand away. I could feel the waves of emotion bouncing off of him, could see competing thoughts warring on his face.

'What do you want, Alex?'

'I, I . . .' He looked away and then looked at me again, jaw set. 'I just want to talk, okay?'

'Alright, Casper.' It was nice seeing him grimace. He couldn't pretend he hadn't been ghosting me for the last few days.

'What you ran out of wizard quotes?'

Arse. I stepped toward him and pointed in his face. 'You know what gets me about you? You keep saying how you hate that people know you. You know what, you love being *Alex Jackson*. If anything challenges the idea of what *Alex Jackson* is meant to be like, you bolt.'

'Like you're any better?' he said, flicking his nose at me.

'I don't push people away like that.'

'Horseshit. That's exactly what the med thing is. You wanted to bury yourself in study because that's what you do. That's how you pretend you have this grand noble plan, when all you're doing is hiding.'

I wrapped my arms around myself and glanced away.

'Look . . .' he took a breath, 'I freaked, okay. I just don't know how to be with you.'

I stared. He hadn't really just said that, had he? Like I was some sort of sea demon you had to figure out how to be with, how to love?

'Stuff you.'

He sighed. 'I didn't mean it that way.'

'Yes, you did.' I took a breath, tried to stop my lip from

trembling, 'Look, I'm used to falling for . . . *characters.*' I took a breath. I should have stopped, but the anger was still rising. 'I just thought the Alex I fell for was real.' I paused, leaned forward. 'My mistake.'

I heard how sharply he inhaled, like I'd gut-punched him. We stared at each other, but we'd stacked too many landmines between us to take steps back together. I turned and walked away.

'Tara . . .' He was coming after me. I flinched away from that desperate note in his voice.

No. I wasn't going to settle for a guy who didn't know how to be with me.

'Go to hell!' I called out over my shoulder. I didn't look back, but the footsteps stopped. He didn't call out again. I walked down two blocks, sat on a bus-stop bench, called an Uber. I managed to hold back my tears until it arrived, and I closed the passenger door behind me.

Chapter 20

I rubbed my eyes with the back of my hands and blew my nose. The light was on. Of course Mum had stayed up for me. She knew it was election night. I opened the door, ready to plaster a smile on my face.

'*Azizam, chi shod?*' ('Sweetheart, what happened?') I guess I looked worse than I thought. 'It doesn't matter if you lost, the way you put yourself out there is what counts.'

The way I put myself out there was the problem. 'No, I was one of the people who got elected,' I said, walking to the kitchen for a glass of water.

'What? Congratulations?!?' She pulled me into her arms so hard, my water almost went up my nose. She wore the same confused expression she'd had last year, after I got my ATAR. She sighed. 'It's about the guy you were going to introduce me to, isn't it?'

'Can we talk?' I moved to the couch. She nodded and sat next to me. Might as well tell her I was looking at places with Mitra. A fight with Mum would really cap off the night. 'Look, um, Mitra and I have been looking at apartments together.'

'Oh. You want to move out?'

'Yeah,' I said. 'Mitra can't keep crashing on the sofa bed in the closet.'

'Oh,' Mum said, rubbing her temples, 'of course not.'

'Yeah, I have my savings from summer, which should cover the deposit, and the medical centre is always looking for people to cover shifts – and I figured if I picked up some tutoring on the side . . .'

'On top of studying and Union board?' Mum said, shaking her head incredulously.

'I can juggle,' I said, pushing out my chin.

'I know you can, *azizam*.' Mum grabbed my hand and pulled me down. 'Look, I don't know what happened with the boy, but I'm worried.'

'I know it'll be a big change, but it'll be good for me to get out there.' It wasn't fair, but I knew that was the only way to get her to back off.

She pulled away and nodded. I pulled a pillow into my lap and hugged it, pushing down the guilt.

'Let's talk more tomorrow, okay?' she said.

'Sure.' I threw the pillow to the couch and headed to bed, a list of ways I could deflect conversations about Alex running through my head.

The next day I didn't get to uni early, like I usually did. I got coffee in the city, not on campus, and practically ran to my first class. Every other corner, poster board and bench reminded me of him: of a joke he had told me, of the way he'd checked up on me, how his eyes shaded darker or lighter according to his mood. So my plan was to go stealth. Get in and out. No library, no hanging about, just getting to classes and going home. The idea of bumping into him walking hand-in-hand with that girl . . . well, I just couldn't.

I sat down, grabbed my notebook and pen, and waited for the lecturer. Mitra sat down next to me just as they got up to the lectern.

'You okay?' she said.

I nodded. I could tell she wanted to ask more questions, but the lecturer started talking. I pointed, shrugged apologetically and then started writing down what the lecturer said, word for word. The moment he finished, I shoved everything into my bag.

'Wait up!' Mitra called as I got up. I slowed down and we walked out of the lecture theatre together.

'Sorry, I'm playing catch-up with exams, let's hang later?'

'I get it. Whatever went down with Alex, you're pissed about it. We'll do a few wheelies in Dee and get it out of your system.'

'I'm fine.'

'Right . . . you were a heartbeat away from noting every fucking breath the lecturer took and how long it lasted.'

'There's nothing wrong with being thorough.'

'That's what people say when they're trying to stop anything from getting done.' She planted her hands on her hips and stared at me, 'Look, fine, it's been a tough few weeks. You get a pass for now – just know, we ain't done talking about this.'

The next few days disappeared into a haze of books, bickering with Mum and Mitra, and burnt meals. Any time I tried to cook, I'd decide I wanted to read something, or go get something, then wander away and come back to charred eggplant, or chicken, or pastry. After a couple of days of this, I stabbed one of Mum's Lean Cuisine meals, popped it in the microwave and actually ate two bites before tossing it.

I was on top of exam prep, so I started researching the Union and its history: reading through the board minutes of the last year, reading through the notes from various committees and then downloading the annual reports and going through the budgets line by line.

I was getting the best grades of my life and was totally prepared for Union board. I was doing great, really great. Honestly. The whole cooking thing was just a weird tic. I scraped the chicken I'd turned to charcoal into the bin and started chopping some veggies to make a stir fry.

Mitra walked in and winced at the burnt kitchen air. 'You want to talk about it?'

'The place we applied for turned us down – so we need to check out more places. I'll send you a list later.'

'I meant about Alex.'

I looked from her face to the tomato I seemed to have somehow pulverised. There was no use trying to deflect Mitra at this point. She'd dig in for hours if she needed to. 'I liked him, okay?' I pouted.

'*Really?* I'm shocked, *shocked.*'

I put the tomato in the bin with the chicken and took another one from the fridge. I picked up the knife again. 'You saw him at the election night party with *her.*'

Mitra put one hand on my shoulder and used the other to pry the knife from my hand. 'How 'bout we keep the innocent tomato out of this, okay?'

'He said he didn't know how to be with me,' I said, glaring at her.

'That's a stupid thing for him to say, but – don't kill me – I get it. He's probably used to hook-ups, casual stuff . . . and you're not that. Look, I'd be pissed too, he flirts more than most people breathe. And yeah, the flirting was more intense on election night . . . but he didn't look the way he is with you. I mean, if you're right I'll happily lay into him. I'm just saying . . . the situation might not be as bad as you think.'

'This whole mellow thing doesn't suit you a damn.'

'I know.' Mitra grabbed a can of Coke from the fridge and popped it open. 'All the sex is really taking my edge off.' She winked.

'Ewww.' I threw a tea towel at her, but couldn't help but smile. Somehow Mitra convinced me to watch a *Fast and Furious* movie with her, instead of reading the latest Sarah J. Maas book in my room.

I don't know what it was about watching people drive cars out of buildings and planes (and under trucks) that made me think that maybe – just *maybe* – talking to Alex wouldn't be the worst idea after all.

Coffee?
No, that wasn't right.
Chat?
Not enough.
I miss you.
Too much. Way, way too much.
I stood up, brushed the grass off the white peasant blouse

I was wearing, and started to walk home. It was one of those rare days when I felt actually pretty. My puffy-sleeved blouse cinched in at the waist, hanging loose over my thighs. Tiny roses were embroidered at its hem. It was gorgeous against my jeans. My coral hijab felt super girly and, well . . . I wished Alex could see me in this outfit. I'd been drafting text messages to him since last night and nothing seemed right. Tomorrow. I'd figure out what to say to him tomorrow.

I walked past Manning on my way to grab a bus home. I recognised some of Jess's entourage hanging out in the courtyard. Their eyes bleary from drinking, occasionally calling out or making rude gestures at people who passed. They were sharing swigs from a giant bottle of Coke, and as I drew close, I tensed. I doubted that the only thing in that bottle was sugar water.

I kept my eyes facing forward as I quickened my pace, trying to get past them as fast as possible. I felt their eyes on me, but within seconds, I had done it. I let out the breath I'd been holding.

'Oy, it's our newest board member!' I felt sweat trickle down my back. I didn't turn around. It was daylight and the campus thronged with people. Surely they wouldn't do anything.

'King's Haul!' one of them yelled behind me. *King's Haul?* Why did that sound familiar? I didn't have time to think about it more, because footsteps clamoured toward me and my head whipped back. I stumbled backwards – choking, shrieking. Someone was pulling my hijab, and it caught around my neck like a noose. The safety pins holding it up snapped open, stabbing at my neck.

I clawed at the fabric as the world dipped around me. I couldn't get enough air to scream or shout. I fell backwards and just like that, the pressure was gone – and so was my hijab. I dropped to my knees. Wheezing. Shaking.

I saw a ruffle of yellow skirts, big blue eyes. 'Are you okay?' a woman asked, reaching out. I lurched away, running my hands over my head, not quite registering that I was feeling my hair under my fingers instead of my pretty coral scarf. 'Help is coming,' she said, squeezing a phone to her ear with her shoulder, crouching next to me.

I turned back to see the guy running, waving my hijab above his head like it was a trophy. I couldn't see who it was. The rest of Jess's crew cheered him on, puffing out their chests and hollering. He pushed aside anyone who tried to grab my hijab from him and flicked off anyone who yelled out.

Oh, hell no.

I didn't think. I just ran. People were shouting all around me, but I didn't care. With every step, he came into sharper focus and I picked up momentum, charging at him. He raised his hand, keeping my hijab out of reach, half-turning towards me. Instead of jumping for it, I threw my body into his, using every ounce of strength I had. He went down and I yanked my hijab from his hand as he fell.

Someone grabbed my shoulders. A male voice hissed, 'Don't you touch him!' Then I was flung backwards.

'Leave her alone!' someone shouted as I crashed against the concrete. My head cracked with a sickening noise. My body heaved in response.

'Oh my God, oh my God . . .' Someone was hovering over me, but they were too blurry to make out. 'Everything is going to be okay,' said the voice, as sirens screamed and the world went black.

I squinted against the harsh fluorescent light, and turned away.

'Tara – ' Mum's mascara-streaked face slowly came into focus. I felt my hand in hers.

'What happened?' I tried to sit up, but an IV in my hand pulled me back.

'Now, look.' Mitra's voice calmed my rising hum of panic. She was slumped in the corner, cracking her knuckles, tapping her foot against her chair, obviously freaked out but still giving me that smug smile, trying to pretend she wasn't. 'I thought we had a deal between the two of us that riot-starting was solidly *my* department.'

'How long was I out?'

'About two hours? You woke up before, had some food, then fell asleep. You don't have a concussion, *khoda ra shokr*.' ('Thank God.') Mum ran the back of her hand against the side of my face.

'Yeah, it's kind of embarrassing fainting like that.' Mitra was smiling, but I could tell from her tone that she was pissed. I tried to laugh, but everything hurt. The pain reeled in the memories.

'A guy pulled off my hijab,' I whispered, staring at the ceiling, hoping one of them would tell me it wasn't true. I felt so small and wanted to pull the blankets around me, to hide.

'Don't think about it now,' Mum said, running her hand over my hair.

A nurse swooshed back the curtain and strolled in holding a clipboard. 'Had a bit of a scare, did we?' She had a sing-song voice and a morphine smile. 'Not to worry, let me just unhook you from these things and you can get on home. You might want to take the back exit? There are a few cameras out front.' She and Mum shared a nod, like they were part of a covert team.

Why were there cameras in front of a hospital? Had someone famous just given birth? My head was too foggy from painkillers to process it. Mitra handed me a sweater. I stepped out of bed and pulled my hair into a bun. I wished Alex was here. The thought of him made my stomach knot and I shoved it away.

'I need to find a hijab.'

Mum winced and looked away.

Mitra chucked her bag on the bed and rifled through it. 'This was the best I could do.' She pushed a swaddle blanket printed with foxes at me. I hugged her.

Mum grabbed my stuff, and with Mitra on one side and Mum on the other, the three of us hobbled out of the curtained room and into the corridor.

I froze as I saw cops. What the hell was going on? Had there been some kind of attack? I shook my head and winced at the movement.

'I want to press charges against whoever assaulted my son – no, I will not calm down – Larry, hold on – I want to know who pushed him.' A man in an expensive suit was holding an iPhone to his ear, dividing his attention between whoever was on the other side of the call and the police officer in front of him. His hair looked like a stainless-steel scourer and I was sure I'd seen it before.

'Is that . . .' I peered at the other side of the hall, making sure I was seeing clearly '. . . Carl Maddison?'

Mitra shrugged. Her grip on my shoulder got a bit firmer. The presence of one of the richest men in Australia explained the journos.

The officer was an older gentleman, tufts of white hair poking from under his hat. His glasses kept falling down on his nose, and each time Carl Maddison yelled, he would push the frames back into position. We were still a good twenty metres away, but as we got a little bit closer, we could hear what the officer was saying, too.

'Sir – I'll be able to answer that much sooner if you let me have a few words with your son – '

'You're not going anywhere near him until our lawyer gets here – Larry, if you're not here in five, I'm cutting your retainer!' Carl Maddison was still having two conversations at once. I caught the officer's eyes and smiled at him softly. I felt bad for the guy who was getting yelled at for trying to do his job. The officer held my stare, then turned back to Carl.

'Tara Lutkari?' I turned. The second officer, with his friendly smile and chubby cheeks, was a dead ringer for Santa Claus.

'Constable Moss, is it?' Mum stepped in front of me, reading his name off his badge.

'I just have a few questions for your daughter, Ma'am.'

What did I do?

'Is there a charge I'm unaware of?' She said it so casually, like she was asking about the weather. Constable Moss shook his head. Mum nodded, reached into her handbag and pulled out a card. 'Well, if that changes, or if you come into the possession of a subpoena, you can reach me at my firm, Morrison King Birch.' She handed him the card and smiled as his eyebrows twitched. 'Good? Good. Evening, officer.' Mum took my hand and marched us into the lift and all the way to the car park, without turning back once. I'd only ever seen Mum type and file papers when I had to go by her offices. I had never really seen her *lawyer* before.

'Leila's a badass,' Mitra whispered as Mum marched towards the car. I jumped a little when the car alarm beeped off.

'Yeah, she really is.' I smiled and then turned to Mitra, 'All the women in my life are.' Noosheen. Leila. Mitra, Sam, Anaya – maybe I'd make that into a poster.

We got into the car. Mum readjusted her mirror and asked me if I was okay twice before starting the engine. She was holding onto the steering wheel so tight, I was worried she was going to snap it in half. When we stopped at a red light, she rubbed her left temple. 'I know you've had a big day, but there's something I need to tell you.'

Surely there was no way this day could get worse. She glanced over at me and sighed. The light turned green. 'Your father is on his way.'

Turned out I was wrong. 'Why?'

'I had to tell him what happened, Tara.' Her voice was like a paper cut. I stared out the window, watching the bright lights flicker as we drove through the city.

'Everything will be back to normal by the time he gets here anyway,' I said, closing my eyes. It would still take him another day, even if he was already on a plane from LA.

'I hope so.' Mum didn't sound convinced.

We pulled onto our street and I leaned forward. There were a half dozen people on the footpath in front of our house, some of them in suits, holding microphones, others in jeans and T-shirts, hauling cameras over their shoulders, or around their necks. They looked completely out of place on our quiet street. What the hell was going on? Mum pulled into the garage and some of them started pointing at us and running towards the car.

Mum swore, slowed down, reached into the dashboard and pulled out a pair of black sunnies. 'Chuck these on, it'll make it harder to know it's you.'

I pushed the sunnies over my face as the crowd started pounding on our windows. Mum navigated through them like having a mob of journalists in our driveway happened every day. She pulled into our garage and clicked the door closed.

'What's going on?' I pulled off the sunglasses.

Mum had buried her face in her hands, taking deep breaths.

'The guy who attacked you, who tore off your hijab – it was Steve Maddison,' Mitra said as she slammed open her car door.

I shook my head, still woozy with painkillers. Mitra opened my door and helped me up. I was shaking now, trying to take everything in.

'Things aren't going to go back to normal, are they?' I asked. Neither of them said anything as we walked into the house.

Chapter 21

I had no idea what time it was when I opened my eyes, but the bright light told me the morning was almost gone. Maybe if I slept a bit longer, the whole thing would fade into a bad dream. I turned over and buried my face in the pillow. Minutes passed. It was still real. And I was still awake.

I sat up and cringed. Every part of my body was sore, like I had run a marathon without training, or even stretching. I pulled my arms over my head, willing my muscles to loosen up, but they didn't. I guess they had good reason to be on edge.

I opened the door and heard the sound of the news, as well as Mum and Mitra furiously whispering at each other. I turned into the hallway. They were both on the couch, looking like they hadn't slept, neither of them wearing a shred of make-up.

'We have to tell her,' Mitra said, frustration etched into her voice.

'Tell me what?'

They jumped. Mum grabbed the remote and clicked off the TV, while Mitra leaned back into the couch and ran a hand through her hair.

'Let me fix you some breakfast,' Mum said, darting to her

feet and running into the kitchen, slamming pots onto the stove like she hoped the noise would drown out the tension. I walked to the couch, crouched next to Mitra and gave her a questioning look.

Mitra sighed, shook her head and turned to Mum. 'Leila,' she said.

Mum raised a hand. 'Not on an empty stomach.'

There was nothing either of us could say to that, so we just sat and listened to the banging, chopping and sizzling, watching Mum move about the kitchen until she handed us each a plate topped with a cheese omelette, and sat down opposite us with her own matching plate. We ate in silence.

Mitra took the plates, washed them and put them away before coming back into the living room. Mum's arms were crossed. She looked like she had aged ten years since last night.

'Please?' I asked, looking at her. She looked up at me and I felt my chest hollow out. Maybe I should just go back to bed.

Mitra sat down next to me and took my hand. 'Ready?'

I nodded and Mitra flicked the remote. YouTube appeared on the screen. I didn't even know our TV was linked to the internet – Mitra must have enabled it at some point since she moved in. The setting on the paused video was recognisable as our uni campus. I braced myself. Mitra pressed play.

'Sydney University is still investigating a race riot that happened yesterday, with more than eight students injured. The Maddison family has yet to comment on the shocking video of Steve Maddison appearing to spark the violence. A warning to viewers that some of this footage may be distressing.'

I took a breath and heard myself rasp. My legs started to shake. I wanted to turn away, but couldn't.

The segment cut to a grainy video that looked like it had been shot on someone's phone. The camera turned to Steve. He swigged from a giant Coke bottle as a voice behind the camera repeated, 'He's gonna do it man, I can't believe he's gonna go for it.'

The video showed him slowly stalking me, before grabbing my veil. 'Holy shit, did you see that?' The voice was gleeful. I felt numb as I stared at the footage of myself falling, choking, screaming. 'Bet she's a screamer in the sack too,' another voice slurred. They laughed and hooted as I fell on the ground, as Steve waved my hijab in the air.

Mitra swore next to me, clenching her fists at her side. Tears rolled down Mum's cheeks. 'Enough, turn it off,' she said.

Mitra took the remote, but I shook my head. 'No.'

The footage rolled on as I raced towards Steve. 'Oy, what does she think she's doing?' a voice said. And then the footage cut out, as if whoever was filming dropped their phone. Mitra clicked off the TV.

'Is it . . .?'

'Everywhere? Yep.' Mitra said.

I pulled my knees to my chest and closed my eyes. 'What do I do?'

'Get some sleep, your dad's going to be here in the morning,' Mum said.

I looked up at her and nodded. I hadn't seen Dad in years, wouldn't really know what he looked like now, if not for Instagram. I bit a fingernail. What would he say? I was too tired to imagine and thanked Khoda for that small mercy.

I almost asked Mitra to hand over my phone, but I didn't want to deal with all that, not yet. Just thinking about what people could be saying about me, how they'd be talking about the whole thing, was enough to make my stomach spasm.

I shuffled back to my room. I didn't want to break down in front of them, didn't want to worry them any more than I already had. I closed the door, collapsed on my bed and closed my eyes.

The footage of the attack kept replaying in my head. I'd run for Union board to stop being the bomb-threat girl. But how was I ever going to get away from *this*? I'd never be able to make everyone in Australia forget what they'd seen. It didn't matter who I was, what I did. This was always going to be my story. What was the point of trying then? What was the point of anything?

I could picture it now. Going back to uni – the pitiful glances, the whispers behind my back, the random people wanting to talk to me about that video. I tried to shove the thoughts away, but they tightened their grip. How long would it take before people stopped asking me about the attack? A year? Two? Ten?

Then another thought hit me like a broadsword. What would happen if I ran into Jess's crew again? Would they avoid me? They couldn't try pulling something like that again, would they? Besides, Jess was on Union board, we were colleagues now. I started crying, feeling hollowed out and useless. I'd tried, but I wasn't like Katniss, Hermione or Buffy. I had run for Union to help make things easier, not just for me, but for Roshan and others. Instead, I'd made it all worse. I crouched on all fours, pressed my forehead against the carpet and cried.

I rubbed my tears away, pulled out my jah-namaz and started to pray. I was thankful these chats with God were scripted, because I had no words left. If I had been on my own, I wouldn't have known what to say or ask for.

It was late afternoon. I was huddled in bed watching a re-run of *Project Runway* on Mum's old iPad, surrounded by empty cups of tea and snacks that Mitra and Mum had brought me. They took turns to check in on me, every half hour. So when Mitra poked her head in to my room ten minutes after Mum had left, I knew something was up.

'It's shit timing, but we gotta talk to you.'

I nodded and walked out to the living room with her. Mum was sitting on the couch in front of the TV, looking worse than she had in the morning.

I sat on the floor. 'What's up?'

Mum slid down next to me, put a hand over my shoulders and kissed the top of my head. '*Azizam,* I know you're still coming to grips with everything, but we need to have a chat about what you want to do – if you want to say anything.'

'No.' I stood up and headed back to my room. I had tried, and hadn't just failed. I'd made things spectacularly worse.

Mitra stepped in front of me. 'That bastard put out a video. Do you want him to tell this story for you?'

'I don't care.' I pulled myself to my full height. I still had to look up at her.

'Really, you don't care about this?' She pulled up another YouTube clip of the news.

'In breaking news, Steve Maddison has given a tearful apology over his apparent role in the race riot at Sydney University. Here's the footage – ' The anchor cut to a video of Steve Maddison in front of a pale background. He looked faded, like a shirt that had hung in the sun too long. At first his words were robotic. 'I want to apologise for my actions. I let down my family, my friends and myself. People have been calling me a racist online.' His voice cracked. He tipped his face forward and looked up with tears in his eyes. 'I'm sorry . . . I'm sorry, that's just not me, I believe everyone deserves a fair go . . .'

'Yeah, I'd cry too if I was a fucking racist who'd been caught,' Mitra said, giving the TV the finger.

'They probably spent thousands on that video, made it look deliberately impulsive. It's what I would have done if he was my client,' Mum said, looking pale.

The news anchor appeared back on the screen. 'The education minister weighed in on the debate today.' The picture of the education minister appeared on the screen, along with his tweet: *It would be a shame to expel a talented young man from university and dim his bright future, given his apology for what was clearly a terrible mistake.*

'Turn it off,' I said, wanting to throw up. I wrapped my arms around myself and stared at the ceiling. They had money, a brand, and the most powerful institutions in Australia in their circle of influence. I might be fighting Goliath, but I wasn't David. I didn't have mad slingshot skills. I wasn't going to get out of this with my dignity intact.

'You're not alone in this.' Mitra fiddled with her bangles and flicked her curls. 'There's a petition online demanding that Steve be expelled and that the university launch an inquiry into the colleges. Well, it's hit 300,000 signatures. People are on your side, they're just not sure what to do to help . . .'

I shook my head. It didn't matter. I'd gotten heaps of people to see me, *really* see me during the Union board campaign – and within a matter of seconds, Jess's crew had turned me back into a meme. They'd find a way to wreck whatever I wanted to do.

'This ain't just about you. Do you think anyone who looks like us feels safe for a damn second in that university now?' Mitra said, her voice breaking.

'Then let one of them fight this one. I'm out.'

Chapter 22

'Trying to impress your dad?'

I threw one of my scarves at Mitra. 'No, I'm just on edge.' I looked over my outfit, shook my head and yanked off the dress.

''Cause you're trying to impress your dad.'

I glared at her as I pulled on some black jeans and a pink sweater and smoothed my black hijab. He was going to be here in a few minutes, so this would have to do. 'What are the chances that this goes well?'

Mitra shrugged as she sat up on my bed, ''Bout the same as Kyle Sandilands making it through a broadcast without saying something offensive.'

'You're really not going to stay?'

She stretched and shook her head. 'Leila's already pissed and that woman is straight-up terrifying when she's mad. Course I'm getting the hell out of here. I'll be down the road. Buzz if you need me.'

I gave her a massive hug at the front door before she left. Mum walked into the living room wearing perfectly tailored navy pants and a white sleeveless blouse. Her hair and make-up were immaculate. She looked radiant – certainly not like she'd been freaking out and not sleeping. Apparently, I wasn't the only one who wanted to look good for Dad.

The doorbell rang before I had a chance to say anything. Mum fiddled with her hair and dabbed on some gloss before she opened the door.

I didn't know how to greet Dad when he walked through the door with his Louis Vuitton duffle bag. Was I meant to shake his hand or hug him? I opted for an awkward wave. He looked ridiculous, with blonde highlights in his black hair and oversized aviators hanging from his tight black V-neck.

He reached out and beckoned me forward like I was a distracted waiter. I tiptoed toward him. He pulled me into a hug, and I almost choked on his sharp cologne.

'*Dokhtaram.*' ('Daughter of mine.') It sounded more like a deed of ownership than a greeting. He turned towards Mum, put his hand over his chest and bowed his head just far enough to make it clear that he was half greeting and half mocking her.

'*Beshin*, Hamed.' Mum gestured towards the couch for him to sit. Dad marched through the house with his sneakers on. He dropped the duffle next to the couch, glanced up at me and patted the space next to him. I sat on a nearby dining-room chair instead.

'How was the flight?' I asked.

He shrugged. '*Ashghal.*' ('Trash.') He fluttered his hand in a dismissive gesture. 'Why are you wearing hijab? Who here is haram?'

I tucked a stray hair into my hijab and patted it possessively. 'I like wearing it,' I said. *Especially around you.*

Mum walked out of the kitchen with a pot of hot tea and our fancy tea set, painted with the face of a mustachioed man, who I imagined was looking disapprovingly at Dad.

'Have some, Hamed.' Mum set the tray in front of him, but didn't pour for him. It was a massive burn. Maman Noosheen would have told her off for being so rude. He reached out and poured himself a glass, sat back and took a sip, without so much as offering to pour for anyone else.

'This is a nice little beach house,' he said, shaking his head while adjusting his gold-plated watch.

'How's . . . whatshername? Your secretary?' Mum asked, mimicking his motions. I looked over at her and smiled. Mum would have made an excellent high school mean girl.

Dad tucked up his shirt sleeves. 'Huma? We're engaged. She says hello. She's having a spa weekend with Jennifer Aniston.'

'How nice!' Mum's voice was an octave higher than usual.

'*Okay hasti*?' ('Are you okay?') He looked directly at me.

'Yeah, I'll be fine.'

He nodded, then pulled his duffle bag into his lap, unzipped it and pulled out a black box. I resisted the urge to roll my eyes. The last thing I wanted was some kind of flashy gift to compensate for him not knowing me.

'I was saving this for your birthday, but given . . . I thought you'd like it now.' He held out his hand and I leaned forward to take the box. I looked up and he nodded, so I took off the lid with a fake smile already plastered on my face. Then I saw what was inside and my smile collapsed into something real.

I ran my hands over the worn stethoscope, and opened the card tucked into it. It had been Victor Chang's, and there was a photo of him wearing it. I bit my lip and looked up at Dad. He remembered that I wanted to be a doctor. Tears stung my eyes. Had I totally misjudged him?

'Thank you. This is . . . it's incredible.' My breath caught on the words as I fought to stay composed. He shrugged, and I fidgeted with my hijab. 'Thank you for coming to make sure I was okay. It means a lot.'

'I had to reschedule two surgeries this weekend. Let's just say that with the Oscars coming up, my clients weren't pleased.' He put his tea down and looked at me, before twisting his face and turning away. The change in him was so quick that if I hadn't been holding the stethoscope in my hands, I would have been sure I'd imagined it. 'I can't even look at you in that thing.' He turned to Mum. 'Why haven't you fixed this?'

Mum put up a finger to stop him, '*Dorest harf bezan*, Hamed.' ('Talk properly, Hamed.')

He looked at me, sneering. 'People think I beat her to wear it, they think I agree with this *ashghal* [trash].' He pointed towards my hijab. 'People don't come to my practice because they think I support that homicidal regime.'

'I'm sorry,' I said, looking at my feet. I wished I could melt away.

'*Einam feministeh*?' ('Is this feminism?') He directed this at my mother, steamrolling on. 'You like her wearing a symbol of terror?'

'Hamed,' Mum said, standing.

'It's not a symbol of terror,' I said, looking up at him, trying to stop my lip from quivering.

'You think it's okay for her to wear something so anti-woman?'

'*Gomshoh*.' ('Get lost.') Mum pointed to the door. I looked at my parents, from one to the other, and wondered how they'd ever been a couple. I hated the idea that I was the thing they had in common.

'Leila – why don't you understand? I'm trying to protect her!'
He was leaning forward now, yelling, his face red. 'Listen, Tara.'
He lowered his voice and looked at me in what I think was an
attempt to be earnest. 'There's nothing left for you here. No
matter what, you're always going to be the girl in that video – '

His words hammered into me. I felt like he had just shoved
me into Tamora Pierce's chamber of the ordeal. He'd just found
my worst fear and threw it at me – the same way the chamber
did. Unlike Alanna or Kel in the books, though, I didn't walk
out as a knight. I just curled into myself, feeling small.

'My friend, he does admissions at UCLA – the best medical
program in the world. You take that thing off, and with your
grades and the recommendations my friends will write you,
you can learn medicine from the best.'

I stared at him, mouth open. I could go to America, have a
clean slate somewhere where I wouldn't be the girl from the
video, or the girl in hijab. Just Tara, the girl who wanted to be a
doctor. I didn't know what to say. It sounded like the answer to
my prayers. While a part of me was screaming *yes*, another part
of me was shrieking *no*. I couldn't just leave uni, abandon the
Union board and put myself an ocean away from Mum, Mitra
and home.

'I'm at the Hilton. Let me know your decision by tomorrow
night. My flight home is the next morning,' he said, standing
up. He walked past the photo frames and stopped at the photo
of my grandfather at the rally in Iran. He laughed bitterly and
turned to me. 'You know the story of this photo?'

'Hamed, don't – ' Mum's voice was shrill.

Dad glared at Mum, '*Bahs Kon,* Leila. [Enough, Leila.] Tara,
you should know about your blood.' He pointed at the photo.

'That was an anti-hijab march. Your grandfather died at a march defending women from that thing.'

What? My grandfather had died at an anti-hijab march?

It couldn't be true. I looked at Mum. She was shaking, clenching and unclenching her fists. I pulled out Maman Noosheen's tasbeeh from my pocket and pressed it into my palm. Had I been letting her down all this time? Had I let them all down? I looked up at Mum, then at Dad, hoping one of them would tell me this was all a joke.

Mum grabbed his duffle bag, opened the door and threw it out, '*Gomshoh*, Hamed! *Gomshoh*!'

Dad put his hands in his pockets and shrugged at her, turning back to me. 'I love you so much.' He put his hand on my shoulder and leaned down so that we were eye to eye. 'But I can't keep watching you throw your life away. If my flight leaves and you're still wearing that *thing* . . . we're done. I won't have it in my life, Tara. I won't.' I couldn't stop the tears then. I jumped when the door slammed shut.

'Don't listen to him.' Mum pulled me aside and was suddenly kneeling in front of me. I kept my eyes on the floor, and she grabbed my chin and tilted my head up so I was looking at her. 'That march wasn't anti-hijab – it was against *compulsory* hijab.' Her mascara streaked down her face. 'I didn't grow up with kids' stories, Tara. Your grandmother put me to bed at night telling me about my dad. She told me a hundred times that your grandfather went to that march because his own mother had her chador ripped off by Reza Shah's cronies. He thought women should make up their own minds about the hijab – be free to practise their faith in peace.'

She ran her thumbs over my cheeks, wiping away my tears.

'He would have been so proud of you. You're so like him, it scares me sometimes.'

I buried my head in Mum's shoulder and sobbed. I had no idea how long we sat there, holding onto each other and crying for everything that had changed and everything that had stayed the same.

Chapter 23

'Do you think it was worth it?' I asked Mitra, squirting extra chocolate sauce on my ice cream and tuning out *Project Runway*. Mitra raised an eyebrow as she sprinkled extra chocolate chips on her sundae. I had another mouthful of ice cream, taking a second to pull together my thoughts. 'He died protesting something that ended up happening anyway. It just seems like such a waste. Do you think he still would have gone if he knew he wouldn't come back?'

Mitra studied her bowl for a moment, moving her ice cream around so that every bit was covered in chocolate chips. 'That's the wrong way to look at it. He could have had a heart attack that day, or walked into a truck. He showed up for a thing he believed in – the rest ain't his fault.'

'I guess.' I put the bowl down and glanced at the TV. Tim Gunn was telling a hyperventilating designer to *make it work*. 'You think I should go to LA?'

Mitra reached out and took my hand, 'I don't give a damn what you wear, and if anyone blames you for wanting a fresh start, I'll kick their arses.'

'But you wouldn't do it.'

Mitra shrugged. 'I don't know.'

I knew her well enough to sense the lie. I'd never seen her walk away from a fight, especially one where she knew she was right. I grabbed one of the pillows on the couch and hugged it. But what did I think? I stared at the TV as I let the question settle.

'You could have my room if I went,' I said.

'With that creepy-ass skeleton staring at me all day? No thanks.'

'What do you have against Rumi?'

'Just to be clear, if you stay and we move out, Mr Bones stays here. I'm not going to wander out of the bathroom at night and have a heart attack seeing that thing in your room.'

I looked back at the TV. Tim Gunn had moved onto another designer, put on a look of mock horror and said, 'I'm concerned. I really am.'

That was the thing. In my stories, the good guys usually won – they had to give it their all, make sacrifices, but they got there. Maybe that wasn't the point though. Maybe it wasn't about winning, but about doing the right thing. I mean, if we waited to be sure we'd win before we acted, would we ever do anything?

I set the pillow aside and paused the episode. 'I want my laptop and my phone.'

Mitra looked at me for a moment, frowning. 'Are you sure?'

I nodded. Mitra went to her bag, pulled out both things and set them down in front of me, before grabbing the remote and turning the TV back on.

I smiled at her. She was going to give me my space and pretend to watch *Project Runway*, but stay close enough that she could make sure I was okay. I loved her for it. I switched on my phone and it vibrated for ten minutes straight with a rush of messages. There were seven from Alex. I didn't read those ones. I could still remember what he said to me on election night. *I don't know how to be with you.*

I was broken, sure. Maybe loving me was complicated. I could live with that. But I wasn't going to be a coward.

I thought about my grandfather fighting for women to be able to choose to wear the hijab; heard my dad's taunt from this morning. But what Baba Joon had believed in was women making their own decisions. That's what he stood up for. The government hadn't listened to the protestors, but so what? His legacy was bigger than that. It was about courage, love and freedom. What he did meant something. It made me want to stand up, too – even if I was afraid.

I flipped open my laptop and took a breath before opening Facebook. There were dozens of messages: some from friends, some interview requests and quite a bit of hate mail. I scrolled through my feed. Anaya, Linda, Kate – all had written furious posts defending me, and they weren't the only ones. Most of the posts had attracted a flurry of comments. People were arguing about the incident, trying to make up their minds. After all, he had apologised, hadn't he?

I closed Facebook and opened my Gmail. There was a bunch of junk, a few more media requests and then there was the vice-chancellor's name. I paused, leaned forward and clicked. It wasn't the usual form letter, but a brief note saying he was sorry about what had happened. He wanted to talk to me about the incident.

I took a deep breath, opened a new tab and searched for the petition that Mitra had mentioned. It had already gotten a bunch of media coverage and a bit of backlash, but it also had hundreds of thousands of signatures. The petition in support of Steve didn't have even half the numbers. I read through the text and smiled. It was smart, sensible and striking – whoever had started it wasn't afraid to take sides.

I signed the petition before turning to Mitra. 'Do you think Sam can come over for breakfast tomorrow?'

'Sure.' She nudged me and smirked. 'I guess it's game time, then?'

'We don't need to do this today if you need more time.' I turned toward Mum's voice. She looked gorgeous, of course, as she always did. But I could tell, from the little details no one else would notice, that she was stressed out: no lipstick, a few stray strands of hair, the chipped nail polish on her left pinky.

'I'm ready to talk about how we deal with this, just like I'm ready to have your boyfriend stay with us if that's what you need,' I said. We hadn't talked about Jonathan in weeks, but I was sure they'd been talking. I wouldn't have been surprised if he was already in Sydney and dying to see her. I hated seeing her so sad. She needed support that I couldn't give her. She smiled – actually *smiled* – for what felt like the first time in weeks and opened her arms to me. I stepped into them and thanked Khoda for the hundredth time that I had her.

There was a knock at the door. Mitra opened it and Sam strolled in. I introduced her to Mum and the four of us huddled on the couch.

'So you wanna fight this thing?' Sam said, her arm thrown lazily around Mitra's shoulders.

I nodded. 'The vice-chancellor sent me an email. He wants to talk.'

'You're going to need back up.'

Sam lifted her hand to silence me as I opened my mouth. 'The four of us aren't going to cut it. When you go in there and talk to the VC, he needs to know we mean business. Good thing I have years of practice getting his attention.' She paused, leaned forward and gave me one of her *don't bullshit me* looks. 'I'll fight this with you if you're going to see it through. There's no point if you're planning to jump on a plane and walk away from everyone who fought for you to get on Union.'

'Lay off, alright?' Mitra grabbed Sam's shoulder and pushed her back into the chair, glaring.

'Have you thought about it, *azizam*? There's no shame in either decision,' Mum said, her words almost a whisper. Just getting the words out seemed to exhaust her. Sam snorted and Mitra growled at her.

The time crunch wasn't their fault. Dad was getting on a plane tomorrow. I had to tell him what I wanted to do tonight. Yes, we barely talked. But the idea of being actively disowned still stung.

I looked around at each of them. Yes, I'd probably always be the girl in that video, but this was my home. There were a lot of arseholes out there. But I had plenty of people who'd stood by me, fought with me. Even elected me as a student leader. The truth was, I wasn't alone. I never had been.

'I'm going to stay,' I said.

It felt the room relax around me. Mum smiled. Mitra smirked at Sam as if to say, *I told you so*.

'Always knew ya had fight in ya,' Sam said, giving me that

nod that teachers give you in high school when you ace a particularly hard test. 'Let's get to it, then.'

We spent the next hour talking through plans, going through talking points and figuring out what our next steps were. It was physically exhausting, the same way a workout was. I felt totally worn out at the end of it, but in the way you do when you know you've just accomplished something.

'Look, we're gonna have to call in Alex. Hell, at this point the press would even find it weird . . . *OWWW!*' Sam rubbed her ribs where Mitra had nudged her. 'You haven't told her?' Sam glared at Mitra.

'She's had a bit on her plate,' Mitra snapped back.

'What?' I said, reminding them I was still in the room.

'Alex was the one who started the petition. It went viral because he started sharing stories about other King's Hauls, and how this wasn't a one-off,' Sam said.

'But, he lives with them . . .'

'Not anymore. He moved out into a share house with a bunch of old high-school mates.' Had he really done it – stood up to his friends, stood up for himself, instead of trying so hard to be what everyone else wanted him to be? *Alex Jackson* the brand? Was he okay being just *Alex* now? My insides felt all jumbled up at the thought.

'He was at the hospital, too. Leila and I didn't think you were up for seeing him,' Mitra said.

'Got us coffee, stayed with us the whole time till you woke up, and then disappeared. Didn't push it at all.' Mum said. *Oh, so he met her, after all.*

'But, the night of the election – '

'Mitra told me about that. Look, Tara, nothing happened.

Sure, Don Juan couldn't live up to Alex's reputation. But he was all about casual hook-ups before. Nothing wrong with that. You know how he is about letting people in. It was always different with you – you got under his skin. I've never seen him smitten before. I don't know what happened, but my gut tells me he freaked and shoved you away. Look, I talked to Hailey – the girl he was all cosy with election night – and she said nothing happened. Don't get me wrong – total dick move. But,' she shrugged, 'I figured you'd want to know.'

I grabbed my phone and started reading through the texts he had sent over the last few days.

I hope you're okay.

Please, please be okay.

I'm sorry, I knew about that stupid game. Like I told you. I should have spoken up about it before. If I had, maybe this wouldn't have happened.

You were right. About everything.

I know I have no right to say it, but I miss you.

I miss you so much

God, Tara, I'm so sorry.

If my chest felt like it was caving in before, it collapsed altogether now. He'd shown up to the hospital, started the petition, reached out. I looked over at Sam. 'Do you know where his new place is?'

Chapter 24

Mitra pulled up outside a classic inner-city terrace house, its wrought-iron front fence matching the railings of its tiny upstairs balcony. It was one of the rare terraces that renovators hadn't yet painted pastel. Its cream walls were cracked, its wrought-iron and windowsills painted a sun-faded green that had probably gone out of fashion before it even dried. 'You sure about this?' Mitra asked.

I nodded. She smiled and tapped her fingers on the steering wheel. 'Look, if anything happens, I'll be round the corner at Sam's.'

I got out of Dee, walked to his door and bit my lip. What if he wasn't home? What if one of his roomies answered the door? I took a deep breath, made a fist and then knocked: once, twice, three times.

I heard footsteps shuffling behind the door, getting closer. The doorknob turned and there he was, staring at me.

'Tara?' His voice was raspy, like he hadn't slept for a long while.

His hair was wet, the ends curling, falling into his eyes. He pushed a hand through it, before brushing off the stained shirt he was wearing.

I stepped forward, closed the door behind me, looped my arms round his neck and let my head rest on his chest. For a second, he was totally still and I thought I had lost him – *really* lost him – but then his hands clamped around my back and he pulled me closer, squeezing me so tight that my bones ached.

'Alex,' I said, holding his face in my hands, 'don't ever try to put me on a plane again.'

He laughed at the *Casablanca* reference and pressed his forehead to mine, so that he was staring right into my eyes. 'I'm so sorry, after you left my place after we . . . well, I kind of lost it. I convinced myself that since you hadn't said you were falling for me too, maybe you'd just gotten carried away. That you'd regret everything . . . and I . . . I couldn't stand the idea. Then somehow I figured even if you did have feelings for me too, that I'd screw it up somehow, end up hurting you anyway . . . The stuff you said on election night, you were so spot on . . .'

'You were right too – ' I took a deep breath, brushing a curl behind his ear ' – about me hiding behind med, using it as an excuse to not let people in. I'm done hiding.'

'Me too,' he said, taking my hand and leading me to the tiny living room, crammed with furniture that looked like it had been scavenged from a roadside. 'Can I show you something?' he asked, as he took me up the stairs to his shoebox room. He had a mattress on the floor, a clothes rack, his laptop and a projector. I sat on his bed. He grabbed his bag from the milk crate he was using as a bedside table and dug something out.

'Remember when I said you had to be all in for the election?' He handed me a little velvet box. I looked up at him and flicked the lid off. 'Well, I did some reading and this reminded me of you.' Inside was a silver ring with an inscription on the inside: *Life before death. Strength before weakness. Journey before destination.* It was a quote from the Stormlight archive – mottos of new heroes figuring out their honour code. I noticed he was wearing a silver ring too. I reached out and traced it with my finger.

'Don't freak – they're not engagement rings. I just want you to know I'm in. All in. If you'll have me.' I pulled the ring off his finger and looked at the inscription inside. *I will do better* – I'm pretty sure that was a quote from the flawed hero of the series.

Okay, so he didn't have a magic amulet or a kingdom – but he'd rejected his dodgy friends and stood up for what he believed in. For me. I kissed him on the cheek and let him slip the ring on my finger.

'Of course I'll have you,' I said.

Two days, a hundred flirty texts with Alex, a bunch of meetings and a couple of good old-fashioned freak-outs later, I was back at uni.

'Your dad still hasn't replied?' Mitra said.

I shook my head. I wanted Dad to reply: even if it was to lash out or yell. I'd messaged him with my decision yesterday and heard nothing but radio silence since. His ignoring me made his parting threat feel real. I didn't exist for him.

I paused to rebalance the box, filled with pages of petition signatures. A part of me was still amazed that over 300,000 people agreed with what we were asking for: that Steve be expelled and an inquiry launched into the colleges. I tried to focus on my aching back, on the ground in front of me – on anything that wouldn't remind me of the day, the moment, when Steve had attacked me.

'What if no one shows up?' I asked. I wished I'd let Mum come with us.

'If you're hoping no one's going to hear your speech, I'd start praying that a Kardashian pops out a baby in the next hour.' Mitra nodded towards the lawns in front of the quad.

I followed her gaze and shuddered. There were already about a thousand people there, with placards and my old campaign T-shirts. Worse, a couple of TV crews were setting up. We were half an hour early, which meant that there was no way this wasn't going to get even bigger.

'I think I'm going to be sick.'

'Nah you won't, 'cause if you did, someone would record it and you don't want that meme floating round the net.'

Brutal but helpful. I could feel the tension rolling off Mitra as we walked past the police vans. She made a point of not looking at any of the cops swarming around campus. Given that the fight originally broke out here, it wasn't surprising they were out in full force. When I saw the stern-looking mounted officers, I couldn't help but clutch the box of signatures tighter.

We walked to the lawns, where a makeshift stage had been erected. Sam waved us over. I squared my shoulders and marched towards the front of the rally. People swarmed from all directions and the crowd kept bulging. I noticed some journalists were waiting near the front, microphones in hand.

Sam steered us towards where the speakers were hanging out. Most of the Union board members were huddled close to the stage, along with some of the key volunteers from my campaign. Seeing them somehow made everything real, pulled me back into memories of the campaign. Then I remembered falling, waking up at the hospital, seeing the video for the first time. I stumbled, and Mitra grabbed my arm.

'You're okay.' It wasn't Mitra. It was Alex. I wanted to feel his arms around me, but we'd agreed to avoid any PDA. Neither of us wanted our relationship dissected online.

I opened my mouth to thank him, but a roar of boos and hisses went through the crowd and photographers started running past us. I turned around and almost screamed.

About fifty people, some of them wearing Australian flags for capes, had marched to the opposite side of the road, holding giant signs: STAND WITH STEVE. I raised myself on my toes to see if I could spot Jess or Steve, but neither of them was there.

A row of cops promptly settled in between the two rallies, forming a human barricade. There was shouting, swearing and flipping each other off on both sides. A cluster on our side started chanting, 'RACISTS OFF CAMPUS!' while the counter-rally burst into 'AUSSIE, AUSSIE, AUSSIE, OI, OI, OI!'

Seeing them sharpened my resolve. I stood up straighter. I'd dressed in all-black that morning, with a grey hijab. It felt like my armour and the petition felt like my crest. This was where I rallied the troops and led the march into battle. I had never imagined being the one to wave the banners and lead a charge, but I could do it.

'I'm going to kick this off before people lose it,' Sam said, squeezing my shoulder and throwing a questioning look at Mitra before grabbing the mic and jumping on stage. The crowd cheered her.

Everything felt like it was in slow motion: Sam standing

on the stage, Mitra and Alex standing next to me, a crowd of people nodding, waving or pointing at me. My heart was racing and then everything felt like it was spinning. I was going to throw up. I knew it. But the idea of that image being splashed on the internet made me swallow the bile in my throat.

'You okay?' Alex asked. He moved a hand towards me and let it drop to his side as a journalist walked past. The worry in his face, in his voice, was so clear I could have sensed it with my eyes closed.

'Yeah.' I rolled my shoulders and tried to stand as tall as I could. He didn't say anything, but didn't look any less worried.

'You're up next,' Sam called from next to the stage. I turned to look at the crowd, which had exploded – thousands of people were crammed onto the lawns. I closed my eyes and ran through my speech in my head, clutching my tasbeeh. I imagined I had wings. That my outfit really *was* armour and that my tasbeeh could unlock spellbinding magic. It sounds silly, but it worked. I felt the tension leave my body.

I heard Sam say my name and the crowd applauded. Sam stayed on stage and extended a hand to help me up the stairs. I flashed her my most grateful glance, walked towards the mic – and froze.

Cameras flashed. Journalists furrowed their brows. I heard a few coughs through the crowd. I opened my mouth, 'I . . . I . . .'

This was it. I was going to melt down in front of everyone, and it would be captured and replayed a hundred times over. I felt all the magic powers I'd imagined for myself evaporate. I was just a girl, totally overwhelmed and in over my head.

I felt the colour drain from my face, my knees weaken. Then I closed my eyes. And when I opened them, all I could see was my grandparents standing in front of me.

'I'm here because what happened last week isn't okay – not here, not anywhere.' I could almost feel the crowd leaning in, listening. I shut them out, clenched my tasbeeh and focused on the image of my grandparents. It was like tapping into a power source. I felt magic pulse around me.

It's really hard to ignore thousands of people when they all start applauding, hooting and hollering. I took a breath and waited for the cheers to die down, then kept going. 'It's not just about what happened in that video. There are way too many stories about people on this campus being bullied, belittled, berated and bashed for what they believe or how they look. Today is where it stops.'

The crowd roared.

'This place has always been about learning and curiosity, with the promise that if you work hard, you can do well. Yet since the first day I walked through those gates, my hijab has defined my experience here more than anything else. I know that I'm not alone. I know that Indigenous students, international students, LGBTQIA students and women experience similar things. It's time we stop pretending that the walls of this campus can keep out thousands of years of history – and systems that have been built to divide us, by belittling those of us who happen to carry some mark of *other*.'

I took a breath. The crowd was with me – I could feel them hanging off my every word, like I really *had* spellbound them.

'At the same time, this place is filled with people who are doing their best to learn from history, to reach out instead of letting old ways divide us. Today is a great example of all of us coming together to create the university we want and deserve. Here's the thing: we can't grow, we can't keep learning and building, without justice, without holding each other accountable.'

The crowd cheered and started chanting. 'JUSTICE! JUSTICE! JUSTICE!'

'The thing that keeps me going, the thing that got me out of bed today, was knowing that my story isn't just one of hurt. There are people who have lashed out at me on this campus, but there were many more who stood by me, supported me and believed in me. We are already better than this. We will pull together and be stronger because of it. And I want to thank you all for being the type of people who dare to do the work to make that dream of a better future into a reality.'

Applause rang in my ears. Cameras pointed towards me from the audience. I just nodded and walked off the stage. Sam hugged me at the edge and Mitra grabbed my waist, picked me up and twirled me around.

'I thought you were going to throw up out there, but damn girl, you owned it,' Mitra said, putting me back down.

I wasn't an assassin or a queen, but maybe I wasn't a Muggle either. Maybe I did have some magic and I was just starting to learn how to use it.

Alex passed me a water bottle and gave me a smile that made me want to kiss him, despite all the journos around. I took a gulp of water, and with the adrenaline fading, suddenly felt exhausted.

'Come on, let's find you a chair before you collapse,' Mitra said, putting an arm around me and steering me away from the stage and the journalists who had started to head straight for us.

I huddled on a bench, wedged between Mitra and Alex. The next speaker was a girl who was a bit older than me. She talked about how a group of guys had broken into her room during a King's Haul game – how this was normal, happens every year. The speaker after that was from the Muslim Society. She talked about how last year, someone had put a pig's head in the prayer room. It was gross, all of it. And it wasn't new. What had happened to me wasn't a one-off. That was what made me really angry.

'You ready?' I jumped at Mitra's voice and noticed the stage was empty.

'Yes.' I was ready to take this to power, to demand change, to stand there not just for myself, but for all the people who'd gone before and all who would come later. We walked to the big arched doors that led to the vice-chancellor's office.

Two security guards and three cops stood outside the door. One of the security guards looked from me to Mitra and then to the boxes in our hands. 'Only you,' he said to me, putting his hand on the doorknob but not opening the door.

'No way she's going in there alone,' Mitra said, taking a step forward. Two cops stepped into her path. I looked back up at the security guard who had spoken. He looked bored, which was impressive given the cameras, the flashes and the masses of people around us. He wasn't going to budge, that was clear.

'Fine,' I said. Mitra whirled towards me, but I shook my head. She pressed her lips together and turned back to the guard.

'Here then.' She let the box she was holding fall onto the floor in front of the cops' feet. 'At least help her carry this up then, will ya?'

For a second I thought the guard was going to ignore her,

or one of the cops was going to grab her. Instead, the other security guard picked up the box. The two of them nodded at each other and opened the door. I walked into the hallway, and once the door slammed closed behind me, I took a breath. I was well and truly in the dragon's den now.

Chapter 25

The hallway that led to the vice-chancellor's office looked like something out of *Harry Potter*. There was a giant mahogany staircase, and the walls were lined with portraits of old professors looking stern in their academic robes. Bright colours flickered into the hall through the stained-glass windows. I took a deep breath and walked up the stairs, shuddering every time the steps creaked under my feet.

Maybe, just maybe, the vice-chancellor would turn out to be a Dumbledore and everything would be okay.

A floor-to-ceiling window framed by a sandstone arch poured light into the room at the end of the staircase. I flinched under the brightness. In the middle of the room was a small desk, with a stack of colour-coded files and a large Mac desktop. Behind the desk sat a stern woman with glasses on a chain around her neck, a collared shirt done up to the very last button and lips that seemed to be frozen in a dissatisfied purse.

'Ms Lutkari?' the woman said, tilting her head and raising her eyebrows. I nodded.

'You're on time.' She brushed invisible lint off her royal blue pencil skirt, grabbed the petition box from the security guard behind me and rested her hand on the doorknob. 'Follow me, please.'

I half expected to be shish-kabobbed by a booby trap of poison-tipped arrows as I walked into the vice-chancellor's office.

It looked more like a library or a regency sitting-room than a modern office. The vice-chancellor sat behind a large desk on one of those ridiculously high-backed executive chairs, a paper notebook in front of him and a gold-plated fountain pen in his hand. Two amber leather armchairs were on either side of his desk. There was a window on the wide side of the room that looked out onto the Quad and the rest of the walls were lined with books. Their musty smell suggested they hadn't been dusted, much less read, in a long while. Even his laptop was leather-cased. Sitting closed on his desk, it looked like an encyclopedia.

The vice-chancellor had a Harrison Ford vibe: white-flecked hair, square jaw and the nonchalant arrogance of a sixty-something Hollywood actor.

He hadn't looked up from his notes since we walked in. The only acknowledgement of our presence was a tensing of his shoulders. 'Thank you, Maggie – ' he said, as he fingered his storm-coloured tie. I heard Maggie put the box on a bench and click the door shut. Was I meant to sit down or say something? The whole thing felt like a test. All I could do was shuffle my weight from one foot to another.

I put the petition box I was carrying on the floor and stretched slightly. There was an antique-looking globe next to me. I let my fingers graze it. The globe clanked as it spun towards Europe. I hissed in horror – did I break it? No. Instead of spinning, the top of the globe slipped backward, falling on hinges that revealed a cleverly concealed bar. The liquor inside was all top-shelf: Johnny Walker Blue, Glenfiddich. The freshly cut limes hinted that the bottles got more use than the books.

'Do sit, if you're done – ' I jumped at his voice. He was staring at me now, frowning.

'Sir.' I sat in an armchair, keeping my back as straight as possible.

'Miss Lut-*kari*.' He seasoned my name with disdain, so it sounded like, *little girl*. He pronounced my last name with perfectly practised precision. 'I have heard much about you – ' He drummed his fingers on the table as if trying to calculate the exact number of times he'd heard my name. 'I hope you have recovered from the unfortunate incident – ' He stopped tapping his fingers and interlaced them as he leaned back in his chair.

This guy was no Dumbledore.

Something in his tone made my stomach twist. Fine, I could play this game. I could turn formality into a weapon too. 'Can't say that I've fully recovered, no.'

He pursed his lips and leaned forward, like I was suddenly worthy of attention. 'The whole dreadful business is most unfortunate. Some consider it one of the darkest moments this university has known.'

'Only some?'

'The matter is being considered very seriously.'

'The same way a pig's head showing up in the prayer room was handled?'

He shook a finger at me. 'I've condemned those actions, met with the students – '

I scoffed. 'What about a security camera, a door code, or

something remotely useful to stop it from happening again? *The incident* you mentioned isn't the first time that kind of thing has happened here. I came here to be a doctor. I deserve to be able to study without being attacked. So do the students who live on campus in the colleges. So does everyone else.'

'Jess Wilkey sat in that same chair and said the same thing.' He smiled. 'An abandoned bag on a day when the whole nation was on high alert. The taunts she's received, the emails . . . and even a few incidents where you seemed to encourage such behaviour while running for Union.'

'Are you saying –?'

'An investigation has been completed. We will be issuing an apology to you personally. The Maddisons will issue an apology. Steve will voluntarily engage in sensitivity coaching and the family will be donating a substantial amount to the department of Islamic Studies. Steve will be suspended for the remaining semester, but allowed to sit exams.'

'No!' This couldn't be happening. 'This wasn't a one-off.'

'Procedures, dear girl, aren't biased.'

Like hell they weren't. I noticed the hint of a smile on his lips and felt my stomach turn like I was dropping into a rollercoaster's dip. 'You didn't ask me to come so you could tell me the results of the investigation.'

'I would suggest you review these documents.' He opened a drawer, pulled out a manila folder by its very tip and flung it towards me.

I glared at the folder for a moment, reaching tentatively towards it as if it were a snake. Inside were my admission papers and a copy of the university's code of conduct. 'I don't understand.'

'You agreed to uphold the reputation of this institution on admission. As I mentioned, the investigation didn't cast a particularly favourable light on anyone.' He paused, catching my gaze and resting his chin on his fist before continuing. 'Given that, if you now, in light of your claims having been addressed, continue to besmirch the name of the university, like you did just below my window today, your enrolment can be annulled.'

I pressed my lips together. My back had started to ache from holding it so straight. I held his eyes and swallowed my sneer.

'Of course, I'm sure you are as keen as other parties to put this whole matter behind you.' He flicked his hand like he was dismissing any other possibility as foolish. 'That said, in light of your contributions to the university and our commitment to diversity – we'd be honoured to feature you in the upcoming alumni newsletter and general recruitment drive.'

Why don't you shove it? I took a deep breath, and unclenched my hands from the sides of the armchair. My fingers ached from how hard they'd been clasping the seat. I stood up and nodded. 'I also have something for you.' I reached out to the box next to me, pulled out the petition text and put it on his desk. 'Over 300,000 people have signed that petition.'

A muscle in his jaw twitched and I couldn't help but smirk. 'Vice-chancellor.' I dipped my head at him, turned and marched out of the room, letting the door slam behind me.

I had failed. I'd walked into the dragon's den, been singed by fire and left empty-handed.

Mitra was next to me in a heartbeat. She wrapped an arm around my shoulder and navigated me into Dee, where Sam and Alex were already waiting. I closed the door and leaned back against the front seat, closing my eyes. If it wasn't for the rumbling in my stomach, I could have slept for days.

'Sounds like we need to get you some tucker,' Mitra said, fastening her seatbelt.

Alex's hand reached around the seat to squeeze my shoulder, I leaned back into it, grateful to feel his warmth.

'Top line now, full debrief later?' Sam said, as Mitra turned on the car and pulled out of the parking space.

'He threatened me, but said if I kept my mouth shut I'd get to be on a poster.'

'Bastard.' Mitra shook her head and I could see her tightening her grip on the steering wheel. I didn't ask where we were going, I just glanced out the window. I wasn't even thinking about the rally or the meeting with the VC. It felt like my brain had too many tabs open and was about to crash.

A few minutes later, Mitra pulled up outside a tiny Thai restaurant in Glebe. It was one of those places with student specials and a bright neon sign. A waitress in jeans and a white shirt said hello and welcomed us the minute the door chimed open. The place was deserted but every table had been set out with orange plastic tablecloths and sturdy white plates. An FM radio station played in the background.

'It's almost like we're on a double date,' Alex said, sliding in next to me and holding my hand under the table. Mitra snorted, then yelped. I couldn't hold back my smile. Sam had obviously kicked her under the table.

'I bet the VC's knickers are in a twist 'cause those cowards are hightailing it back to the mothership,' Mitra said, flipping over her vibrating phone, ignoring whoever was calling. She looked from me to Sam. 'Well, tell 'em.'

'It's on Instagram. Jess and Steve are moving to London.

He's taking a year off to *find himself* – ' here she dramatised air quotes ' – and she's studying at Cambridge.'

'They're still together?' I shouldn't have been surprised. But when Jess had apologised, I thought she got it, at least a little.

'Together? I'd bet Dee that she'll be flashing around a rock the size of Mars in a few months to try and get people to forget that they're both racist knobs.' Mitra's phone buzzed again.

Well, at least I didn't have to worry about sitting through Union meetings with Jess. Would her spot go to the person who got the most votes out of those who didn't make the cut, or would they hold a special election?

'Let's just eat.' Alex pulled me closer, kissing my temple. I let myself lean into him for a moment and straightened as the waitress sauntered over, carrying laminated menus. I nodded thanks to her.

'Oh and the house I was showing you last night is open at noon this weekend.'

I nodded at Mitra. Now that both of us officially had employers who could vouch for our ability to pay rent, we were ready to apply for houses again. I'd arranged with the medical centre that I'd start working weekends and nights, and was trying not to think about how I'd juggle that and study. Maybe I could read my textbooks behind the reception desk? I sipped some water. I'd think about that later. For now, I was just going to focus on what was happening.

'So, what happened while I was with the VC?'

Sam poured water into four coloured plastic cups, then shrugged. 'Not much. We packed up the gear, dismantled the stage and had a quick huddle with key people. There's meant to be a follow-up call tomorrow.'

I rubbed my eyes and felt myself sag in my seat. I wanted this mess to be over. Every time I felt like I was at the finish line, it suddenly shifted.

Mitra's phone buzzed again. It was starting to make me twitch. She didn't seem to notice, though. She leaned back lazily and looked up at the waitress. 'We're going to get a beef pad thai, a tofu pad see ew, a green curry and some fried rice with prawns . . . oh, and the appetiser set to start, with a few extra spring rolls.' The waitress nodded and took our menus. Mitra looked from me to Alex, then to Sam. 'What?' she said, as we watched her send another call to voicemail.

'Who's calling you?' I asked.

'Fadi. He probably lost his car keys or something.'

I frowned. Mitra's brother had been known to call at odd hours with totally inane requests, but this felt different. I couldn't remember him calling this many times in a row. Her phone buzzed again, and this time I reached over and grabbed it.

'Hey Fadi.' I pushed the phone to my ear and ignored Mitra's eye-roll.

'. . . Tara?' My heart started beating faster at the catch in his voice.

'Everything alright?' I glanced at Mitra.

'Dad's in the hospital. Is Mitra there?'

My stomach sank. 'I'm so sorry, I'll put her right on.' Mitra was already holding her arm out and drumming on the table with her other hand.

'What happened?' Her face crumpled as he gave her the news. Sam reached out for her, but Mitra pushed her away, turning away from us. 'I'm on my way.' She was practically out of her seat, then stopped and went paler than I'd ever seen her. 'What do you mean I shouldn't come?' It came out as a whisper. The hurt in her voice wrenched my heart. 'What fucking article are you talking about?'

Sam threw me a worried glance, pulled out her phone and started googling. Mitra covered her face with her hands and her shoulders slumped. 'Fuck,' she whispered.

The waitress came over with our starters, noticed our faces and then practically ran back to the kitchen. Alex leaned over and asked if he should cancel the food. I nodded and he walked over to the waitress, who was flipping through a magazine on a stool at the back of the restaurant.

'Oh God.' I looked over at Sam. Her hand was covering her mouth as she stared at her phone. Tears in her eyes, she looked over at Mitra with something between heartbreak, fear and concern.

If something made Sam cry, it was bad. Really bad. I reached for the phone, even though I was one hundred per cent sure I didn't want to see whatever was on it. Alex knelt beside me. 'What . . .?' he said, before he caught sight of the headline and hissed.

It was worse than I could have imagined. The headline screamed: *Does she look 'Muslim' to you?*

I didn't read the article, but I scrolled through the photos. They were mostly of me – there was one where Alex and I were huddled close together smiling flirtatiously, at Manning the first day we met, a jug of beer in front of me. Someone had obviously gone through my Facebook feed. I didn't want to think about who. I added double-checking all my privacy settings to my mental to-do list. And then there was a photo of the campaign stall: me handing out leaflets, Sam and Mitra kissing in the background.

I looked up at Alex. He was pale, his lips a line of worry. I wanted to call the newspaper and yell. Coming after me was one thing, but outing Mitra? I glanced over at her and clenched the phone in my hands.

'Look, I'm heading over – don't argue. I'll be there in twenty.' Mitra slammed her phone on the table and then buried her face in her hands, shaking.

I walked over and crouched in front of her. 'I'll drive.'

Chapter 26

Mitra chewed on her nails, aggressively wiping away tears. Her fingers came away smeared in foundation, while liquid eyeliner streaked down her face. We'd been driving for ten minutes now. I had turned on her music, but she'd just turned it off and gone back to staring out the window.

I switched lanes and glanced back over at her. She was shaking her head a little, like she was saying *no*, over and over.

'What did Fadi say?' I wanted to hug her so badly, I almost pulled over.

She leaned her head back against the chair. 'He said a few family friends saw the article, emailed and called Dad about it. He left work livid. By the time he got home, he was so worked up that Mum called in the ambos. He's worried if I show up, it'll make him worse.'

I started to say that of course her parents wanted her there, but stopped myself. An ache grew in my chest. I hated not being able to reassure her of something so basic. I took a breath and reached out for her. 'I love you and I'll be here.' She just nodded back.

We drove the rest of the way in silence. After I parked at the hospital, the two of us sprinted to the ER, nurses watching in alarm as we dashed past corridors and burst through doors. Fadi was sitting on one of the plastic chairs in the waiting room, his head in his hands.

Mitra stormed up to him. 'Where are they?'

He looked up at her slowly and patted the seat next to him. Mitra kept standing. He sighed and said, 'The doc said Dad's gonna be okay, they're just keeping an eye on him for a few days.'

It was like someone had punctured Mitra, draining all her air. She fell into the seat beside Fadi, and a sob exploded from her. He wrapped an arm around her shoulders and pulled her close, rubbing the tears from his own eyes.

'This is bullshit,' Mitra said, wiping her nose on her sleeve.

'You think I like this?' He paused and looked away before turning back to her and taking her hand. 'I love you. I don't give a damn about who you hook up with.'

Mitra let out a sob. 'I should've told you. I didn't . . .'

I walked over to the vending machines. The coffee would be rancid, but the tea should be doable. I got two cups and brought them over. Mitra and Fadi took the tea with small nods. Mitra squeezed the bridge of her nose. I kept looking over at the emergency doors, wishing her mother would walk out, fold her in a hug and tell her it would be okay.

'Mitra, Fadi . . .' I looked up and saw the next-best thing. Amoo Ali was here. '*Kojast*?' ('Where is he?') Fadi told him the room number and Ali nodded and walked towards the door before looking back. '*Khob*?' ('Well?') Fadi shook his head. For a second, Amoo Ali frowned. Then his face sagged, like he had realised why they weren't coming with him.

He rubbed his face with both hands, and when he stopped, he

looked like he had added another five years' worth of exhaustion and age to his face. *'Jayee narin.'* ('Don't go anywhere.') Then he walked through the emergency doors.

I sat opposite Mitra and Fadi, and tapped my foot against the leg of my chair until Mitra ordered me to quit it. I started to crack my knuckles. I half expected shouting to erupt from the ER. Given how tense Mitra's mum must be, and that her dad was officially not speaking to Amoo Ali, I wouldn't be surprised if she kicked him out too.

'You think he'll talk some sense into them?' Mitra asked.

Fadi shrugged. *'Inshallah.'* ('God willing.') From the sound of his voice, it sounded more like, *if God intervenes.*

'Why aren't you in there?' Mitra nudged Fadi.

He shrugged and tapped his heels together but didn't answer the question. Mitra leaned forward and opened her mouth, but decided against it at the last second. She leaned back into her chair.

I crossed my legs and tried to make myself as small as possible. I had no idea what to do or say. I closed my eyes and started praying: for Mitra's dad, for her parents. For them to be able to heal and really *see* each other again.

Half an hour later, Amoo Ali was back. A frown pulled at the corners of his lips, and he somehow seemed to have shrunk. His flak jacket looked too big on him and his slouched shoulders made him look smaller. He caught our eyes and waved us outside to a small eating area. He sat on the only table in direct sunlight and tipped his head back, closing his eyes like a lizard recharging.

'How is he?' Mitra asked.

He opened his eyes, like Mitra had awakened him from an

hour-long nap. He fingered his chin like he had a beard, even though he didn't. A corner of his lips twitched up into a hint of a smile. '*Alhamdulillah, yek moe ro sarash fargh nakardeh.*' ('Thank God, not a hair on his head has changed.')

Fadi snorted and Mitra smiled at him. I felt the knot in my chest start to unravel. Just seeing Amoo Ali here was enough to know everything was going to be okay.

Amoo Ali took a pack of cigarettes from his coat pocket. He didn't offer them to anyone else. He pulled out his lighter and drummed the fingers of his free hand on the plastic table between us as he took a deep puff. '*Sunday digeh free hastin?*' ('Are you free next Sunday?') I loved the way he threaded his sentences with Farsi and English together.

'Yeah, why?' Fadi asked, his face pinched as if he'd sucked on a lime.

'*Daram Doomad Misham.*' ('I'm going to become a groom.')

Mitra's eyebrows shot so high that for a second I thought they were going to fly off her face. 'What?'

Amoo Ali's smile cracked open, making him look a decade younger. He swayed his head like he was listening to music.

Fadi chuckled. His shoulders pulled away from his ears. He leaned forward, as if to conspire with Amoo Ali. 'Who's the chick?'

Amoo Ali stilled at the question. His lips pulled back down into a frown and he looked away from us, taking a few deep puffs of his cigarette. He looked at Mitra, sighed and then squeezed her hand, only turning back to Fadi after he let it go.

'You know Mahmoud?' he said.

Fadi nodded. 'Yeah, of course.' The garage co-owner. Mitra looked at me. I shrugged back at her.

Amoo Ali took another puff of his cigarette. His hand shook. 'Mahmoud . . .' He stopped, rubbed a hand over his forehead and took off his jacket. 'Mahmoud is my *partner* . . .' Tears sparkled in his eyes, as he paused, letting the emphasis sink in. I swallowed a lump in my throat. '*Siey saleh*. [Thirty years.] I asked him to marry me, he said yes.'

He took Mitra's hand again, leaned over the table and kissed her knuckles. '*Man o bebakhsh*. [Forgive me.] If I had said something earlier, maybe . . .'

Mitra looked like she was about to burst into tears. She took his hand in both of hers and looked him straight in the eye. 'Just 'cause you're gay doesn't mean you can play Dariush or some other depressing as hell music at the wedding, alright?'

Amoo Ali laughed and clapped her on the back. I looked over at Fadi. He was twirling his phone, his face blank.

'Fadi?' Amoo Ali looked over to him too.

Fadi threw his phone on the table and frowned back. '*Mobarak*.' ('Congratulations.')

Amoo Ali smiled and put out his cigarette. His lips quivered. He let out a sob and doubled over, burying his face in his hands as his whole body shook. Mitra was next to him in a second.

He hugged her and pulled away, shaking his head. '*Okayam, Okayam* . . .' ('I'm okay, I'm okay.') He paused for a second, his face crumpling with emotion again. '*Fekr nemikardam joloyeh khoonevadam doomad besham*.' ('I didn't think I'd become a groom in front of my family.') He took out a handkerchief from his pocket and blew his nose before pulling it together.

I wiped away my own tears. I'd always respected the quiet strength of Amoo Ali, but now, knowing what he must have gone through, I realised I'd underestimated his courage all this time.

'Hey.' I felt some of the day's tension melt from my shoulders.

'You alright?' Alex stepped in and closed the door behind him.

I shrugged. 'I'm sorry about the article. Have your parents said anything?' They couldn't possibly be thrilled that I'd dragged him into a scandal.

Alex shrugged. 'Mum was pissed that she hasn't gotten to meet my girlfriend yet.'

I rested my head against his chest, closing my eyes and listening to his heartbeat. I thought of Amoo Ali. Alex and I'd had to be careful about how we interacted in public the past few days and I was already relieved it was over – I don't know if I could have done it for decades.

We settled in on the couch and I curled against his side. I filled him in on everything that had happened with Mitra's parents and at the hospital. He sighed and drew circles on my palm with his finger. 'How is she doing?'

'She's with Sam and not out doing wheelies, so that's good. I keep dragging her to open houses to keep her mind off stuff.' I nuzzled closer to him. 'How are your folks taking you moving out of college?' Somehow, we hadn't really talked about it – not properly. We'd been in crisis mode pretty much since we'd gotten back together. I felt the sigh vibrate through his chest and I looked up at him.

'Dad convinced them to hold my spot and put down the deposit for next year as well. We had a big blowout. He thinks I'm overreacting.'

'I'm sorry, I'm sure the story today didn't help.' I scratched his chest. He put his hand over mine and squeezed it.

'They'll come around. I am the golden child, after all.' He gave me one of his toothpaste-ad grins before taking my hand and kissing it. I pulled away and swatted his shoulder.

'Movie and ice cream?' He nodded. I tore myself away from him and headed over to the kitchen. I gave him the biggest helping of ice cream and squirted extra chocolate sauce onto his bowl.

'Have you got the furniture for your new room yet?' I curled back into his warmth.

'Nah, haven't had a chance yet.'

The idea of him sleeping in a sad little room with a mattress on the floor made me shudder. 'Want me to go to IKEA with you?'

His eyebrows shot up. 'You'd do that?'

'What?'

'I mean, there's serious and then there's IKEA.'

I laughed at that and his smile flipped my stomach. He leaned down and kissed me, then he pulled me to him. 'Movie, you said?' He reached for the bowl of half-melted ice cream. 'I think next weekend we should plan on having a *Godfather* marathon.'

'Aren't those movies, like, three hours long . . . each?' I said.

'Which is like, what, half as long as a *Lord of the Rings* movie?'

'We can watch *The Godfather* after you finish reading *Throne of Glass*. That was the deal. Remember?' I said.

'Fine, I'll pop into a bookshop tomorrow.'

I flicked on my computer, then looked up at him. I couldn't wait to hear his reaction when he figured out that *Throne of Glass* was a seven-part series.

Chapter 27

Mum opened the door, threw her keys onto the side table and froze as she spotted Alex and me snuggled up on the couch. Something was bugging her. I could tell by her loose ponytail and total lack of accessories: no earrings or necklace. She never left the house or her office without being perfectly assembled, unless something was on her mind.

'Hey,' I said, smiling and moving a heartbeat away from Alex. It was weird seeing the two of them in one place. They had met at the hospital, so they knew each other, but the whole thing still felt awkward as hell.

'Hello,' she replied, smiling at me like she was in on a secret. I knew she was cool with Alex, but this still felt like a test.

Alex straightened next to me and shut the laptop. 'Evening.' He glanced back at me like he was trying to decide if he should stay or give us some space. I squeezed his hand and he relaxed back into the couch.

'How was your day?' Mum asked as she headed into the kitchen. Where the hell did I start? Mum must have noticed the pause, because she poked her head back out and asked, 'Am I going to need a glass of wine for this?'

I nodded. She let out a breath, took off her blazer and reappeared with a glass filled almost to the brim. So I told her about the rally, the meeting with the vice-chancellor, the article that had outed Mitra, Mitra's dad being in hospital, and Amoo Ali's wedding. She was halfway through her red wine and shaking her head by the time I finished telling her about the day. She didn't say a word, but grabbed her phone and started texting.

'What are you doing?' I asked.

'Telling Mitra I love her.'

A warm wave went through me. I loved that she thought of Mitra as a daughter. She turned her attention back to us. 'I can look at legal options around the article if you like.'

I had to stop my mouth from falling open. Mum always got a bit bulldozery when she was feeling protective. Her asking what I wanted, rather than just acting in what she assumed was my best interest, made me want to run over and kiss her.

I looked at Alex. He didn't let go of my hand.

'It's been rough, for sure,' I said. 'Really appreciate the offer, but heaps of people condemned the article already and I'm worried if we try to take it down, it'll give the trolls more fire.'

Mum nodded and took a sip of her wine. 'Have you two eaten yet? I can order pizza.'

My stomach rumbled and Alex chuckled. 'That'd be great!' I said. Mum reached for her phone again and Alex excused himself to go to the bathroom. I looked at her. Between the dishevelled (for her) look and how quickly she'd let go of legal action against the paper, I was certain something was up.

'Everything okay?' I asked.

She looked at me, paused, then fiddled with her phone

like she was stalling, hoping Alex would come back. Yeah, something was totally going on. I waited until she'd ordered the pizza before prodding again.

'I'm just tired,' she said, not meeting my eyes.

'Mum . . .'

'It's nothing. It's just, a lot of things are changing.' She rubbed the bridge of her nose before looking up at me. 'Jonathan, my colleague in Melbourne, he's moving to Sydney.'

'Oh.' I wondered if he was one of those guys who lived in a suit, like I'd always imagined.

'*Oh*?' Her eyes went a little wider, her lips pulled down. I couldn't tell if she was upset or angry.

'Is he moving in here?' It wasn't an angry question, just curious. I smiled at her, so she'd know it.

'God no, I need my space! He's getting his own place in the city.' It was weird talking to her about her dating life, like she was a mate and not my mum. We didn't do that. 'You'll probably see him round a bit, though.'

'That wouldn't be so bad,' I said. Watching her face light up in response . . . well, it was something else.

'We need to talk about you and Mitra moving out though.' She raised a hand and I closed my mouth. 'I know you keep telling me you want to take a leap, but the last few weeks have been a lot and with your study and Union board, taking two jobs on top of that – or even one, frankly – just doesn't sound sustainable.'

'It's not just about me,' I said.

'I know, so hear me out, I have a plan.'

I had expected maybe ten people to turn up to the working bee. But when I arrived at the indoor basketball court, there was close to fifty. Anaya, Linda, Kate and the key crew from the campaign had all shown up, of course. Some were screen-printing T-shirts, others sitting in a circle going through plans. A few texted away on their phones, call sheets on their laps. I recognised a handful from the rally too.

I grabbed Sam's hand and pulled her close. 'When you said people agreed to the strike, what did you mean exactly?' I looked up at her in awe. I didn't know how she did it, I really didn't.

'The workers' unions are in, the Union board is shutting down facilities, the student council is in and a bunch of students have said they're walking out of class.' She smiled at my shocked face.

I found Mitra on the floor, painting a banner. I knew she wasn't doing great. Between the gold sequinned jacket, matching sneakers and bright blue eyeshadow, it was hard to look at her too long. Then she waved at me and I noticed a giant bandage on her wrist.

I panicked and grabbed her hand. 'What the hell?' It took all my self control to whisper the words. If Mitra had tried to do what I think she did . . . I had to clamp my jaw to stop myself from screaming.

She smirked. I was about to lash into her about it not being funny, when she unfurled the bandage. I scrunched my nose. She had tattooed *live fast,* on her wrist, though it was hard to read through the swelling. I took a breath. At least she hadn't added the *die young* part of the quote. 'It's very you,' I said, surprised at how neutral my voice sounded.

'I wouldn't, by the way,' she replied, looking straight at me with all the bravado in the world. 'I thought about it for a second, then decided screwing Sam was too much fun.'

'You should still talk to someone about everything.'

'Yeah, Sam dragged me to my first appointment this morning, after I disappeared last night and came back with this.' She waved her wrist at me. 'Therapist chick was like a forty-year-old version of you. Wouldn't let me get away with shit. Not that I cried or anything.'

'You know you can chill, right? Stuff like this isn't exactly rest.'

'You really want me on the road right now?'

No, I really didn't want her driving. I punched her shoulder like we were joking around.

Sam crouched next to us and I felt another wave of gratitude go through me. I was going to buy that woman a cape to accessorise her superpowers. 'Do you think the strike will get the vice-chancellor to back down?' I asked.

Sam caught my eye and held it for a moment. 'It's worth a shot.'

'Can we do anything else?'

Sam ran a hand over her hair and pursed her lips. 'It's a long shot, but if any major donors say something, I think the university board would have to pay attention.'

I nodded. Money. It always came down to money – and for this to work, we'd have to take more money out of the university than Steve's family had put in. 'I'll get on it then.'

I pulled out my laptop. It didn't take long to find the names I was looking for. I had no idea who any of these people were and the more I looked them up, the more desperate the whole thing felt. They all seemed like they'd be linked to Steve's world.

I wanted to close my computer and join the others in painting shirts or banners, but I couldn't. Sam was right. We had to try everything to win this thing. I googled the next name and my breath caught. A partner at Mum's firm. I grabbed my phone.

'Hey Mum . . . I'm okay, yes, I promise – look, I need a favor. Do you know Robert Shatterton? Well, there's a strike on campus in two days and we're looking to see if any big donors would pull their support until the uni launches an inquiry into the colleges. Do you think Robert would do it? Great! Thanks for asking him. Can I send you the list and see if you know anyone else on it? You're the best! Love you.'

I hung up the phone, grabbed my computer and printed the list. I went around the working bee, talking to union officials and the people who had volunteered on the campaign. I talked to the other student groups who were there, from the women's rights activists to the Christian and Jewish groups making solidarity signs. From them, I got leads on two more donors. So when I circled round and noticed six students I hadn't seen before, I was feeling particularly confident.

'Hey, I'm Tara – I don't think I've met any of you before,' I said. The guys were in polo shirts and khakis, while the girls were in Lululemon active gear.

'Diane.' One of the girls shook my hand. 'And this is John, Lee, Paul, Ben and Ellen.' They all smiled at me. I looked down at their sign. LIBERALS AGAINST RACISM.

'Yeah, we get that look a lot,' said Ellen. 'I don't really believe in strikes as a rule, but I want to make sure that people see Liberals standing up against this nonsense too.'

My cheeks flared red. Had my surprise at their being here been so obvious? 'I'm so glad you're here and thank you for the help. I have a question – do you know anyone on this?' I passed around the list and explained what we were trying to do.

They all looked through it carefully, then Diane smiled, 'I know Reggie McLaren, he's one of my Dad's mates. I'll give him a call – I don't know if he'll say yes, but I'll ask.'

'We miss Alex at college,' said Paul. 'There's a lot of us who want to see that place shaken up.'

'I'll let him know you said hi,' I smiled.

A few minutes later, Diane bounced into the room again. 'I'm amazing!' she announced, throwing her arms out wide like she was doing a solo on Broadway. 'He said he'd write a letter saying he was pausing his donations until this mess was sorted out. He knows a few others who donate too and he'll ask them to do the same tonight.'

I stared at her, my jaw on the floor. I tackled Diane with a massive hug and then ran around high-fiving the group, not caring if I looked insane. We had done it!

'What's going on here?' Sam asked from behind me. I twirled around and announced our big win. I couldn't tell what was better – actually seeing the impact we were having, or Sam's shocked face.

Chapter 28

We got to the main entrance at campus and I froze. My skin felt clammy, my mouth was dry and goosebumps lined my skin. It was strike day.

'What?' Mitra said, hands on her hips, brows raised.

'What if it isn't enough? What if it doesn't work?' I whispered.

She rolled her eyes at me. 'You gonna bail on Union board?'

I glared at her. 'Of course not.' I wasn't about to let anyone push me out of here. I had made a promise to serve the Union and I was going to keep it. Hell, if I was going to be a surgeon and hold people's lives in my hands, I'd get through this. I had to.

Mitra started marching to the front lawns and I followed her. Different organisations had set up rows of tables to hand out buttons, leaflets, calico bags and T-shirts for everything from ending fossil fuels to abortion rights and union membership – there was even a stall set up for anyone who wanted free hugs or water. Past them, the front lawns were packed with at least double the number of people from the last rally. There were heaps of cops too.

The last time I'd felt this kind of vibe was Welcome Week,

when the festival had been on full blast. Seeing this many people here for the strike, in such a spirit of joy, was something else. I looked up at the stage. At least I wasn't giving a speech today. Sima was speaking instead, on behalf of the Muslim Society. Just thinking of her made my heart swell. After *that* article was published, more than a few people in the Muslim community had been uncomfortable with the idea that I dated and had outright condemned my actions. Sima was one of the first to publicly denounce the article. I knew she didn't approve of my relationship with Alex, so the fact she'd stood by me meant the world.

Mitra had been right, more than I wanted to admit. While heaps of people from the campaign had showed up for me again, there were also so many others showing up for the first time. They were here because they believed in what we were doing, and knew that the only way we could win was if we stood up together and called for change.

Tears pricked my eyes. It didn't matter what the vice-chancellor did. Whatever the outcome, we had started to build something new, acted together to bring the university closer to what we all wanted it to be. We walked past a stall that was blasting electronica, so I grabbed Mitra's hand and twirled her. She threw me a grumpy look for about two seconds and then started dancing too.

Within a few seconds, hundreds of people were dancing with us. Throwing my head back, feeling blood pump through my veins, I felt incredible – even though I probably looked ridiculous. I felt a hand on my waist and turned to see Alex smiling at me.

'And I was worried you'd be freaking out about how today

was going to go . . .' he whispered in my ear, as he pulled me to him so that we were dancing together.

I went up on my tippy toes so that my lips were at his ears. 'I love you.'

His froze, his hands tightening around my waist, his smile evaporating. 'What?' It was more of a grunt than a question.

'I love you!' I said it louder, my smile growing. Even if he freaked out, it felt great to say it.

He pulled me out of the dance and walked me to a quiet corner, behind the library where no one could see us. What the hell? My heart was pounding. Okay, maybe I *wasn't* okay with him being freaked out. Was he going to tell me it was too soon? I looked up at him, but he wouldn't look at me.

'Tara, I . . .' He grabbed my hand and pulled me to him. My body slammed into his, and he held my shoulders and gave me a look that weakened my knees. Then he was kissing me. I wrapped my arms around his neck, pulled him as close as I could.

He broke the kiss, his cheeks and neck flushed. He pressed a finger to my mouth. 'I love you too.' He took a step back and took my hand. 'Let me get you back out there before Sam comes after us.'

I giggled at that and followed him back to where everyone else was. I waved at Mitra, who wriggled out of the dance party we'd set off and joined us in zigzagging our way through the crowd towards the main stage. I wasn't on the speaking roster, but I was on Sam's back-up list in case anything went wrong.

'Can I help?' I asked, the back of my neck prickling at having left her to do so much of the work.

'Nah, the coordinating team has it covered. I'm really just

holding this because it makes me feel better.' She lifted her clipboard. 'Rima is managing the stage. She insisted I was burning out and . . . well, she didn't give me much of a choice.'

'So you listen to this Rima chick then, huh?' Mitra wrapped an arm around Sam's waist and kissed her collarbone.

'She must be less distracting than you are.' Sam flashed her a mischievous smile. They were never going to stop being nauseating.

'Show time,' Alex said as the MC walked onto the stage and the crowd started to roar.

I shoved a plastic cup into the garbage bag I was holding, then stood up and stretched. The strike had been more successful than any of us imagined. We were too jacked up on adrenaline to go home yet, so we'd each grabbed a bag and were helping to clean up.

I looked up and vaguely recognised an older woman in a pale pink suit loitering by the car park. She'd shown up at the candidate debate and had been there when we were 'fixing' the graffiti on campus too.

I held her gaze for a moment and then she started walking towards me. I let the garbage bag drop and wiped my hands on my jeans.

'Hi there – ' she said. I was caught off guard. She didn't sound like a professor. Her tone had an assertiveness to it that most academics had been trained out of. She leaned over and offered me her hand. 'I'm Edith.'

I shook her hand. 'Tara.'

'I want to share something with you, but need to know that

what I tell you won't end up in the papers tomorrow. Can I have your word?'

Who was this woman? Did she think we were in some sort of Bond movie? 'Sure,' I shrugged.

'I wanted to let you know that this afternoon I led a motion to rebuke the vice-chancellor. We didn't have the votes for his resignation, but it was close. There's nothing I can do on how the Maddison affair was handled to this point, though you should know that some *heated* conversations were had around that.' She looked me in the eye and that's when it hit me. Why she looked so familiar. I had seen that stare on every official letter from the university. This woman wasn't an academic: she was the chancellor.

'Do you think he'll change?'

'It's not a matter of *if*, but of KPIs, now. If he doesn't meet certain benchmarks around diversity numbers and implementing new guidelines around campus safety and sensitivity, he won't survive the next vote.'

It wasn't what we'd asked for, but it was something. 'Thank you for letting me know.' It was the only thing I could think of to say.

She turned to leave but I took a step forward. 'Thank you, for speaking up. Not everyone would have.'

She gave me the kind of nod that a hard-ass teacher gives you when they're impressed. And then she left. I stood there, food wrappers in my hands, floored.

Sam and the others were scattered across the campus. I ran over to Sam and texted the others. Soon, the four of us were sitting on the lawns. I told them about the conversation with the chancellor. They were all quiet for a few moments after I finished.

'Well?' I said, looking at Sam.

'Smells like a trap to me,' Mitra said, pulling blades from the lawn.

Sam shook her head. 'Nah, it sounds plausible. They're giving him and the university a chance to save face without doing nothing. It buys them time with donors. It makes sense.'

'But, it means it's working, right? We're getting through to them.'

Sam shrugged. 'Maybe. It's more than I've seen them do before, so that's something.'

Alex wrapped an arm around me. 'So we keep going then?'

'Like we had anything better to do anyway.' Mitra tugged out a giant weed and I couldn't help but smile.

Chapter 29

I wiped my forehead with my sleeve after I dropped another box into our garage. I couldn't believe it had been a month since the election.

The shelves that lined the garage walls were usually empty. Mum hated clutter, and to her, there wasn't a difference between throwing something out and putting it in the garage. But today, there were four new boxes on the shelves, with more coming, as we cleaned out the closet room.

Alex and Sam wandered up, each carrying four boxes, breathing like they'd run a 5k. I shook my head. 'Competing over how many boxes you can carry? Are you both five?'

'Six, at the very least.' Alex winked at me, drenched in sweat.

'So what's the plan?' Sam said, moving to the empty kitchen and throwing me one of her best sceptical looks as she wiped her forehead.

'I think that's everything. I guess all we need to do now is put together the bed. We gotta get a move on – she's going to be here in an hour.'

The two of them helped me put the boxes on the shelves, then we walked back into the living room and down the hall into what used to be our closet room. Mum had bought us both wardrobes for our bedrooms, and we'd moved our clothes out, taken down the chandelier and given away the sofa bed on Gumtree. I leaned against the door and remembered all the times Mitra and I had dressed up in here, had chased each other around with make-up.

'She's gonna love it,' Alex said, as he grabbed the drill. 'Are you sure about this, though?' He lifted up a Hot Wheels track.

'Yes,' Sam and I said together, and we all laughed. Sam and I tore at the plastic that had been wrapped around Mitra's new headboard. We'd gotten her a double bed, in a dark wood that I hoped Mitra would like. Once we'd assembled the bed, Alex helped us bring in the mattress from the hallway and lay it over the slats. Sam and I pulled the fitted sheet tight. It was the same yellow as Dee, as was the flat sheet we layered on top.

'What do you think?' Alex said. He'd mounted the Hot Wheels track on the wall, the bright orange plastic surprisingly complementing the yellow bedspread.

Sam grabbed a shiny green toy car, put it at the top of the track and let it fall. It zoomed through the loop and onto the floor. 'Perfect.'

We cleared the room of trash and then looked over it again – her bed, a side table and empty shelves we'd painted black that morning. It came together, but still looked bare.

'Chill, Mitra will have stuff all over the floor and sequins on the walls in about two minutes,' Sam smiled.

The door opened and the three of us jumped out into the hallway, ready to yell *SURPRISE!* before we realised it was just

Mum, carrying big green grocery bags. Alex hurried over, took the bags and carried them into the kitchen.

'You know, I could get used to that,' she said to me as she walked past. I was glad she was here. The closet was Mum's favourite room in the house. Giving it up to make sure Mitra had a proper room . . . well, it was a lot.

'Who left the door open?' Mitra's voice boomed down the hallway.

'SURPRISE!' we yelled.

Mitra glanced at each of us in turn. 'What, is there a gas leak in here? My birthday ain't for months.'

'This is better than a birthday present,' Sam said, grabbing Mitra's hand and pulling her to her new bedroom.

Mitra walked into the room, looked around and turned back to me and Mum. 'I don't understand,' she said.

'I'm at work most of the time, and have been spending a fair amount of time in the city. I saw some of the places you were looking at and . . . I want you both to be able to concentrate on your studies, without having to work two or three jobs to just scrape by.' Mum scrunched her nose and shook her head. 'Of course you can't keep living on a sofa bed. We wanted you to know that we want this to be your home too.'

'I . . .' Mitra paused, her bottom lip quivering, 'There's a Hot Wheels track on the wall – ' she grabbed a car and fiddled with it. 'I . . . I don't know . . .'

'Wait, if you're going to get mushy, I need to get a camera – ' I said. Mitra laughed, walked over and took Leila's hand in both of hers. 'Thank you, *vagehane* [really].' Then she looked at me. 'You too.'

'*Beya* [Come],' Mum said, 'We have desserts to make. Mitra, put on something *Gheri*.' Gheri is one of those Farsi words that doesn't have a good English equivalent: it's something between dancing, shimmying and flirting.

Mitra plugged her phone into a new sound system she'd installed for us a few weeks ago and blasted Iranian wedding anthems: classic upbeat pop songs that almost made it impossible to sit still.

Alex grabbed my hand as we wandered into the kitchen. He kissed my knuckles before letting go so we could unload the baking supplies.

'So, the plan is pistachio cupcakes, baklava, cake yazdi, sholezard, and I'm picking up the zolibiya tomorrow.' It took about twenty minutes to grab all the utensils and pots we'd need to put together the dessert table for Amoo Ali's big day. 'Sam and Mitra – the two of you are on the baklava and sholezard. Tara and Alex, you're on the cupcakes and cake yazdi. I'll be on clean-up duty so that everything keeps moving.'

Sam poured a packet of rice into a saucepan, Mitra started greasing a baking pan with butter and Alex blasted the food processor we'd jammed full of pistachios. Already, the kitchen smelled amazing.

The doorbell rang. 'Fadi's here!' Mitra said, cleaning off her hands with a dishtowel and heading towards the door. A minute later, Fadi danced into the living room.

'Hey, hey, hey!'

'The cheapskate showed up with presents,' Mitra said, holding a casserole dish covered with aluminium foil.

'Nah, they're from Mum.'

All the colour drained from Mitra's face. 'What?' she whispered, setting the parcel down on the kitchen counter like it was radioactive.

'She said you didn't know how to make baklava, so she made a batch for Amoo Ali's wedding. She also gave me this to give to you.'

Mitra's hand shook as she took the small box and sank into a couch. Within seconds, Sam was kneeling on the carpet beside her. She slowly unwrapped the box and flipped it open. Inside was a framed drawing of a girl driving a yellow car. 'She kept this?' She looked up at Fadi, who just nodded. Mitra turned to Sam, 'I drew this when I was five and told her this was my dream car.' She sniffled, dabbing a tear away, and hugged the drawing to her chest.

I was happy for Mitra, so happy for her. But I'd be lying if I didn't admit that a part of me hoped Dad would reach out to me like this one day. That he hadn't walked out of my life forever.

'Look, I know how great it is that I showed up, but the waterworks are a bit much, yeah?' Fadi said. He slipped next to Mitra and poked her in the hips. She elbowed him back.

It was a first step. I looked over at Mum, who was obviously trying not to cry. Alex kissed my head as he stood behind me and wrapped his arms around my waist.

I reached into my pocket and squeezed my tasbeeh, sending up a prayer of thanks. There was a long road ahead: getting into med, changing uni for the better. But I wasn't scared of the struggle anymore. After all, wasn't that where the magic was?

AUTHOR'S NOTE

If you're reading this – thank you!

Love it or hate it, you took the time to read the book and that means the world. This might sound strange, but I also want to say – go for it. Go for what? Well, whatever it is you've always wanted to do but have been a bit afraid to. I've always loved writing and for much of my life, I believed I couldn't write – not well, anyway. Now, I have a published book that real people like you have read! I'm not going to say it'll feel awesome every step of the way. It'll be hard, you'll have to dig deep, you'll want to quit a million times, but if you stick with it – you'll get there. Chances are, you'll need help on the way. I know I did.

Which gets me to all the people I need to thank who made this book possible.

First of all I want to thank Ilya. Without the late nights, the extra childcare shifts and the eternal belief that I could make this happen – this book wouldn't be in your hands right now. Anton and Yasi – I can always find joy and perspective in your company, and it makes me so much the richer for it. Mum, I love you so much and couldn't have done this without you. Also, Yanna – here it is, I promised you'd be able to read it soon.

Danielle, thank you for being the best agent ever. I'm so grateful for your constant belief in me, your patience and your general badassery. Thank you to Margot Lloyd – for seeing the potential in this book, for giving me fantastic feedback that really helped bring out the story.

Jo, I was so nervous about the idea of editing this book – but with you it felt easy. Your edits were so insightful, so spot on and so kind – you created a safe haven for me to create in and this book is so much better for all your work. Also, thank you to Poppy Nwosu and the whole Wakefield team for all your support!

It's hard to write a novel without a squad and I had one of the best writer's groups around. Thanks, Jen Crichton, Deb Eldridge and especially Jo Mackenzie – who read the whole novel and gave me excellent pointers and feedback.

Thank you to Cathie Tasker, for being an incredible mentor and teacher, to Rachel Hills and Sarah Ayoub – for having my back and going out of your way to support me. Emma Ruby-Sachs – your tough love, mentorship and knowing that someone like you thought I had talent meant so much.

Special shout out to Sofia Madden, Allen Tieu, Alex Hurden – and the lovely Julie Holmes, for taking the time to talk to me for research for this book.

Thank you to all my friends at the Castle: Bron, Ben, Taren, Downstairs Nick, Viv, Jignasha, Mark, Tom, Upstairs Nick, Meg, Nick Lee, Danny and Mia, for indulging me when I was highly sleep deprived and declared I was writing a book. Especially to Chrissy, for all the dancing, joking and supportive memes you created to help me know I could do it.

See? If you want to do the impossible – go for it. Just find the squad to help you get there. After all, that's how all the best stories start.

Wakefield Press is an independent publishing and
distribution company based in Adelaide, South Australia.
We love good stories and publish beautiful books.
To see our full range of books, please visit our website at
www.wakefieldpress.com.au
where all titles are available for purchase.
To keep up with our latest releases, news and events,
subscribe to our monthly newsletter.

Find us!

Facebook: www.facebook.com/wakefield.press
Twitter: www.twitter.com/wakefieldpress
Instagram: www.instagram.com/wakefieldpress